Barb Wire

D1247673

*Also by Walt Coburn
in Large Print:*

The Secret of Crutcher's Cabin
Coffin Ranch
The Square Shooter
Guns Blaze on Spiderweb Range
Law Rides the Range
Violent Maverick
Branded

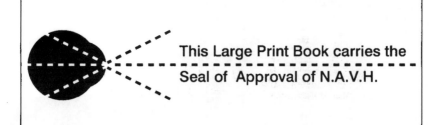

This Large Print Book carries the
Seal of Approval of N.A.V.H.

Barb Wire

Walt Coburn

WHEELER PUBLISHING

Published in 2002 by arrangement with Golden West Literary Agency.

Wheeler Large Print Western Series.

The text of this Large Print edition is unabridged.
Other aspects of the book may vary from the original edition.

Set in 16 pt. Plantin by Al Chase.

Printed in the United States on permanent paper.

Library of Congress Cataloging-in-Publication Data

Coburn, Walt, 1889–1971.
    Barb wire : a novel of old Montana / by Walt Coburn.
      p. cm.
    ISBN 1-58724-334-2 (lg. print : sc : alk. paper)
    1. Montana — Fiction. 2. Large type books. I. Title.
PS3505.O153 B37 2002
  813'.52—dc21   2002033054

Barb Wire

CHAPTER I

THE HOLD-UP

When the Nighthawk planned a train hold-up, he made a thorough job of it.

Dusk of a chilly May evening, on the east end of the Lodge Creek Bridge. . . . The Nighthawk chose the month of May because the grass was high in the coulees and the water-holes were full. Heavy rains had swollen Lodge Creek so that the trains slowed down to a scant five miles an hour to cross the bridge.

The spot, a few miles east of Chinook, Montana, lies thirty-five miles as the goose flies in the spring, from the Canadian border. Also, by the same method of reasoning, a stout horse, traveling at a circle lope, will carry its rider southward into the Bear Paw Hills before the Chinook posse have gathered their wits enough to pick up fresh sign.

Relay of fresh mounts lay north and south of the railroad, for the gang always split after a division of the loot. Every man in the gang knew the country as a scholar knows his book.

It was beginning to drizzle. The men in the brush pulled their yellow slickers about them. But not a button was fastened, because they wanted easy access to their Colts. Cigarettes were held in cupped hands as they listened to the instructions of the Nighthawk.

"Zeb, you better flag 'er to a stop. Ben and Slim uncouple the express car. Tug and me'll take care uh the engine crew and run 'er acrost the bridge. Shorty and Pat guard the bridge and drop any fool that tries tuh cross it when we pull the express car yonderly. Them as kin swim the crick and git to us, kin have my cut uh the proceeds. Even a fish couldn't get across Lodge Crick, high as she is to-night.

"Damn this rain, it'll make our sign clear as a sheep trail. Remember, when we scatter, keep to the ridges and rocky country where yuh won't leave much of a trail. Whitey, you and Tex handle the first class Pullman coach, both uh you bein' sorter ladies' men. And all you boys mind this. No fool shootin'. If some jasper goes fer a smoke-pole, try not tuh hurt him so's he'll up and die on us. All we want is that cash in the express car safe. No killin'.

"Keep yore faces covered. Yonder she comes, cowboys. Git a last draw outa them cigarettes and hide yore purty faces under a mask. Light the lantern and git on the tracks, Zeb. Lay low till she stops, gents, then climb aboard."

Aboard the Pullman, an ebony-hued porter shoved a grinning face into the smoking compartment where young Buck Rawlins of the 7UP, a newly appointed stock association deputy, and two traveling salesmen were playing

8

a monotonous game of draw poker.

"We's slowin' down for de Lodge Creek Bridge, gemmen. Betta cash in yo' chips, Mista Rawlins, so's I kin bresh yo' off befo' we pulls into Chinook. I'm tendin' to dat lady in lowah six now. Git you-all when you come into yo' section."

The blond-haired girl in lower six was staring gloomily out the window into the black drizzle. Since dusk, Mazie West had been wishing she were back in New York, doing her "twice a day" at her third from the end, front row position, chorus, of *The Prince of Paris*. She wrinkled her nose at the grinning porter and sniffed. The train jerked to a stop.

"Another cow on the track, George? Or does the engine need some more water? Or has that flirty brakeman got a heavy date with some jane that lives around here?"

"Rains done made the road-bed soft, miss."

"This rheumatic engine needs a soft bed."

"Yas'm. I reckon you-all better lemme bresh yo' now, miss. We lands in Chinook in mighty short time now."

"I hope there's a rowboat handy to take me to the hotel."

"Ah done tole Mistah Buck Rawlins that you-all gittin' off here. He'll take keer uh you, sho' nuff."

"This Rawlins sketch is the big, good-looking boy that tried to drink all the hard liquor in Chicago just before he got on the train? Then spends the rest of the time sobering up on a quart per

9

day? Say, that Johnnie will be worked to death taking care of himself. He needs a nurse."

"Shucks now. Missy, that boy kin — Lord he'p us!"

The porter's hands shot upward and stayed there. Mazie West smiled wearily at his rolling eyes, then suddenly saw what the trouble was.

A man stood at the end of the aisle. A tall man in a big hat and dripping yellow slicker. A black silk handkerchief covered all his face save a pair of narrowed eyes. He held a blue-barreled .45 in each hand.

"Take it easy, folks," drawled a voice from behind the handkerchief. "We ain't robbin' nobody in this car. All we're after is some dough up yonder in the express car which the boss an' the boys aims tuh git without no ruckus. Jest keep yore hands in sight an' reachin' sorter upward."

Mazie West cast a quick glance toward the other end of the car. A second masked and slicker-clad man was herding five men down the aisle. Buck Rawlins, grinning easily, walked in the lead, hands elevated. Behind him came the two frightened traveling salesmen and a tall, dapper-looking man with slender blond mustache and shiny hair. Mazie remembered seeing this man get on at the last station.

Lastly came the heavily built, scowling deputy, his new badge shining mockingly in the light. The masked man's .45 was boring into his shoulder blades.

"You three dudes lay down on the floor an' stretch yore arms out ahead uh yuh. You there, Rawlins, take this law officer's gun off him and throw it out the window. No monkey-shines while yo're doin' it, either, Buck!"

The hold-up man backed away, gun swinging idly to cover the ground. The tall bandit with the two guns leaned idly against the doorway.

Mazie stole a scared glance at the deputy. His jaws were clamped until the muscles twitched and the light of battle shone in his eyes. Buck Rawlins, unruffled and grinning, was taking the deputy's gun.

"Shoot it out with 'em, Rawlins," whispered the deputy in an undertone. "You got a even break."

Mazie West crouched in her seat, scarcely daring to breathe, her wide gray eyes fixed on Buck's tanned face.

"If I had better than an even break," Buck announced, "I wouldn't shoot. I'm not paid to kill road-agents."

With a careless shrug of his wide shoulders, he tossed the gun through a closed window.

"You — you yellow quitter!" whispered Mazie hoarsely.

Buck, a trifle red, looked around and down into the girl's tense face.

From outside came the spasmodic sound of rifle shots. The big man in the slicker shifted uneasily on his feet. Then the chugging engine pulled the express car slowly across the bridge into the black night. Somewhere in the Pullman a frightened child was crying.

"Better change your seat, lady," said Buck. "There's somewhat of a draft from that window I just busted." One of his elevated hands lifted his new high-crowned Stetson and he bowed mockingly. The bandits chuckled. There were more shots outside.

"Ain't that there college uh yourn lettin' out early, Buck?" drawled the tall hold-up man.

"Nope. They let me out early, that's all," came the careless reply. "Harvard will get along somehow without me. I was fired."

"The ol' man'll put yuh to ridin' fence fer that. Tell him, when yuh git home, that there's two 7UP saddle hosses trailin' with them Long X broom tails in the Larbe Hills. Hey, you with the hair growed out on yore lip, lay quiet! Yeah. One of 'em's a chunky built brown that looked like ol' Bogus. The other'n is a strawberry roan. Likely lookin' pony."

"Thanks. You boys picked a bad night."

"She was clear as a bell when we left the Bear Paws, damn it all. A man can't figger on too much luck, though. Come mornin' they'll pick up our sign if the rain don't wash it out. But we'll be a long time gone by then. I'm plumb sorry tuh make you lose that there gun, Mister Deputy. Looked like a good 'un. You kin pick it up, come daylight."

"Go to the devil!" growled the officer.

The locomotive was backing up now, shoving

12

the express car. There came a jolting as the train was re-coupled. This was followed by a shrill whistle.

"If yuh got a bottle along, Buck," drawled the tall man, "feed that porter a big shot. I reckon he's done passed out, he's so scared. Remember us to the boys at the 7UP. Ladies an' gents, *adiós.*"

As mysteriously as they had appeared the two slicker-clad men slid out the doors and into the wet night.

"You can take your valuables out from behind the seat now, lady," grinned Buck. "The bold, bad men have gone."

"That big gent," muttered the stock deputy, "is Tex Arnold. The other one Whitey Rance."

"And outside are the Nighthawk, Zeb, Shorty, Pat and a few more," added Buck. "But what of it? If I were you, I'd forget it, pardner."

"Forget, hell! I'm leading a posse after 'em when we hit Chinook."

"Yeah? Better stick to your last, shoemaker."

"Meanin'?"

"Meanin', my friend, that you're green on the job or you wouldn't make a crack like that. The stock association don't pay their men to cold trail the Nighthawk."

The traveling salesmen and the dapper man with the mustache were on their feet now, brushing dust from their clothes. The latter stepped forward, not unconscious of Mazie's presence.

"Had an automatic in my pocket," he explained, tapping his hip. "But the rough-neck saw me when I reached for it. Otherwise, I'd have done something." He adjusted a beautiful lavender tie and cast a sidelong glance at Mazie, who smiled up at him.

"You mighta took a chance, Rawlins," complained the deputy, "when yuh had it."

"Him take a chance?" put in Mazie West, scornfully. "Say he's one of their gang, mister. A blind guy with one eye could see that. Didn't he team with 'em from the rise of the curtain? I'll say he did. You better make a pinch right now, mister, if you're any kind of a wise dick. Here comes the flirty pet of the Mister Great Northern himself and his hand's done up in a bloody rag."

"They're bringin' in a dead man!" gasped one of the salesmen. "A member of the gang."

The conductor, followed by a group of excited men, pushed into the car. They carried something limp in a dripping yellow slicker.

The grin left Buck's lips as he shoved aside the man in the lavender tie and strode down the aisle. At Buck's heels came the stock deputy.

Buck took one look at the blood-smeared features from which a sodden handkerchief had been removed. Then he made his way to the smoking compartment, looking very grave.

"I was hid under the car," boasted the conductor. "Dropped him as he stepped off."

"Tex Arnold," announced the deputy. "You got him through the back of the head."

"I can name my own run when I get back to St. Paul," chuckled the conductor.

The deputy was glaring at him coldly. He pulled his coat lapel aside and showed his badge.

"I take charge uh the body. Let's have yore gun, mister. It'll be needed at the inquest. And say, when yuh ask fer a new run, put in fer a Eastern route, mister. Tex has friends that will shore be rearin' tuh hang yore hide on the fence. They don't like folks that does their killin' from ambush."

Mazie West, listening with both ears, was becoming more bewildered each minute. What manner of men were these Westerners, anyhow? First, a college man, son of the wealthiest cattleman in Montana, to quote the porter, chats with a highwayman. Then an officer sneers at a trainman for shooting one of the bandits.

"To think," she inwardly groaned, "that I give up a perfectly good job to come out here on a one-way ticket. Chinook, be good to your new female farmer!"

The train jerked, then crept along the track at a snail's pace.

Mazie took a seat at the far end of the car and stared at the dripping black square of windowpane, tears in her eyes.

Back in the smoking compartment, Buck Rawlins and the stock deputy sat beside the stiffening body of the dead bandit. Buck had gotten a sheet from the frightened porter and covered the body that lay on the floor. Thin rivulets of water trickled from the yellow slicker, across the carpeted floor.

Buck brought a bottle from his grip and poured his companion a drink.

"I've ridden circle and stood night guard with Tex," he said, in a low tone, "when he was just a big, good-natured cow hand. He deserved a better break at the end, no matter what he's done."

The deputy nodded.

"Wasn't it Tex Arnold that saved that breed kid from drowning in Milk River a year ago last spring, and come damn near drownin' hisself?"

"Yes."

"Then he killed that tin-horn over a poker hand and joined the Nighthawk."

"The tin-horn had a lot of friends to buy off juries. Yes."

"I done changed my mind about follerin' that bunch with a posse, Rawlins. Here's happy days."

"To old Tex. May he find fat meat in his Shadow Hills. Drink hearty."

CHAPTER II
FIGHTIN' TALK

Then swing your rope slowly and rattle your
  spurs lowly,
And give a wild whoop as you bear me along;
In the grave throw me, and roll the sod o'er
  me,
For I'm a wild cowboy and I know I done
  wrong.
            — The Cowboy's Lament.

Tuley Bill Baker lit his stub of cigarette and reached for the bar bottle.

"As I was sayin'," he told the bartender with an air of solemnity, "this here jasper down on the Pecos was hell fer experimentin' with crossbreedin'. He's got a one-eyed sand-hill crane which he's plumb fond of and calls Henrietta. So he takes a fifty foot, four strand rawhide rope an' coaxes Henrietta to set on it, feedin' her on red-eye licker an' jerkie meanwhile. Now what d'yuh reckon come uh that there experiment?"

"A crop uh wallyloo birds," guessed the bartender, who used to ride broncs for ten dollars a head.

"No, sir. Worse'n that. Henrietta wakes the

ranch early one mornin' by shore heart-rendin' cryin'. They run out to her nest an' finds her millin' aroun' suthin' speckled. They fights her off with their hats an' gits a squint at this here speckled varmint. It's smokin' of a cigareet an' wears a Chihuahua spur on its off foot. It growed into a man an' the man sets yonder."

"Cutbank Carter?" inquired the barkeep, nodding vaguely.

"Ol' Cutbank Carter. The speckles still shows on his face and hands an' his strawberry roan hair is done slipped some on top, but otherwise he don't look no purtier than he did that mornin' I saw Henrietta peckin' at him."

"Have a drink," suggested the man behind the bar.

"Don't care if I do. Roll outa that chair, Cutbank, and belly up to the mahogany. The house is buying one."

He accompanied the invitation with a yip that brought Cutbank's six-foot-three frame out of the big chair with a leap. Blinking, Cutbank's hand groped in the region of his right hip. The bartender promptly slid out of sight behind the bar.

Tuley Bill Baker, short, bald and heavily built, stood leaning idly against the glass cigar case.

"Bust this here seegar glass, big feller," he announced coldly, "and it sets yuh back a year's wages. Quit clawin' fer yore hardware an' have a drink with two white men."

"Yuh danged li'l' cow-hocked, short-backed,

18

knee-sprung idjit!" complained Cutbank nasally. "Yuh like tuh get yorese'f shot up a batch. Settin' up all night with Tex Arnold's corpse done raised hell with my nerves. I bin dreamin' about speerits."

Cutbank steered a course for the bottle and dropped his voice to a whisper. "Seen ary sign uh the boss, Tuley?"

"She come an' went," lied Tuley Bill easily. "She seen yuh laid out in yonder chair, snorin' plenty. I done told her we'd pull out fer the ranch when yuh got sober enough tuh set that thing yuh call a hoss. She was shore ringy, too. She 'lowed that the Rollin' M didn't pay top wages to broken-down waddies that's so stove-up they can't hold their licker like a white man orter. If I was in yore place I'd mosey on over to the Chinook House an' have a medicine talk with her. Mebbyso you kin keep her from firin' yuh. I dunno."

Tuley Bill winked slyly at the barkeep. Cutbank helped himself to another drink and attempted a grin that was a miserable failure.

"I reckon yo're lyin' plenty. Never knowed yuh to speak the truth when yuh could make a lie do the work. I'm boggin' down here till I git plumb primed tuh leave. Mebbyso a eighteen-year-old gal kin buffalo you, but I'll tell a man that Colleen Driscoll can't run no whizzer on ol' Cutbank Carter. Not by a damn sight, gentlemen an' feller citizens.

"I'm a rattlesnake, I am. A wolf an' a grizzly! I

cut my fust tooth on a gun barrel an' my drink is panther blood. My trade is tamin' bad-men an' I kin scratch the buckin'est hoss that ever crossed the flats."

He gulped another drink and glared about, then his thin, nasal howl rent the air as he once more voiced his toughness and double-barreled nerve.

"I've fit Injuns, hung greasers, licked sheriffs, shot — Oh, gosh, we're done fer!"

Cutbank's voice had suddenly shrunk to a thin whisper. He shoved the bar bottle toward the astonished saloon man.

"No, sir, I tell yuh, I ain't drinkin' a dang drop, so yuh needn't go coaxin' me. Tuley kin guzzle the stuff if he's fool enough, but not fer ol' Cutbank. I told the boss I'd —"

"That you'd hit the trail for home early yesterday morning."

The voice, cold and uncompromising, came from a tanned girl in worn riding clothes who stood in the doorway. A wide-brimmed Stetson swung in a small brown hand and she slapped it against her dust-covered riding breeches.

Colleen Driscoll, slim, athletic, capable, ran the Rolling M horse and cattle outfit for her father, who had been blind for many years. She had a way with men and horses that made both her eager slaves. A mop of jet black, thickly curling hair was cut short for convenience, rather than fashion, but it made her all the more attractive. Dark blue eyes, thickly fringed, looked at you with a disconcerting level gaze. Her nose was short, her chin firm, and the glow of Montana sunsets had put a color in her cheeks that no one could ever mistake for make-up.

Now, as she stood in the doorway of the Last Chance Saloon, frowning with disapproval at these two old cow-punchers who loved her as a daughter, she made a ravishing picture.

Buck Rawlins, close behind her, gazed at half-averted cheek with admiration that bordered on worship.

"Cutbank!" said Colleen crisply.

"Yes'm." Cutbank resembled some long-stemmed plant after a hard wind. One of his huge freckled hands pulled at his hat.

"You were yelling about Injuns, greasers and fighting. Don't let me interrupt you. Go on with it."

"I'd — I'd finished, ma'am."

"Then begin over. From the very start, so Buck and I won't lose any of it. All ready now. Begin."

"Shucks, I done fergot."

"I'm a rattlesnake and grizzly —" Colleen prompted. "Go on from there."

"My gosh, ma'am, I —"

"Make him sing 'er!" chuckled Tuley Bill, then reddened as the girl sent him a withering glance.

"Your turn's coming, Tuley. Hurry, Cutbank. You're keeping me waiting."

"I *gotta?*" groaned Cutbank.

21

"Or go to jail for shooting out the new street lights last night. The sheriff's rearin' to jug you. From the teething part, now, to the sheriff licking and greaser killing. Otherwise, I don't pay your fine."

In a sickly replica of his former cry, Cutbank raised his voice in his howl of challenge to a shooting, fighting world. He looked positively ill when he finished, and avoided Buck's grinning presence.

"Now, Tuley," said Colleen sweetly, "you put on your little act. Take off your hat, so that the scar will show, and tell us how the Comanches were scalping you when you were so badly shot up that they thought you dead. How you grappled with three bloodthirsty braves and killed them with your bare hands, then scalped them."

"But, dagone it, I —"

"As a matter of fact, a horse threw you when you were drunk. You lit on your head in a stack of hot branding irons and got branded on your sparsely vegetated dome. But the one you were telling that saloonful of awed homesteaders last night was more colorful. All set, Tuley? Go! And don't mumble your words. Set him on that card table, Buck, so his voice will carry farther. Loudly and clearly, remember."

"Dagone it, now, Miss Colleen, I was jest tellin' it a mite scary to them scissor-bills an' —"

"You were lying horribly. I heard you, clear across the street. Speak your piece. And every time I signal with my hat, duck your head and how so that every one can get a look at the scar."

A few idlers were gathering at the windows and door. Among the crowd on the sidewalk stood Mazie West and the man with the lavender tie who had been on the train. He was dressed in well-tailored, expensive riding clothes and carried a rolled blue-print map under his arm.

"Our friend Rawlins of the 7UP, Miss West. That's Colleen Driscoll with him."

"They seem to be having the time of their young lives. Do the Western women usually hang around barrooms, Mr. Marley?"

"She seems at home, doesn't she? Product of a select New York girls' school, too, I've heard. We might as well be starting for your new ranch. The roads are a bit rough and I may have to change a tire or two on the way."

"In them swell pants?"

"I was speaking figuratively. My driver does all that sort of thing."

They passed on down the street.

Others crowded into their place, peering at the odd scene inside the saloon.

"Darn yore picture, Buck Rawlins," growled Tuley, wiping beads of nervous perspiration from his red face as he got off the table. "Yo're the cause uh the whole dang thing. Me'n Cutbank'll git yuh plenty some day fer this."

"So that's it?" frowned Colleen, turning on Buck. "Just where do you fit into this degrading affair, Buckie boy?"

"Quit calling me 'Buckie boy' and otherwise

lay off me. These two old longhorns are loco."

"Give the boys some beer and make mine soda pop," Colleen told the bartender, who had known her since she was a baby and had slipped on a fresh apron in her honor. She turned to Cutbank.

"Did Buck rib you boys into shooting out those lights?"

"Noooo. But he done coaxed us into layin' over in town tuh he'p sit up with Tex's corpse an' lend a hand plantin' him to-day. He 'lowed Tex was entitled to a swell plantin' an' me'n Tuley was the only two waddies in town. We'd worked with ol' Tex afore he turned bad."

"So he kept my wagon-bosses in town while my two round-up outfits laid up at their camps, doing nothing? Buck Rawlins, your dad is right. You'll never amount to a hill of beans. Instead of settling down and making that grand old man proud of you, you carouse around, get fired from school, and jim up my outfits to bury a train robber. As a success, you're a thorough failure. Then you have the crust to ask me to marry you. You need a governess, not a wife, Buck Rawlins!"

Buck flushed crimson and gazed at the toe of his shop-made boot. With an angry stamp of her foot, the girl turned to walk out, then halted, gazing at an overall-clad young giant who barred her way.

"Look out, Bill Murdock," chuckled the irrepressible Tuley. "Let our boss pass."

"In a minute." Big Bill Murdock, son of Angus Murdock, the sheep-man on Wild Horse Creek, looked like some young Scottish chief as he stood there clenching and unclenching his fists. His eyes traveled from Colleen to Buck.

"Howdy, Bill," Buck greeted him. "Thought you were still at Yale."

"Well, I'm not. I thought you were at Harvard, if you want a come-back to your small-talk. I suppose you two have been laughing over your cow-man's idea of what you term humor. But if you want my opinion, I'm telling you it was a despicable trick. I'm no sheep lover myself, Rawlins, but I'd figure I'd sunk mighty close to the bottom of the scale of humanity if I wantonly slaughtered them, scared a haif-witted harmless Swede sheep-herder, and burned his wagon.

"I might overlook the fact that you destroyed fifteen miles of fence that was on my own land, but I can't forget the sheep and the herder. I'm not going to law, because that's not my way of settling injuries. Pull off your coat, Rawlins, and I'll show Colleen Driscoll that her partner in crime isn't so much of a bully as he thinks he is. Shed that coat, you dirty, sneaking coward!"

Buck Rawlins, white about the lips, slowly took off his coat and laid it on the bar. Then he stooped and unbuckled his spurs. These and a short-barreled single action .45 were laid on the coat.

"I don't know what you're talking about, Bill. But I don't let anybody, much less a sheep-herder, call me a sneaking coward. Better slip out the back door, Colleen. This won't be pretty."

"Bill Murdock," snapped Colleen, "you aren't drunk. I hope you haven't gone loco. You two boys cut this out and you, Bill, explain yourself."

"That's hardly necessary under the circumstances," growled Bill, rolling his flannel sleeves to bare his powerful forearms. "The herder recognized a 7UP man and two Rolling M riders in the crowd that tarred and feathered him. Rawlins is right. This won't be any tea-party. Better fade out of the picture."

Hot, angry tears welled to the girl's eyes. She was half angry, half frightened. Twice before she had seen Buck Rawlins and Bill Murdock fight.

The first time was when they all three attended the little log school at Black Coulee. They had fought because Buck called Bill a sheep-herder. Boys of fifteen, they were then, but it had taken three men to pull them, bleeding and badly beaten, apart from each other's grip.

The second time was when they were leaving for college. Cutbank and Tuley knew what she did not, that they had fought over her. Since early boyhood, they had imagined themselves in love with Colleen Driscoll. It had gotten to be a habit with them.

That had been the hardest, fairest, bloodiest fight that Chinook had ever seen. Now she looked at their set faces and dreaded the coming conflict.

Bill Murdock, big as a grizzly, cool, clumsy, powerful. Buck, lithe and active as a panther, with the build of a middle-weight and well scienced in the art of self-defense. There would be no quitting on either side. No words wasted as they beat one another into bloody, bruised pulps.

"Cutbank! Tuley!" she appealed to the two cow-punchers. "Stop them!"

"Yes'm," came the uneasy consent. "How?"

Then a big-framed, white-mustached man shoved his way through the fast-gathering mob that blocked the front door. Pinned to his vest was a sheriff's badge.

At his heels strode a tall, raw-boned negress clad in overalls and a man's shirt. On her head was a battered slouch hat. "Ike Niland," came in a relieved tone from the bartender, "and Fancy Mary. Them hot-headed young fools'll shore calm down now."

"What's the rip?" rumbled Ike, the sheriff, pushing between the two would-be combatants.

"Lawzee, honey," came Fancy Mary's soft drawl, almost a crooning song as she put a long arm about Colleen's shoulders. "Them young skalawags orter be hoss-whipped, makin' you-all cry. You come along with ol' Mary, missy."

She half led, half carried the protesting girl through the side door marked "Ladies' Entrance."

"Now, boys" — the old sheriff smiled in a fatherly manner — "what the dickens ails yuh?"

"Somebody killed a lot of Murdock's lousy sheep," Cutbank put in, when neither Buck nor Bill spoke up. "He aims tuh blame Buck an' the Rollin' M spread."

"Figgered that was it. Yo're shore wrong, Bill. You'd know yuh was, if yuh wasn't on the prod. I don't know who done it, but I bet all I got them two outfits never had a hand in it. That ain't Driscoll's ner Rawlins' way uh fightin' an' you know it, young feller. Now you two young colts shake hands an' we'll all have a drink."

"On the house," came the bartender's hearty seconding. "Bury the hatchet, gents."

Bill Murdock grinned feebly. "I suppose I was somewhat hasty, Buck. I lied when I called you a sneaking coward. Knew I lied when I said it. Shake?"

"You're damn right, Bill. Now let's get the drift of this business."

"Somebody," explained the young sheep-man, "cut our new drift fence on Alkali Creek. Fifteen miles of new fence, all five wires cut between every post. The herder was camped on the creek and heard his dogs bark in the night. Thinking it was coyotes, he stepped to the door of his sheep wagon and fired his Winchester into the air.

"They were on him like a pack of wolves. Tarred and feathered him, killed the dogs and a lot of sheep, then fired his wagon. They wore gunny-sack masks, but he recognized Bob Doran of the 7UP and the two Listen boys

28

from the Rolling M."

"I fired Jeff and Jake Listen two weeks ago," said Cutbank. "And it wasn't more'n ten days ago that Bob Doran hit me fer a job. Old man Dave Rawlins had fired him fer usin' a spade bit on a bronc."

A man who stood well back in the crowd wormed his way out and on to the street. He headed for a building with a sign over the door. The sign read, "Creighton Marley, Real Estate. Let me Locate your Homestead."

"Who, then," asked Bill Murdock, "had it in for our outfit bad enough to cut that fence?"

"Perhaps it was someone that wanted to cause trouble between the sheep and cattle outfits," suggested Buck in a low tone. "The country's full of nesters that look onery enough to pull such a deal."

"Two of 'em located in our horse pasture," added Bill. "Tough-looking babies. If they're farmers, I'm a preacher. Five of the skunks near the Driscoll home ranch and I heard they had made the crack that it would go hard with the man or gang of men from the cow outfits that crossed their lines. It looks to me like they were grafters. Hoboes that moved in here, hoping we'd give 'em a piece of change to move out.

"They all pack guns and have whisky on their places. There's trouble coming, Buck. You may be kept busy, Ike."

"Say," asked Buck, "how come you aren't trailing the Nighthawk, Ike?"

"They sent five men down from Helena on a special train to take up the chase. Wired me to organize a posse and have 'em ready. Uh course, by the time them five man hunters got here, the trail was shore hard tuh foller account uh the rain washin' out the sign. Now they're sashayin' around the hills like so many stray sheep, most uh the nesters in the posse plumb scared tuh death fer fear they'll jump one uh the Nighthawk's men."

"Who is this Creighton Marley, Ike?" asked Buck.

"He's the dressed-up dude that's locatin' these here nesters on every pinnacle in this section uh the State. Some of it's good land. Some of it won't raise nothin' but greasewood an' boulders, jackass rabbits an' tumbleweeds. They say Marley's loanin' money right an' left to 'em, takin' fust mortgages on their places. Must be loco."

Cutbank and Tuley exchanged a meaning look and Cutbank jogged Buck's elbow.

"Hadn't we better drink this here likker afore she gits stale, Buck?" he suggested.

"The boss'll be showin' up directly," added Tuley Bill.

"And we'll all catch hell again, eh? Here's how. Then let's get old Tex buried." Buck raised his glass.

"One drink to old Tex, eh, Ike? To the Tex we used to know, when we all bucked blizzards and stood night guard together. He didn't have a preacher to pilot him across the Big Divide, but I reckon that when he came to where the trail forked, he took the upper one. I know a lot of God's laws that Tex Arnold never broke."

It was an unobtrusive little procession that bore the rough pine box through a drizzling rain to the graveyard just beyond the town. Cutbank and Tuley, Bill and Buck carried the rude coffin. Carried it on a sling made of their lariats, their horses traveling at a slow walk. Ike Niland rode in the lead, his yellow slicker buttoned tight. He carried a package in his arms.

Beside the grave which Cutbank and Tuley had dug, they paused. Cutbank kicked aside an empty whisky flask and gave Tuley a quick look. Then they lowered the coffin.

Ike took the burlap covering from his package, revealing two huge bunches of red roses. No cards accompanied these floral offerings. "From Colleen Driscoll and Fancy Mary," the sheriff said in a low tone. Then he dropped the flowers in on top of the pine box.

A week ago, had Ike Niland met Tex Arnold, they would have burned gunpowder. Now he was paying last tribute, not to a fallen enemy, but to a friend with whom he had once ridden along dim trails.

These men who stood bareheaded in the rain had, in burying Tex Arnold, cow-puncher, forgotten Tex, the outlaw. It was their way. They knew no other.

Mazie West would not have understood. Nor

would the thousands of Mazie Wests and John Wests whose shiny barb wire was being strung across Montana's open range, have understood. How could they who had never ridden all night under the stars, singing to a sleeping beef herd, or fought white death in a blizzard, or grinned carelessly at death in a hundred violent forms, how could they understand the great hearts of the men who looked upon them as invaders?

In the days that were to come, Ike Niland, enforcing that law according to his lights and the words of his oath of office, was to find himself on the side of those invaders. Something of that thought must have come into his mind now as he gazed across that open grave to a group of men who were tacking barb wire to freshly set fence posts, for his lean jaws set till the muscles bulged, albeit there was a mistiness in his eyes.

"So long, Tex, ol' pard," said Cutbank. And the wet sod thudded dully into the grave, crushing the red roses.

CHAPTER III

SQUATTER ON THE 7UP SPRINGS

My ceiling the sky, my floor is the grass,
My music the bawling of steers as they pass;
My books are the brooks, my sermons the
*   stones,*
My parson the wolf on his pulpit of bones.
                    — Old Cowboy Ballad.

Colonel Bob Driscoll sat on the long veranda, his huge arm-chair tilted against the log wall so that his scarred, white-bearded face caught the last rays of the setting sun. Every evening, the weather permitting, the blind cow-man sat thus.

Beyond, on a grassy knoll, stood a little white cross. A white wooden cross that marked the grave inside its picket fence. There lay his wife, the only woman, save his daughter, who had ever seen old Colonel Driscoll's softer side.

Years before, a renegade band of Sioux had quit their reservation and along their blood-spattered trail lay the Driscoll ranch. They had stolen a bunch of his horses, killed his wife, and left him for dead, an ugly hatchet gash across his eyes. But Bob Driscoll was destined to live and care for the infant daughter the marauders had overlooked.

A wild young cowboy, whom Fate was later to turn into an outlaw known as the Nighthawk, took the trail of these renegades, ten in number. He rode into Fort Musselshell five weeks later with four prisoners. Tied to his saddlestrings were six Sioux scalps. That was one of the reasons that no cow-puncher ever rode in a posse that was after this quick-shooting, hard-riding Nighthawk.

The blind cattleman's quick cars caught the thud of a horse's hoofs.

"That you, Colleen?"

"It sure is, Dad. A day late getting back from Chinook, but couldn't make it sooner. I'll be back as quick as I get Sapphire taken care of."

She gave her blue roan horse his head and rode to the barn.

She was back in a few minutes, perched on one arm of his chair, loading her father's pipe.

"Yuh made the loan at the Valley Bank without trouble, I reckon?" he asked, when he had lit his pipe.

"No, Dad," came the reluctant reply, "I didn't. I was going to lie to you about it and keep you from worrying, but I knew you'd drag the truth from Cutbank or Tuley. I couldn't make the loan, Dad."

"Wasn't old Hank there?"

"He was. So was that snippy son-in-law of his."

"Snodgrass?"

"Howard Snodgrass. Silk shirt, creased pants,

English shoes, and cigarette-holder. The idiot, I felt sorry for Uncle Hank. He's simply bullied to death by his wife and daughter and Howard. They were very cordial, had me to dinner, and I played with Maud's two youngsters. But the weather got cool when I mentioned money. Uncle Hank looks worried, too. Howard says they've loaned to the limit and no prospects of getting any money on the notes they hold.

"I reckon we shouldn't blame 'em, Dad. If we have a dry summer, as we did last year, beef will be in poor shape. The market shows no sign of bettering either. I'm having White Cloud's bunch rounded up and the bronc fighters will get to work on those three we halter-broke and had to turn loose. There's fifty-odd head of those White Cloud broncs and we may be able to turn them at a decent price. I —"

Colleen broke off suddenly, biting her lip.

"What's the matter, honey?" He groped for her hand and held it.

"I got an offer for White Cloud," Colleen said firmly. "That horseman from Dakota will give a thousand cash for him. It'll help pay round-up expenses."

"Uh-huh," grunted her father, and slowly pulled her into his lap. His hand, passing gently across the girl's cheek, came away wet.

"Uh-huh, we could sell White Cloud. But we won't. If a daughter uh mine was tuh sell a hoss that she'd raised on a bottle an' growed up with, I reckon I'd jest nacherally take that young 'un

35

an' whup her. He's sired some uh the best ponies that ever turned a cow er brung a drunk cow-puncher home of a snowy night. He's about plumb useless now fer a stallion, bein' as we need new stud stock, but ol' White Cloud'd make a shore good pension hoss, hangin' aroun' the lower pasture."

Colleen showered his scarred face with kisses, then nestled in his arms like a child.

"It's grand of you, Daddy, to let me keep that white elephant. I hated to see him leave his range. We could trade him to Dave Rawlins for Stardust and he'd be happy over on the 7UP range."

"I'd sooner see my hoss dead than eatin' 7UP grass!" snorted old Driscoll, bristling like an old timber wolf. "Yuh know dang' well I'd shoot that Dave Rawlins on sight if I could see tuh line my sights."

"I forgot," fibbed Colleen, smiling to herself.

It had been five years since those two hot-headed old stockmen had quarreled over some trivial thing. The bitterness in Bob Driscoll's heart had grown with his months of loneliness. The Driscoll ranch house seemed strangely void without the booming laughter of Dave Rawlins, who had visited his old friend Bob with faithful regularity, winter and summer, until that quarrel. More than once, old man Dave Rawlins had made overtures of peace, but the fiery old Colonel would have none of it.

"Buck's back home. Fired from college, Dad."

"That's where the college was plumb fortu-
nate an' Montana loses. Keep that young rascal
off my range er I'll have him run off like a sheep-
killin' dog, hear me? When I punched cows, they
wouldn't let a young idiot like him drag a rope
acrost the range. We was cow-men, not college-
learnt hellions that think shootin' up towns an'
ridin' into saloons is punchin' cows."

"When was Ike here, Daddy?"

"Last week. What's that got tuh —"

"You and Ike sure do enjoy gossiping about
Buck Rawlins and Bill Murdock and the other
young men that ride this range," laughed the
girl. "You thought Buck was about the fastest
cowboy north of the Pecos until you and Dave
Rawlins quarreled. You won't let Bill light
within shooting distance of the Rolling M because his dad raises sheep. Dad, if you keep on
this way, you'll be a cranky old man."

"And you are gittin' dadblamed sassy, young
lady. Yuh ain't too old fer me tuh spank and
I'll —"

"You'll weaken, you wonderful old fraud.
You're like one of these summer storms. All
thunder and no lightning. Besides, if you spank
me you don't get a word out of me about the
train hold-up."

"Eh?" snorted old Driscoll. "What's that?"

"The Nighthawk struck again at the railroad.
Second time in the last year. Gosh, that man's a
good hater, Dad."

"He figgers he has cause tuh be. From a kid,

37

he was stubborn thataway. They'll cut him down one uh these days, pore devil."

"They got Tex Arnold. Remember Tex?"

"Soft voice? Usta sing Sam Bass of an evenin' at camp? That the gent? Wore bell spurs?"

Thus did the blind cattleman, out of his life of everlasting night, tabulate a man whose face he had never seen. Colleen nodded.

"I rode as far as the Red Barn with Mary," Colleen went on. "She didn't invite me to stop there, so I came on. But I'd have given a new hat to get a look at the man who owned a sweat-marked bay gelding that was in Mary's corral."

"Mary," said old Driscoll sternly, "is as good a negro as I ever knowed, and down in Texas, where I was raised among 'em, I've knowed some shore white 'uns. The only thing black about Mary is her hide, honey. But don't never go visitin' the Red Barn, savvy? It's her business if she runs a saloon an' stage station an' lets some hard citizens hang aroun' there. Mary kin handle 'em. But it ain't no place fer a girl."

"I've never stopped there, Dad. Mary never would let me. But I'm dying to get a look at the Nighthawk's face and I bet a new pair of boots that was his horse in the corral. A man that can hate as bitterly as he hates the railroad people must make a grand lover."

"If I didn't know you was as level-headed as a well broke work mule, I'd be scared yuh'd try tuh run off with some gent like that. Yuh talk like a school kid but act like an old hand at a round-up."

"Level-headed as an old mule. Ain't yuh the flatterer, though?" Colleen's bantering tone belied a look of wistful yearning that filled her eyes.

She was gazing across the distant hills, bathed in the gold-dust of sunset, toward the 7UP ranch. When a girl has to manage an eighty-thousand-acre ranch, it leaves her little time for romance. Colleen, fresh as a full blown rose, yearned for that romance that was her birthright.

She looked down at her shabby riding breeches and dusty boots.

It had been weeks since she had worn any of the flimsy, fluffy frocks that hung in her closet. Now, swept by a quick wave of loneliness for lights and laughter and gay crowded places, she bit her lip to keep back the tears.

It had not been so bad before her father had quarreled with Dave Rawlins. Buck came often with his father and the two youngsters had some good times dancing to phonograph music and playing heated games of "rummy" with Cutbank and Tuley Bill. Colleen had always discarded her overalls for skirts in honor of their "company." Now, since old Bob Driscoll's fiery temper had driven away his friends, this girl was exiled with a blind man who lived in his past mostly, seeing only with the eyes of memory into those bygone days.

"Level-headed as an old work mule!"

With a quick, abrupt movement, Colleen was on her feet.

"What's wrong, honey?" asked her father.

"Wrong? Wrong? Nothing, Daddy." She fought to keep the bitterness from her voice. "I'm going in to get ready for dinner. I want to see what I look like in a skirt."

She gave his flannel-clad shoulders a quick squeeze and kissed him on top of the head.

"Maud Snodgrass was saying she hadn't seen me in anything but pants for the past year. She thinks I'm a mess, anyhow, and because I jolly her smirking fashion-plate of a husband, she's jealous and makes comical cracks about my clothes. I suppose I did smell like a stable and probably brought her a few fleas from the hounds. But we should worry, eh, Dad?"

Old Driscoll snorted angrily. "I'd like to see her run a cow outfit like you do."

"Exactly, Dad," came Colleen's dry reply. "That's the idea, to a gnat's ear."

A few minutes later there came the splashing of water and the girl's voice raised in frivolous song.

"Most girls," mused old Bob Driscoll, filling his pipe, "would hate a ranch. But 'honey' loves it as much as I do, the dadblamed li'l rascal. Now what's that a-comin' yonder?"

Along the road, kicking up a dust cloud, came an automobile. It snorted to a halt and from it emerged a man in tailored riding clothes.

"Mr. Driscoll," he announced himself, "I'm Marley. Creighton Marley. Dropped in for a minute to have a little chat about that three hundred and twenty acres of bottom land you hold on Sand Creek. It is, at present — ah — I say, now!"

Marley was staring at a vision that had suddenly appeared in the doorway. A vision of cherry red chiffon. No butterfly, emerging from its dusty cocoon, ever made a more startling appearance.

On several occasions, Creighton Marley had met Colleen Driscoll. Always, she had worn shabby riding clothes, a man's Stetson, and flannel shirt. Once he had met her at the Snodgrass home and in comparison to the pink and white Maud, who was attractive in a soft, polished-mannered way, Colleen had seemed horribly shabby.

Now, eyes wide with astonishment, Marley was having no little difficulty in regaining his poise. Creighton Marley prided himself on his poise, as he prided himself on his other fancied or real attractive qualities.

"How do you do, Mr. Marley. Dad, this is the gentleman whom I told you I met at the Snodgrass dinner a few weeks ago," she explained as she gave the visitor a cool, brown hand and motioned him to a chair.

"The land shark?" growled Driscoll. Marley squirmed.

"The man who opened the land office, Dad. Sharks are either fish or pawnbrokers. You'll stay to *supper*, Mr. Marley. It's supper, not dinner, out here in the uncouth West, you know."

Marley smiled uneasily. He had a premonition

that the invitation hinted of a threat to repay him for his rudeness to this girl that evening at the Snodgrass home.

He mentally kicked himself for being all sorts of a fool. This girl was a beauty. A rearing, tearing, howling beauty and he had been such an idiot to judge her at those previous meetings by her clothes.

Perhaps, if he stayed, and played the game as only Creighton Marley could, he could turn the handsome curly head of this ranch girl.

"Thanks, awfully," he nodded. "I'd be glad to stay."

Something that sounded like a snort came from old Bob Driscoll. Marley reddened.

He reached for a cigarette.

"What became of the flip little blond you had in tow when I saw you in Chinook, Mr. Marley?" Colleen smiled.

"Some dizzy blond, what?" chuckled Marley. "Used to be a chorus lady. I left her at her new farm. She insisted on staying out there in a tent until her cabin is built. Attractive, after a rather loud, crude manner, but common as mud. Some of her grammatical errors made one feel like shrieking."

Another faint, snorting sound came from old Driscoll, who rather prided himself on the fact that he had never gone to school in his life.

"Colleen," he rumbled, without moving his head, which was turned from them, "suthin's afire."

"I think," she replied, "that it's Mr. Marley's cigarette that you smell."

"Ever try chawin' tuh break yorese'f uh them ready-rolled things, young feller?"

"One of Dad's stock jokes," smiled Colleen sweetly. "He always pulls it on every one. Where did you locate the blond?"

"Above the Rawlins ranch, on the creek. Lovely spot."

"But the 7UP owns every foot of the creek, including the spring?"

"So Rawlins imagined," nodded Marley. "But there's been a mistake made in the old filing. Mazie West's three hundred and twenty takes in the 7UP spring and first water rights."

"What?" Old Driscoll was on his feet, fists knotted. "Yuh say somebody squatted on the 7UP spring? It kain't be done!"

"But it has been done," insisted the land man coolly.

"Young feller," said old Bob Driscoll hotly, "I was with Dave Rawlins when he took that big spring, some years afore you was born. Hester Rawlins, Dave's wife, planted with her own hands, the roses that grows at the edge. That was after me'n Dave an' two cowboys stood off a Gros Ventres war party on that spot.

"I don't give a hoot what the land office maps say, Marley, savvy? All I know is that Dave an' Hester Rawlins crossed many a hundred mile uh Injun country tuh git to that spot and they settled there. Yuh ner no other damned slick

43

tongued skunk kin cheat ol' Dave outa it. Now git in that rattlin' thing that brung yuh here an' git offen my place. I've heered a plenty about you an' yore ways uh doin' business, yuh dang dude mannered he-woman! Honey, fetch me my scatter gun."

Marley, red and hot with anger, looked at the girl. Colleen was laughing.

"It's lucky for you that you are an old man and a blind man," snapped Marley. "I'm not in the habit of being insulted."

"It's lucky fer you, young feller, that I'm blind. Otherwise I'd quirt yuh offen the place. Git, afore I set the houn's on yuh!"

"Look here," blurted Marley. "Nobody can use that tone with me and get away with it. I won't stand for it."

"Just what," inquired Colleen easily, "do you intend doing about it, Mr. Marley? If you get within arm's reach of Dad, he'll just simply pick you apart to see what makes you run. You came here, primarily, to tell Father that those roughnecks that you located across the ridge on Sand Creek are there to stay and that the law will punish any one who puts those five men off their homesteads.

"You are armed. Your chauffeur is armed and ugly-looking. You intended to bully a blind man, didn't you, Mr. Marley? Then you saw me in this dress and thought you'd go at it from a new angle. Flatter the poor little ranch girl who dresses up to eat her evening meal with her blind

44

daddy. Kid her along with your manners of a polished gentleman, and later make love to her. I know your sort. I know it very well."

Marley, his handsome face suffused with anger, stood with clenched fists. He looked as if he might even strike the girl whose eyes blazed like angry sapphire lights. While in his rawhide-seated armchair, old Bob Driscoll sat motionless, his face stern and hard, save for the ghost of a smile that played about his straight-lipped mouth.

He was proud of this daughter of his who was a son as well as a daughter when need be. Colleen could hold her own in any company and against odds, to boot. Bob Driscoll's lack of sight had sharpened his other senses and at times his perception of things going on about him was almost uncanny.

"Two of the boys are just riding in, Mr. Marley," said Colleen. "If I should happen to call them over, I'm afraid you'd get mussed up some and your plug-ugly driver would get some of the toughness drug out of him. The road you followed to get here will take you back. Use it, please. And your next visit will be construed as plain trespassing and treated as such. Good day, Mr. Marley."

"I'm not letting this insult pass," spoke Marley, his voice thick with anger. "I'll make you and your father pay for this."

"Spoken like the villain of the piece, word for word. Now bow yourself out of the scene, please.

Dad's getting restless."

Old Bob Driscoll had begun to lift himself from his comfortable arm-chair. In one hand he gripped a heavy walking-stick.

Marley turned abruptly and strode back to his car. Colleen, her hand on her father's arm, watched the car rattle away in a cloud of dust.

"The young coyote," growled old Bob Driscoll.

"Yes. Coyote is the word, Dad. But even coyotes can make trouble."

And Bob Driscoll's sightless eyes could not see the troubled look on her face.

CHAPTER IV

LAW OF THE COLT

Give me one more day of the old free land,
Uncursed by a road or a barbed-wire strand;
A horse to ride and the sight, as I pass
Of a thousand horns rising out of the grass,
And I'll push back my chair and lay down my
*   hand!*
                                    — The Old Cowman.

Dave Rawlins — tall, leathery, snow-white hair
and mustache, and a pair of keen gray eyes that
looked from under shaggy brows. His flannel shirt
needed mending, his overalls were warped to the
shape of long, hard muscled legs. The silver
mounted spurs on his glove fitting boots jingled a
little as he strode to the door of the 7UP bunk-
house to greet the young cow-puncher who stood,
hesitating a little, smiling uncertainly.

"Howdy, Buck," said Dave Rawlins gravely.
"Welcome home." He held out a strong brown
hand.

"How are yuh, Dad?" Buck gripped the prof-
fered hand and the two men, father and son,
their eyes on a level, eyes of the same gray,
looked at one another. Then a sudden smile
wrinkled the leathery face of the old cow-man.

He swung his left fist into Buck's ribs with a force that made the younger man grunt. He slapped Buck between the shoulders and poked a thumb in his ribs.

"So they fired yuh out uh that fancy college, did they?" He chuckled. "Couldn't make a dude outa the material they had tuh work with, huh? What did yuh do, yuh young idiot? Shoot the lights outa their school-house?"

"Not quite that bad. I spanked a professor for calling me dumb. But he was right, at that. I wasted your money trying to get educated, I'm a bum, Dad."

"Yo're a good cow-hand," said Dave Rawlins grimly, "and we need good cow-hands right now. I was goin' to wire for yuh to come home, but you beat me to it. The boys are rearin' to see yuh. Come on in."

Buck stepped into the bunk-house. There was the odor of tobacco smoke and leather and arnica. The next moment Buck was shaking hands with the cow-punchers who hailed him with profane comradeship. For on the big cow ranch there is no class distinction between employer and the men who draw wages. They are of the same breed, with the same faults and virtues, the same standard of living. They laugh at the same jokes and smoke from the same sack of tobacco.

Buck was hoorawed by the cowboys about having been away to a dude school back East. They fired questions at him and he gave them replies that brought gusts of laughter.

It was half an hour before Buck and his father got away and walked together toward the corrals. There, with backs against the log corral, squatting on spurred boot heels, they talked.

"I didn't seem to fit in back there at the university, Dad. They didn't talk my language and I couldn't ketch on to their ways. It was like being in prison. I'm not making excuses, understand. I had no business being fired. You'd spent good money to send me there."

"You earned the money, son. Supposin' we forgit it? I'm proud tuh have yuh home, that's all. Mebbyso, ridin' out here, you seen what's goin' on. Buck, things is beginnin' to tighten. Nesters are swarmin' in by the hundreds, locatin' dry land farms on every ridge and in every coulee. They're stringin' barb wire acrost the old round-up trails and plowin' up the old bed grounds. They're a-turnin' Montana grass side down.

"It's the finish here of the cattleman. And while I'd bet my last bottom dollar that they'll starve out in five years, still they're stickin' their plowshare plumb into the heart of the cow country. Even if they're doomed to fail, still that don't help us. We gotta pull stakes and drift yonderly."

"You mean sell out here, Dad?"

"Sell out?" Dave Rawlins' eyes hardened. "We can't sell. Nobody will buy. Without free range, there's no money in this cow business to-day.

49

And the nesters are locatin' every acre of free range. Range that the big outfits have claimed since before you was born is no longer ours. Even some of the land we thought we had title to ain't ours. These smart land locaters have looked up old records and found where the titles are not clear. Without givin' us a chance to clear them titles, they're puttin' in these squatters and homesteaders. Some of the homesteaders are honest farmers, poor devils. Others are a bad lot, little better than tramps."

"There'll be trouble, then?"

"Looks thataway, Buck. Us old timers ain't goin' to run from a pack like that. We crossed the plains in the early days, fought off Injuns and drouth and blizzards to trail cattle here from Texas. We raised our families here. You was born on this ranch, Buck. Yore mother is buried here. We've had good times and hard times together, us old timers. It shore hurts to see this old country cluttered up with barb wire.

"We're too old, most of us, to hunt new range. We'd always figgered on spendin' our last days here, peaceful and happy, while you younger boys taken up the job where we laid down our hands. But I reckon it ain't in the cards. We gotta go on fightin' to hold what's been ours fer forty years."

Dave Rawlins looked out across the hills that were bathed in the last yellow light of sunset. Beyond the hills, covered with spring grass, the blue peaks of the Little Rockies, ragged against the setting sun, a gigantic monument dedicated to the pioneer. There in those mountains that great general, Chief Joseph, had made his last stand. There, in his surrender to General Miles, he had made that tragic speech that has gone down in the history of Indian warfare in the West:

"From where the sun now stands, I fight no more against the white man!"

So, on a bright October morning in 1877, did the great Chief Joseph give the vast prairies and the ragged mountains into the keeping of the pioneer cattlemen. And from that day those cattlemen had held it without the aid of barb wire. Their herds grazed on an unfenced domain. Here they made their homes, reared their families, lived their years in an open-handed, broad-visioned way, uncramped by petty laws, settling their problems with scant aid from outsiders.

They have been called, among other hard names, cattle kings, cattle barons, hard handed autocrats, those owners of Montana's free range. If they were hard, then it was because the need demanded it, and their hardness was the hardness of tempered steel. What could men of weaker stuff have done to build that empire of the West? The weaker men had died along the trail that crossed the plains. Those who survived, both the men and the women, were strong in body, with a courage and tolerance unsurpassed.

Stern men in many ways, yet they were kind of

heart and generous always. No lock barred their door to the stranger. There was food and lodging for the traveler and hay for his horse, nor did they ask a dollar in payment. They asked no man his name or his business. Theirs was a hand held out in friendship to their fellow-man. That hand was never withdrawn until the stranger trespassed on their rights. Then that hand that had so willingly extended could hold a gun. For frontier law was the law of the Colt and the Winchester.

Dave Rawlins was of that stanch breed. He had been one of the Vigilantes who had wiped out the lawless at Last Chance Gulch and Virginia City. He had heard the blood curdling warwhoop of the Sioux. And until now, with the invasion of the nester, he could ride up on the wooded butte behind the horse pasture and claim the land as far as he could see in all directions. Until now, no man, friend or enemy, had ever disputed his claim to that unfenced range.

This fencing of open range was bewildering. Dave Rawlins was hoping that perhaps Buck, who had seen more of civilization, could explain away things that were eating like strong acid into his heart. Perhaps Buck could ease that aching pain of grief. He waited now, through long minutes of silence, for Buck to explain away things that to him were all wrong.

"It all had to come some day, Dad." Buck was also looking across the hills toward the mountains. "That's always the way of things. Frontiers are pushed back. Settlers come and make farms out of the big ranges, and then, after a few years more, towns build up into cities. There are factories and big stores and automobiles traveling the roads where the wagons of the pioneers blazed the way. That's civilization, Dad. That's life. It had to come."

"They come here and squat on my land," said Dave Rawlins without heat. "They butcher my beef, set their dogs on my cattle, run off my horses, steal what they kin lay their hands on. Last week I sent a freight outfit to town fer grub. The boys git stuck in the mud and drop the trail wagon. Two days later they go back to fetch it and find nothin' but the empty wagon. The sons had even took the axle-grease and wrench outa the jockey box. Is that civilization, son?"

"There's thieves among any class of men, Dad."

"Not that kind of a thief. I've knowed road-agents and cattle rustlers and hoss thieves, but none of 'em would rob a wagon stuck in the mud. Not even the lousiest 'breed on the reservation would take stuff he didn't need. He might he'p hisself to a few cans uh corn er a sack uh flour, but he wouldn't gut the whole load. If that's the kind uh folks that's aimin' tuh farm this country, they'll deserve what they'll git."

"I saw Bill Murdock in Chinook," said Buck. "He says that some gents scattered a bunch of their woolies and beat up his herder. Then they burned the sheep wagon. Bob Doran and the two Listen boys was with 'em. Bill jumped me about it. Thought our outfit and some of the Rolling M boys had done it. I'm wondering just how many are in this gang that are getting tough."

"Plenty many, if yuh ask me. And somebody higher up is grub-stakin' 'em."

"That's what I heard, but I didn't hardly believe it. I stopped at Fancy Mary's for dinner. She gave me both ears full while I ate my fried chicken. But her say-so is just what she got from the Nighthawk. He lays it onto the railroad companies. Naturally, he would."

"And mebbyso he's right. For all his hatin', he's got a long sight into things."

"The railroad is instrumental in getting a lot of these settlers in here," admitted Buck, "but they're not petty enough to hire a bunch of toughs to start a thing like that. Nope, Dad, we'll have to look on further. Find out who pays this man Creighton Marley and we'll be getting somewhere."

"Mebby. Mebbyso. Who's that a-comin' yonder in that spring wagon? Looks like that dry lander from over on Big Warm. It is, too."

"That's one of our horses with the empty saddle that he's leadin' behind," said Buck rising. "It's that Cherry horse."

"Joe Phelps rode him away this mornin'. He was goin' over to the reservation to fetch home some stray horses old Set 'em High found over on Peoples Crick. Somethin's wrong, Buck."

In silence Buck and his father waited for the farmer, a big red-faced, blue-eyed Swede, to drive up.

"Howdy, Nelson," said Dave Rawlins. "Where'd yuh find that horse?"

Carl Nelson nodded toward something in his wagon covered by a tarp.

"One of your men, Rawlins. I found him at the gravel crossing up above my homestead. He's dead. Shot in the back. His horse was tied to a tree near there. There's been black murder done."

A 7UP cow-puncher was dead. Murdered. Blood had been spilled and that spilled blood was as if the nesters had declared open warfare.

The gray eyes of Dave Rawlins were hard and merciless as they surveyed the nester who had fetched home the body of Joe Phelps.

"Nelson," he said bluntly, "how much do you know about the killing?"

The big farmer returned the cattleman's stare. "Nothing. I was on my way home. My team shied at something in the brush at the creek crossing. I investigated and found the dead cowboy. The brand on his horse told me he was one of your men so I brought the body here."

"The crossing's about a mile above yore place. Anybody at your place hear a shot?"

"There was nobody home at my place, Rawlins. My wife and two daughters are in Chinook filing on their homesteads."

Dave Rawlins stepped over to the wagon. He

lifted the tarp and looked at the dead man beneath, then gently dropped the cover again. Now he picked up a shot-gun from the wagon bed. Nelson scowled, but said nothing as the cowman broke the weapon and sniffed the twin barrels.

"Ain't you the farmer they call 'Deacon'?"

"I am. By callin', I'm a minister of the gospel."

"Hmm. Yo're the first sky-pilot I ever knowed that packed a gun."

"The gun does not belong to me," said the big farmer. "Are you trying to connect me with this murder?"

"I'm tryin' to find out why Joe Phelps was killed and who killed him. Here's yore gun. Keep it. Joe wasn't killed by a shot-gun, no how. I was just wonderin' why a parson went around with a gun in his wagon."

"If you want the truth about the gun," said Deacon Carl Nelson, his blue eyes bright with fire, "I took it away from a neighbor of mine for fear he might use it to kill certain cowboys who have been annoying my two daughters with their unwelcome attentions. My oldest girl is promised in marriage to an honest, sober, God-fearing farmer. Twice, while I have been gone, these ruffians, drunk and profane of manner, have ridden to my place. My wife and daughters have become badly frightened.

"Louise, my eldest daughter, foolishly confided her fears to Eric Swanson, her future husband. Eric, being young and hot-tempered, rashly threatened to shoot the next man who annoyed them. To prevent bloodshed, I took away Eric's only weapon."

"Who were these cowboys that bothered yore women-folks?" asked Dave Rawlins grimly.

"One of them rode a horse branded 7UP. Eric met them once. I don't know their names."

"My men all have orders to stay away from every nester's place. I'll fire the first 7UP man that opens a scissor-bill's gate. Either this Eric lied or I've got snakes on my pay-roll. And I don't know of a man on my ranch I can't trust."

"Eric is not a liar, Rawlins. He said one of the men rode a 7UP horse."

"The horse might have been stolen," Buck put in. "Hadn't we better unload poor old Joe?"

Father and son lifted the cowboy's body from the spring wagon. Nelson looked at the cow-man with steady eyes, when Dave came back from the bunk-house where they had carried the corpse. "Rawlins, I am afraid this is the beginning of something very serious. This may precipitate trouble."

"I dunno about that, Nelson, but whoever killed Joe Phelps is shore gonna pay for it. How much do I owe yuh for fetchin' Joe home?"

"You owe me nothing but your hand in friendship, Rawlins."

Dave Rawlins shook his head. "When I'm satisfied in my own mind that yo're right, I'll shake hands. Not till then. We didn't ask you nesters to come onto our range. You don't fit in with what we call Montana. When men like you begin to clutter up the country, us cow folks has to move on. Buck says that's the way uh things, and mebbyso he's right. But just now, while us old timers is swallerin' the pill, she tastes almighty bitter. If I shook hands now, I'd be lyin' to you and to myse'f."

"I think I understand," said the farmer, running a calloused hand through the corn-colored hair that was generously sprinkled with gray. "I'll wait, Rawlins. I have always tried to be patient, I will pray for the day to come when the farmers and the cattlemen shall be friends."

Dave Rawlins smiled faintly.

"That day is too far ahead fer me to ketch sight of, Deacon. Will yuh stay for supper?"

"I'm afraid I can't, thanks, under the circumstances. But before I go, I'd like you to believe that I will do all in my power to bring the murderer of that cowboy to justice."

"What if yore Eric feller is the one?"

"If Eric Swanson killed that man, he will give himself up to the law. But I know that Eric is innocent, because whoever did the crime is a coward and Eric is no coward. Good day to you, Rawlins."

"So-long, Nelson. You talk like a white man, darned if yuh don't. Still, the worst trimmin' I ever got in a hoss trade was from a slick talkin' camp meetin' preacher down in Kansas. So, outside uh Brother Van and Father De Smet, both old timers here, I never took much stock in sky-pilots. Neither one uh them is hoss traders. Well, good luck to yuh, anyhow, Deacon. And we're obliged to yuh for fetchin' Joe Phelps home. Joe was a mighty fine boy."

Dave Rawlins watched the farmer drive away into the dusk. Then he turned and walked slowly back to the bunk-house. Tall, stiff-backed, stern-visaged, uncompromising. Shoved in the waistband of his overalls was an old cedar-handled six-shooter. Buck met him just outside the bunkhouse door.

"One of the boys is going to town for the sheriff, Dad. Joe would want to be buried here on the ranch, I reckon. As I came along the road, I saw a tent pitched near the big springs. Who is camped there?"

"Nobody as I know of, Buck."

"I thought I saw Marley's car leaving there. I'm riding over to see if that crook has had the gall to locate one of his ignorant nesters there at the spring. It don't seem likely, but I'm riding over."

"That spring belongs to us, Buck. Nobody kin locate there."

"I know that. I'll move 'em on."

"Go careful, son. No ruckus, mind."

"I'll keep my head, Dad, don't worry."

Dave Rawlins rightly guessed that Buck's primary reason for riding the five miles to the big spring known as 7UP Springs, was to ride off something of the grief he felt over Joe's death. Joe had worked for the Rawlins outfit for ten years, and had taught Buck many things that a cowboy must learn. Buck had always been mighty fond of Joe Phelps.

So it was with a heavy weight in his heart that Buck Rawlins, riding a fresh horse, rode through the purple dusk to the lighted tent pitched at the 7UP Springs. Mingled with that grief was resentment against the nesters.

But there was nobody inside the tent, nobody to give reply to his quiet-voiced, "Hello, there!"

Buck shifted his weight to one stirrup and his hand dropped to the butt of his six-shooter. It might be an ambush of some sort. Then a woman's voice, raised in a cry of startled fear, made him start. The cry came from a hundred yards away, where the wild rose bushes grew in a sweet scented thicket.

"Help! Oh, help!"

And a man's gruff voice, blotting out the girl's. "Shut up, you little fool!"

Buck jumped his horse into motion. A few moments and he was on the ground, jerking roughly at the bulk of a man who held a struggling, fighting girl in his arms.

The man let go the girl in khaki camping clothes and smashed a heavy fist into Buck's face.

"Right back at yuh," gritted Buck through split lips, and he swung a clean hook into the bigger man's mid-section. He followed the hook with a couple of swift, vicious jabs, then side-stepped the other's bull-like rush. Now he stabbed wicked lefts into the big fellow's face. It was too near dark to see much. But Buck was fighting with a boxer's science, timing every blow.

He was dimly aware of the blond-haired girl in khaki breeches and flannel shirt, as she danced up and down, panting inane encouragement. Now Buck measured the other man. He led the big fellow into a blind rush, balanced himself, and swung a long, swift, accurate left. The man went down like a felled beef as Buck's fist thudded against the point of his jaw. Buck rubbed his bruised knuckles and grinned through a smear of blood.

"I don't know just how you got here, lady, or what you are doing here, but if you'll fade out of sight for about five minutes, I'll give this squatter the good old bum's rush. Then we'll see about getting you to town where you belong."

"Omigosh! The boy bandit in person! The train robbers' stage-manager in a new rôle! With all the vast wide open spaces to pick from, I had to draw something like you for this meller-drammer. Well, it's just some more of my punk luck, that's all. Where's your gang?"

"I left them at the robber's cave picking their teeth with bowie-knives. What in Sam Hill are you doing here, anyhow?"

"I'm homesteading, brother. Can't you tell by my trick costume that I'm a farmerette? I think the boy friend there is coming awake."

"He is." Buck stepped quickly to the side of the man and kicked the fellow's hand away from the gun he was after.

"I'll take the artillery, mister. And I'll give you just about one minute to vamoose. I'm not in a good humor right now and us cow folks are putting a bounty on skunks of your breed, so you'd better hightail it while you're all in one piece."

"Who are you, anyhow?" growled the man, rising. "What right you got to gimme orders?"

"Unless you want worse than you got in the first dose, git!"

The big man lurched toward his horse and climbed stiffly into the saddle.

"You ain't won this yet. I know yuh now. Yo're young Rawlins. No, you and yore old man ain't winnin' much. I'll be back."

"When you come, come heeled. Drag it, you big bum!"

Buck waited until the man had gone, then turned again to the girl. "Who is that big tramp, anyhow?"

"I was about to ask that, myself."

"I'll throw his tent and stuff over in the coulee, then I can take you on to the ranch for to-night. Too late to get you to town to-night."

"The tent is mine," said Mazie West. "I've located here. I've a notion Marley sent that heavy-weight out to see that I wasn't bullied. But the big false alarm was tight as a tick and bent on making moonlight love. I'm all right now, thanks. How late do these wolves and coyotes keep up their dirge?"

"You mean," said Buck slowly, "that Marley

located you here at these springs?"

"He sure did, big boy. And I'm staying located, too."

Buck smiled a little and wiped the blood from his mouth. "We've owned these springs since '81, lady. Marley has located you on the wrong homestead."

"Not according to the map I have from the land-office, he didn't. I'm sticking here till a court injunction or whatever it is, moves me on. You can't bluff me, mister."

"I'm not bluffing you, lady. I'm in no mood for arguing, either. And outside of the fact that the land is ours, you can't stay here."

"Who's running me off? You?"

Buck shook his head. "You're alone here. You're at the mercy of every tough that happens to ride this way. Men like that big hunk of meat that just rode away. You don't savvy just what you're up against. Pack your duds and climb on behind me. I'll take you to the ranch where you'll be safe."

"You don't seem to clutch the big idea, cowboy. I'm staying right here. I got a gun at the tent. I'm not scared. Again, thanks for giving that big sketch the hook. And good night."

"You can't stay here, hang it!"

"Try to put me off and I'll call the law. I know all about the Rawlins outfit. You're in with that gang of outlaws and you think you can run the country. Well, I'm not running. Wrap that up with your tobacco and smoke it. Good night."

Abruptly, she turned away and strode quickly to her tent. Buck reined his horse and rode back toward the ranch. His exasperation gave way to a grin. He admired the girl's grit. Well, he'd fix her.

Back at the ranch Buck routed an undersized, very bald headed, astonishingly weasened old cow-puncher from his blankets. A squeaky volley of picturesque profanity followed the rude awakening.

"Onion," said Buck softly, "I got a great job for yuh. How'd you like to ride herd on a pilgrim girl for a few days? There's a darn fool female camped at 7UP Springs. She thinks she owns it. She's yaller-haired and pretty as a valentine. Honest. All you have to do is sit on the hill and throw lead at anybody that bothers her. It's your job, whether you want it or not. It's the chance of a lifetime for a heart buster like you, Onion."

"Drunk again, are yuh?" complained Onion Oliver. "Go play yore fool jokes on somebody else. I'm sleepy."

"This is no joke, Onion. And if she ain't pretty as a magazine cover, I'll give you my top horse. She's all alone there at her camp. You're to stay far enough off so's not to scare her. Come morning, you might ride down and show her how to make flapjacks. And don't let any of these prowling bad-men hurt her."

It took half an hour of fast talking to convince Onion. But in the end, Buck won him over. But the old rascal would not quit the bunk-house until he had shaved and put on his holiday clothes.

Despite the fact that nature had dealt him an absurd set of features, bowed legs, fallen arches and a shiny bald head, Onion fancied himself quite a cavalier. No Sir Walter Raleigh ever went further along the trail to gallantry than Onion Oliver. His manners were elaborate and courtly. He was the prime favorite of the maiden ladies and youngsters not yet old enough to ride to the country dances with the younger cowboys. To Onion fell the task of escorting the younger sisters and the old maids. He danced with the fat ladies and the oddly assorted wallflowers and his manner toward the beautiful and the ugly was exactly the same.

Dave Rawlins claimed that Onion Oliver had given away more pinto ponies than any ten men in the cow country, and probably Dave was correct. And the cowboys liked to tell the yarn about Onion whipping a drunken miner twice his size because the miner had spoken rudely to some women.

So it came about that Mazie West had a visitor at breakfast-time. A visitor whose skill at making fiapjacks was marvelous. In half an hour the lonely and bewildered girl from the cities and the ridiculous-looking old cow-puncher who had never seen a tall building were stanch friends. Mazie had given the old cow waddie the story of her life. Onion had laughed with her and when the girl had suddenly burst into tears, the old cow-puncher had dried those tears with the silk neckscarf that some luckless 7UP cow-hand would miss sooner or later.

"I got a calico pony and a saddle that'll just fit yuh," he promised her. "I'll fetch over the pony this afternoon."

And when afternoon came, Onion kept his promise. Not only did he bring a pinto horse and a saddle, but he brought a heavily laden pack-horse. Onion pitched camp down the creek and invited Mazie to supper.

"Onion," she told him, "you're an angel, no less. I'm a sea-going sister at cooking over a gas plate, but between you and me I'd starve on my own groceries if I had to cook over a camp-fire. Even if you do work for that Rawlins outfit, you have a heart of gold, studded with diamonds. That pony is as cute as a Chinese duck and you're priceless."

That was the first time any girl had ever kissed him on top of his bald head. Onion Oliver would have killed lions with a bowie-knife in defense of this girl from the smoky cities.

CHAPTER V

RANGELAND "THIRD DEGREE"

Sam Bass was born in Indiana, it was his
*   native home,*
And at the age of seventeen young Sam begun
*   to roam.*
Sam first came to Texas a cowboy for to be —
A kinder hearted fellow you seldom ever see.
                    — Old Cowboy Ballad.

Four men sat around a poker table at Fancy Mary's road ranch. On the table stood a bottle of whisky. In front of each man was a small glass. The tall man with the straight features and the black hair, patched snowy white around the ears, was dividing a stack of yellow backed bank-notes into seven equal piles. From the kitchen came the savory odor of frying chicken and the whisky-husky voice of Mary singing Sam Bass.

"Posses," said a short, heavy-shouldered man with a two weeks' growth of sand-colored whiskers, "is about the foolishest things, regardless. Them bone-heads is millin' all over the Bear Paws right now, like so many unbroke bird dawgs."

"Quit a-runnin' off at the head, Shorty," drawled a lanky man who could never have come from any other State but Texas; "kain't yuh see the boss is bogged down with figgerin'?"

The dark man who was dividing the money smiled a little. He quit sorting the bank-notes and his eyes, hazel colored, neither gray nor brown, took in the other three with an amused and friendly glance. Time had been when this man had been known as Wade Hardin, cowboy. Now they called him the Nighthawk. In spite of the fact that he was as dangerous a man as ever rode the outlaw trail, there was a perceptible softness in his make-up.

"Zeb," he said in a quiet, rather weary tone of voice, "you was closer to Tex Arnold than any of us. It'll be up to you to see that Tex's share goes to his kin-folks."

"There's only a kid sister down yonder, Wade. I'll see she gits it."

The Nighthawk nodded and finished dividing the money. When each man had taken his allotted share, when Zeb had wrapped Tex Arnold's cut in a silk neckscarf and shoved it in his pocket, when the Nighthawk had taken the two odd piles of money and laid them carefully to one side, he reached for the bottle and filled each empty glass.

Even as he finished that ceremony, there came the thud of shod hoofs, outside. Now the jingle of spurs. Muffled voices sounded out in the bar-room. Each man at the table in the card room had a gun in his hand. Four pairs of slitted eyes watched the closed door that led into the short hallway to the saloon.

The door opened, neither slowly nor quickly. And in the open doorway stood a lanky, leathery faced man whose mouth was partly hidden by a drooping red mustache. His left arm had long ago been amputated between the elbow and wrist and in place of the missing forearm and hand was a wooden stump to which was fastened a sharp pointed hook. His greenish eyes surveyed the outlaws with glittering brightness. They relaxed, sheathing their guns.

"Come in outa the draft, Hook," invited the Nighthawk. "What fetches yuh here?"

"Bad news, Nighthawk. There's a big posse headed this way. Mostly farmers, but a good-sized sprinklin' uh tough men that are squattin' on the best land hereabouts. Hired squatters, most likely, gathered because they are hard and will drift on later, relinquishin' their land to some gent that's got plenty of dough to buy 'em off."

"It's the railroads that's hirin' 'em," said the Nighthawk, his voice brittle with sudden anger. "It's the big railroads that shoved these men in here to rob the cow-men. The railroads is payin' these skunks now to hunt me down for the bounty that's on my hide. Let 'em come. I'm ready. A man could kill a hundred of 'em and not git a one worth two-bits Mex money."

"You shore do hate these railroad folks," grinned Hook Jones. "I never heard the story of how come you had it in fer 'em."

"And mebbyso yuh never will learn, Hook. It's

my personal affair. While I live, I'll deal 'em misery. Some day, mebbyso, they'll hang me or shoot me, but while I'm alive, I'll do my best to hamstring 'em. Let 'em bring on their posse. I'm ready."

Hook helped himself to a drink. "Mightn't it be a better idee to run some, just now? Shootin' it out with them imported gents will buy yuh nothin'. There's plenty for us boys to do here, but it has got to be done keerful. A lead th'owin' party here at Mary's ain't doin' nobody but the coroner any good. I come past the 7UP ranch this mornin'. They're plantin' pore ol' Joe Phelps to-day. Joe got murdered yesterday."

"Joe Phelps? Who done it, Hook?"

"*Quién sabe?* He was shot in the back at the gravel crossin' on Big Warm. Dave Rawlins is mighty upset, and so is Buck. It won't take much more to start another war like that 'un we know about over in Wyoming. Me, I'd hate to see it come. I don't want trouble. I'm doin' good over on my little place. The missus ain't ever bin the same since that Wyoming ruckus. The sound of a gun goin' off skeers her somethin' pitiful. She's never fergot how her two brothers was called to the door and shot down. How she drug their bodies inside and held off them devils with the rifle till I come, at daylight. Her hair had bin black as an Injun's till that night. In a month she was white-haired. That's what it done to her. I don't dast pack a gun.

"And she makes Guy, our boy, read her the

70

Bible every evenin'. She killed three men that night and she kain't fergit it. Guy was born with that fear in him. It ain't his fault that he's scared uh guns and is more like a preacher than a cowboy. Boys, that's what the Wyoming cattle war did to my missus and me. I lost my arm there, and I left my name back there. I came here and took up that ranch at Antelope Springs, thinkin' I'd finish out the game plumb peaceful. Now it looks like trouble is a-comin'. When she busts, I'll be with my friends and I'll do my share uh gun totin'. But I reckon it'll kill the missus.

"Gawd knows what it'll do to Guy. He's throwed in with a gal over on Big Warm. Bin courtin' her fer two months. Her daddy is a nester and a sky-pilot to boot. Fust Swedes I ever come up against. I'm a-tellin' you boys all this because I've kep' it corked up inside me too long. Trouble is a-comin' and I'm from a Texican breed that's bin in trouble since the old days when Texas had a flag that showed one lone star. I'll git into it and I'll pay a-plenty fer the pleasure. And what I'm sayin' now I'm a-sayin' to my friends. I got a heap more to lose than you boys have. I'm askin' yuh-all to ride back into the bad-lands and wait a while. Let the posse come here and find only tracks in the dust. When yo're needed, I'll locate yuh."

The Nighthawk nodded. "I reckon we owe you that much, and a heap more, Hook. What you say now, goes. We'll drag it for the breaks. You know the cabin in the scrub pines on Rock

Crick. When we're needed, ride down there and wait till one of us shows up. We're seein' this game through to the last bet."

The others nodded assent. Every man in that room knew Hook Jones for what he had been ten and fifteen and twenty-five years ago. When he had two hands and when his name had not been Jones. When he had been one of that secret fraternity who rode the outlaw trail.

They knew the tale about how he had ridden into Wyoming to help a man who was his friend. How he had done his share of fighting in one of the bloodiest cattle wars this country had ever known. How he had married the sister of the friend who had been killed, and had taken her, half demented, away from the blood-spattered Johnson County.

And they knew how his one and only son Guy, now nearing manhood, was a coward who preferred books to steers, and whose mildness of manner was meek, rather than manly. He devoted much of his time to study and at the country school where the boys and girls of the cow country rode to learn their three R's, Guy Jones was rated far above the others in mentality. He had a decided leaning toward drawing pictures and painting things on cardboard. He had never had a fight with other boys, even when they plagued him without mercy. So they called him a coward.

But there was one who had never called Guy Jones a coward. That one person was Buck

Rawlins. Buck Rawlins, who claimed no virtues, whose manner of living was untamed. Buck Rawlins, the best rider, the fastest roper, the best all-around cow-puncher in the Little Rockies section of the cow country, was Guy Jones's champion. As unalike as black is from white, Buck Rawlins and Guy Jones. And yet, between them, there was a bond of comradeship and understanding.

Hook Jones had tried his best to understand Guy. He was defending the boy now. But the one-armed Texican whose fame as a gun fighter was known from the Pecos to Powder River had always been ashamed of Guy. He could not understand how a son of his, his own flesh and blood, could be timid. And he had laughed with a strange bitterness the day that Buck Rawlins told him that Guy was the bravest boy he had ever known.

"Brave? Buck, that button is scared of his own shadow."

"Is he? I wonder, Hook. I'd like to lay a big bet that some day you'll be mighty proud to claim Guy as a son that has courage a-plenty. I wish I was half the man that Guy is. I'll bet you my best horse against the sorriest thing you ever screwed a hull on that the day will come when you'll say that Guy has you bested for real cold nerve."

"Calls the bet, Buck, and I hope I have to pay it," Hook Jones had said. "My top horse against yourn."

"You will pay it," prophesied Buck Rawlins.

For Buck had seen into the heart of this youngster of the range whose birth had been marked by a fear of guns and bloodshed. Not fear, exactly, but a loathing.

Since he had been old enough to understand, his unfortunate mother had told that oft repeated tale of the Wyoming cattle war. A grisly yarn, too terrible for the ears of a small boy of sensitive nature. And in his boyhood, Guy's nights had been often burdened by horrible dreams of men killing one another.

He felt a great pity for the frail, snowy-haired little woman who was his mother. And there were times when the boy feared his father because he knew that Hook Jones had been a killer.

Later, when the boy became older, he was less afraid of Hook. And Hook tried in every way to win the love and trust of his son.

Hook Jones nor Buck Rawlins dreamed anything of that which was to happen to Guy Jones. Only Guy, Guy and Olga Nelson over on Big Warm, knew of the grave decision that the son of Hook Jones was to make. A decision that took all the courage a man can be blessed with.

Now Hook Jones drank with the Nighthawk and his men, there at Fancy Mary's road ranch. And half an hour later the big, raw-boned negress was alone there at her place. There was no indication that the outlaws had been there. But the posse of men who rode up to Mary's place were ugly and abusive. No legitimate officer of the law accompanied the crowd of men, who were more like an unruly mob than a posse.

For all that her skin was black, that she chewed and smoked a cob pipe or a long cigar, that she wore overalls, tended bar, handled half broken stage horses, drank her whisky clear and could swear like a mule skinner, Mary had the friendship of every cow-man and common cow-hand in the country.

She would ride all day to nurse a sick person. She never turned away a hungry man. She counted no favor too great to do for a friend. Preacher and outlaw, cattleman and horse thief found the same welcome under the sod roof of her log cabin.

"Them outlaws have been here," snarled the burly, rough-voiced man who seemed to be leader of the mob. "Which way did they ride? Talk up, old gal." And he colored his demand with insulting profanity.

"Yuh-all travel 'long, white man," she told him. "Axe me no questions an' yuh'll heah no lies. Go 'long 'bout yo' business an' lemme be."

"Glaum 'er, boys. Tie the black wench up by her thumbs and we'll see what a good quirtin' will do to'rds loosenin' up her lyin' tongue. Tie 'er up."

Mary fought like a black tigress, but she was badly outnumbered.

But even when the rawhide quirt in the hands of the mob leader had ripped her back till her flannel shirt was soaked with blood, she told them nothing.

75

"Go ahead, whup me, yuh cowards. But fo' every welt yuh-all make on my hide, my friends will put ten welts on yo' back."

She was all but unconscious when they rode away, leaving her lying on the floor, moaning through clenched teeth. They had not neglected to help themselves to all the liquor they could carry away. The place was a wreck when they rode off, singing and shouting.

Mary was still lying there an hour later when Buck Rawlins rode up.

With Buck was Tuley Bill Baker of the Rolling M and Tuley Bill's side pardner, Cutbank Carter.

Buck's face was twisted with rage when he heard the pitiful tale Mary told them.

"I reckon, boys," he told Tuley Bill and Cutbank, "that it is just about time we went into action. Your five squatters from over on Sand Creek are in the mob. The big cuss that is roddin' the spread is the one I tangled with at the 7UP Springs. They're a hard lot and they take their orders from this Creighton Marley. Tuley, you and Cutbank get word to Bob Driscoll and the Murdocks and every other big spread within a day's ride of here. I'll get Mary patched up and then I'll ride on back home. Tell Bob Driscoll and the Murdocks and whoever else you can find that we're meeting at the 7UP ranch to-morrow night to have a medicine talk. Now drag it, you two old warthogs."

"How about a little horn uh likker before we

start out on this long circle?"

"He'p yo'se'ves, boys," said Mary. Buck's ministrations and a stiff drink had revived her and she lit her cob pipe. "Buck, step up to the mahogany."

"If it's the same to you all," grinned Buck, "I'll drink water. I'm off the hard stuff."

They stared at him in wonderment. Tuley Bill whispered loudly in Cutbank's ear.

"Either the young hellion's in love er he's bin nibblin' the loco weed. I never thought we'd live to see Buck turn down a drink. Better keep an eye on him, pardner. He'll stand watchin'. That's what these higher educations does to the flowerin' youth uh the country.

"Mary, I'll take about three fingers uh yore best ridin' an' fightin' likker. We got bad hosses to ride and mean hombres to lick. Can't do it on plain water. Water is good fer alfalfa fields and to swim cattle acrost, but fer internal use it lacks lubricatin' qualities. Pore Buck. He'll be ailin' with rheumatism uh the gizzard if he keeps garglin' that water stuff. Here's yore health, Mary. Cutbank, here's red mud in yore ear."

"Here's salt in yore coffee, Tuley. Mary, here's regards."

And when they had set down their empty glasses and Tuley Bill was stuffing a pint bottle into his chaps pocket, the two old rascals ignored the water-drinking Buck.

"Better get going," grinned Buck, "while you can still travel under your own power. Why the

Rolling M keeps two old soaks like you on the pay-roll has always been a great mystery. Roll along, cow waddies. Ride those ridges."

"If that thing gits violent, Mary," said Cutbank solemnly, jerking a thumb toward Buck, "rap it across the horns with a neck-yoke. So-long."

When they had gone, Buck got a good description of the mob from Mary.

She cleaned and loaded an old shot-gun and stood the weapon against the back-bar. Buck rode away a little later, headed for home.

Buck had almost reached the 7UP ranch when he met Guy Jones.

The boy's brown eyes were troubled and his slender face was grave.

"I had to see you, Buck," he said. "It's awful important. I need a friend to talk to. It's about Joe Phelps, Buck. I saw him get killed."

"Who killed him, Guy?"

"I don't know. I was too far off to recognize the man, but he rode a big gray horse that I'd swear was the same big gray that Angus Murdock always rides."

"And the man on the big gray killed Joe?"

"Near as Olga and I could tell, yes. We were picking berries up there above the rim-rock on the Reservation side of the fence. I saw Joe ride along the trail. From where we were, we couldn't see the crossing. Just saw Joe ride that way. After a time we heard a shot, but we didn't pay much attention. I thought it was somebody hunting

78

sage hens. But I don't like the sound of shooting and it sort of worried me.

"Then, in about twenty minutes, we saw the man on the gray horse ride at a lope toward the sheep camp on Big Warm. The man on the gray horse had come across the creek at the gravel crossing. And that night, when Deacon Nelson got back to his place, he told us about finding Joe's body there."

A frown creased Buck's forehead.

"Deacon Nelson told me that his wife and two daughters were in Chinook that day. You say one of the girls was picking berries with you. How does that happen? Why did Nelson lie?"

"He didn't know he was lying, Buck. He thought Olga had gone with her mother and sister. But instead, I'd met her along the road with a saddled horse and she and I rode into Lodge Pole. The sub-agent there has . . . has authority to marry folks. He married Olga and me. That is another reason I had to see you, Buck. Paw 'lowed if I married a nester, he'd kick me out. Mebby you could make him understand."

Buck gripped the younger boy's shoulder. "Sure thing, Guy. I'll fix it."

But he knew that he could not fix it.

CHAPTER VI

FLAMES IN THE NIGHT

They were dirt roofed, an' homely, an'
ramblin' an' squat —
Jest logs with mud daubin'; but I loved 'em a
lot.
Their latch strings was out an' their doors
wouldn't lock:
Get down an' walk in ('twas politer to
knock).

— Cabins.

They had not expected to find Hook Jones at the 7UP ranch. Hook, red-faced with anger because a 'breed who had just come from the sub-agency at Lodge Pole had told the one-armed rancher that Guy had married the nester girl on Big Warm.

Buck made no attempt just now to breach that black chasm of wrath that divided father and son. But he stood at Guy's elbow while the boy, white beneath the tan that coated his lean face, listened to the vitriolic abuse of the irate Hook. Dave Rawlins sat on the top log of the corral, whittling a stick. His sympathies were all with Hook. He could not ever understand Guy as Buck understood the boy. Nor had Buck ever offered what seemed to Dave Rawlins like a reasonable excuse for his championship of the youngster whom the cow country had labeled "Hook's yellow-backed kid."

"So yuh snuck off an' got hitched to a nester gal, huh?" snarled Hook. "A Swede preecher's gal. Sod busters. Go get a plow an' foller it from now on. I'm shut of yuh. Git outa my sight and don't ever set a track on my place. You . . . you crawlin' li'l' —"

"Hold on, Hook," Buck cut in. "I reckon you've said a-plenty. Let him alone. Just because Guy don't pack a gun and get drunk and mix up in fights, you get the notion he ain't a man. Now, just because he married a decent girl, you cuss him out.

"You say he can't set foot on your place. Perhaps that suits him a lot, too. But this ain't your place, Hook. This is the 7UP ranch and Guy is just as welcome here as the flowers in May. You're saying a lot of stuff that some day you'll be almighty sorry you said. You think that if Guy wasn't gritty, he'd marry against your say-so?"

"A son of mine had better be dead and in his grave rather than be throwed into the nester outfit. He's no better than the lousiest scissorbill farmer that's plowin' up this country. He's a traitor to his own kind."

"He's my friend, Hook. And he's as welcome here as you are. Let him alone."

Whatever Hook Jones was about to say to Buck was never said. Guy, tight-lipped, his face pale and tense, stepped up to his father.

"I'm tired of being called a yellow coward. I'm plumb willing to stay away from you and your place. If it's a disgrace to follow a plow then I'm disgraceful. If it's cowardly to live an honest life, then I'm a coward. I don't need Buck to take my part. I'm standing here alone. I'm not afraid of you and your guns. You tell me not to ever make a track on your place. That goes double. You keep away from the place I'm locating on Big Warm. Stay away from me and mine. I hope I never have to speak to you again, or look at you. Good-by."

Guy turned abruptly and stepped back up on his horse. Hook looked after him in blank astonishment. For this was the first time Guy had ever openly crossed his father. There was something rather terrible about the boy's defiance of the man who was his father, something more than merely courageous in his breaking of the home ties, and the quitting of the only home he had ever known. His break with Hook would make him an outcast in the eyes of the cow folks. And it was more than probable that the nesters clan would not accept him as one of them.

Hook Jones watched his only son ride away. He seemed about to call after Guy, then changed his mind. Stunned, still unable to believe that Guy had so spoken to the father who had always commanded without fear of disobedience, Hook slowly shook his head. Now Dave Rawlins climbed down from the top log of the corral and laid a kindly hand on the shoulder of the one-armed cattleman.

"Come on to the house, Hook, and lift a light 'un. The boy will cool off before the sun sets. I wouldn't be too hard on him, and he won't hold anything ag'in' you. He's got more speerit than ever I give him credit for. The young 'un is right spunky, I'd say."

Hook Jones nodded. "Spunky, that's right, Dave. The boy's gone. Gone for keeps. Said he never wanted to see me or speak to me again. Yep, Guy has done gone. It'll be hard on the missus, losin' her young 'un. I reckon it'll just about kill 'er."

Buck smiled coldly. "Thank yourself for your sorrows, Hook. You and a lot of others have never given Guy a man's chance. I told you he was no coward. Because you've killed a man or two you get the idea that the only brave men on earth are killers like yourself. You can't see how a man like Guy is a lot braver than you are. However, we'll not stand here and argue like a lot of old maids. There's trouble coming and it's coming fast. Hook, when you and Dad have had your drink, I'd like to have you locate the Night-hawk and tell him to stand ready."

Briefly Buck told of the unfortunate deal Mary had had with the nester toughs. Dave Rawlins and Hook listened gravely. "I've sent word out to the Rolling M and the Murdock outfit. We'll all meet here to-morrow night."

"Murdock nor Bob Driscoll won't dare set foot on my place," said Dave Rawlins grimly.

"Dad," said Buck, "don't you think it's about time you and Bob Driscoll quit acting like a couple of school kids? Bury the hatchet. This country needs all of us and we can't do much when you won't get together. We have to be united if we're going to do any good. I'll get Bob Driscoll here and —"

"You'll do nothin' of the sort, young rooster," growled Dave Rawlins. "I don't want that old buzzard near this ranch. When I'm dead, and what's mine goes to you, yuh'll have somethin' to say about what goes on here on the 7UP range. But till I'm in my grave, I'll run the ranch. Yo're a cow-puncher here, don't forgit that. You young sprouts is altogether too important in yore own minds. Come on, Hook, let's likker. Buck, tend to yore chores."

Buck grinned at his father's tall back as Dave Rawlins led Hook to the house. Buck and his father had never had a quarrel. They might argue out a point with some degree of heat, but always there was that easy comradeship between the two. Buck saddled a fresh horse and went to the house to get his Winchester.

"Which-a-way, feller?" asked his father when Buck passed through the room where Dave Rawlins and Hook sat.

"I'm taking a ride, boss," grinned Buck. "Tending to my chores. Be back some time to-night. I'm getting a line on who killed Joe Phelps, I hope. Guy gave me a lead to follow. Any word to send Guy, Hook, in case I meet him?"

"Tell him to go see his maw. And before he goes home, fer him to take a bath in sheep dip. I don't want my place loused up."

Buck broke open a box of .30-.40 cartridges which he shoved into his chaps pockets. He paused at the door.

"So-long, bone-heads," he grinned, and left them.

Buck's way took him past the Driscoll ranch. It was getting dusk and Buck hoped that he might somehow persuade Bob Driscoll into a reconciliation. Also, the young cowboy hoped to meet Colleen and talk to her. He was about a mile from the ranch when he saw yellow flames licking at the dusky sky.

There was a fairly strong wind that would carry the fire across the greasewood to the Driscoll place. Prairie fire, dread scourge of the Montana ranges, now threatened to wipe out Rolling M ranch.

Buck tickled his horse with the spurs. He reckoned that some cowboy had carelessly dropped a match or lighted cigarette. Nor had he any other suspicion until, out of the uncertain light that precedes the night time, a shot ripped past his head.

Buck jerked his six-shooter, thumbing back the hammer. Now another shot droned past him. He shot at the flame of the other man's gun. Then, from another angle, more shots. Buck leaned along the neck of his racing horse. He saw a man on a big gray horse break from the shelter of a coulee. Buck followed, shooting at the re-treating man.

Confusion now, as two other men on horse-back raced into the twilight. There was the odor of kerosene. Buck found himself riding between the fires that had been set. Fires that licked hun-grily at the kerosene-soaked brush and grass.

A sharp, burning pain stabbed at his shoulder. Then, as the rider on the big gray horse showed, cameo-clear against the light, Buck's horse stepped in a badger hole and somersaulted. The young rancher's head struck a rock and in that last split-second before oblivion, he heard a woman scream. . . .

Tuley Bill Baker and his boss, Colleen Driscoll, had done their best to persuade Bob Driscoll into going over to the 7UP ranch. But the blind owner of the Rolling M had taken a stand as solid as a granite cliff, and after an hour's futile argument, Colleen had winked at Tuley and motioned toward the barn.

"As long as Dad feels that way about it, Tuley," she said aloud as she kissed her blind father, "that settles it. Now let's get over to the lower pasture and see how the boys are coming along with those colts. See you later, Daddy."

When Tuley Bill and the girl were at the barn, Colleen laughed knowingly.

"I'll take Dad over there to-morrow, Tuley, in the buggy. He won't know where he's going until he gets there and then it will be too late for him to put up much of a yelp. I'll make Dave Rawlins shake hands with us and call this silly quarrel off. Now let's lope over toward Sand Creek and see if we can smell out any particular brand of orneriness those thugs might be hatching. I'll swing over by the lower gate at the pasture and you ride across the ridge. I'll meet you in half an hour or so, and we'll do some scouting around. Cutbank should be back from the Murdock place in an hour or so, and then we can make more medicine. If I get over to Sand Creek before you make it, I'll be waiting there where the trail drops off the ridge."

So it was that Colleen, choosing the longer but easier trail, was some minutes earlier than Tuley Bill who had to ride in at the head of a rough draw, then choose a trail that climbed the ridge and dropped over into Sand Creek.

Dusk found her riding alone along Sand Creek. More than anything she wanted to bring her father and Dave Rawlins back to that basis of comradeship that had once been a by-word in the cow country.

"As thick as Bob Driscoll and Dave Rawlins," they had said of the two. Now the two old timers would ride many miles out of their way to avoid meeting.

Colleen, planning out a scheme whereby she might bring about a reconciliation, was deep in thought when she saw a man on a big gray horse ride against the darkening sky-line, then turn into a coulee. For a brief moment the girl had a fair glimpse of horse and rider. The horse could be none other than Angus Murdock's big gray. The rider, big of frame, with black Stetson and black coat, must be the sheepman who was of that build and always, no matter how hot the day, wore that long-tailed black coat and big black hat.

Startled, Colleen was about to hail him. What could Angus Murdock, who was not on friendly terms with the Rolling M outfit, be doing here on Driscoll's range? Then, just as she was about to quicken her horse's gait, a big blaze, over ahead in the draw where the man had ridden, made her give a startled gasp.

Now, as if on signal, other fires broke out about a hundred yards apart. Now a rifle cracked. Other shots blazed through the dusk.

She saw a rider on a rangy black horse hemmed in by the fires. Buck Rawlins. Buck, emptying his six-shooter at the men who were shooting at him froin both sides. Now Buck's horse hit a badger hole, upsetting, throwing the cowboy heavily. Fire was crackling around the fallen man as the black horse, up again, terrified by the fire and shooting, loped off. Colleen gave a startled scream as Buck was thrown.

Reckless of her own peril, spurring her horse into that lane of snapping, crackling blaze, Colleen reached the fallen Buck. An instant and she was kneeling beside him.

"Buck! Buck, old boy! Come awake, Buck! Buck, you have to wake up!"

But Buck's head had been too badly rapped by the fall. She tried to lift him. No use. Then she did the one and only thing she could do to save the man's life. Swiftly, with hands that shook with eager excitement, she unbuckled her rope strap. She dropped the loop over his shoulders and under his arms. Then she stepped back in the saddle. Taking her dallies around the saddle horn, she dragged the unconscious Buck to safety.

She was slipping the rope free when Tuley Bill's voice, hoarse with anxiety, hailed her. A moment and the old cow hand, for all the world like some snapping, snarling, grizzled old wolf, rode up out of the blaze-brightened dusk.

"Hurt, Colleen?" was his first question.

"Not a bit. Buck got his, though. Can't tell how bad. There's a bullet hole in his shoulder and his head's all blood. I'll patch him up as best I can. You get busy at the fire. Be with you pronto. If any of that dirty outfit sky-light themselves, let your conscience be your guide. Hurry, Tuley."

"I spotted two of 'em, dang 'em. The two Listens. And none other than old Angus Murdock with 'em. Sheep stinkin' sons!" Tuley Bill rode away, his slicker in his hand.

Now Buck groaned a little and moved. He woke up bewildered, grinned thinly when he recognized Colleen, and tried to sit up.

"Take it easy, pardner," she told him. "Gosh, I thought you were dead, old man. Easy, now."

89

"There's a fire, kid; and we're the fire department. Slickers and saddle blankets and if the snakes haven't set too much of it, we stand a chance. Quit trying to hold me, pard."

"You're groggy," she protested, but he shook her off almost roughly.

"Let's go, sis!" he called, and headed for his horse that now was more quiet.

He jerked the slicker off his saddle. Colleen followed suit. Now they fought, the girl and the two men, with desperate energy. The girl never got far from Buck. She knew that he must be sick and dizzy, that at any moment he might drop in his tracks. The hot blaze snapped at them with yellow tongues.

The heat was like a furnace blast. Slickers whipped the blaze into smoldering embers.

Then another patch of brush, soaked with kerosene, would burst into angry flame. So they fought their unequal battle against the fire. A fire that kept gaining headway, like a sullen, fighting, red-tongued beast, roaring and crackling and hissing its challenge like a thing alive.

Slickers were whipped to shreds. Now they were using saddle blankets. Buck staggered like a drunken man, blood-smeared, one armed. But he would not heed the commands of the other two to rest.

"I'm all right," he gritted.

Now another rider came up on the run. It was Cutbank Carter.

"Yuh never was anything but late in yore

whole miserable life," panted Tuley Bill. "Git off that hoss and git busy."

"Who set 'er? Who set 'er?"

"We did, yuh ol' jughead. We set 'er to warm our gizzards. If yuh got a snort, give Buck a good 'un. The young 'un's about all-in."

Cutbank groaned. "Always, when I git me a bottle, suthin' happens to it. Here, Buckie."

"I'm off the stuff. Don't want a drink."

"Yuh'll take it," snapped Tuley Bill viciously, "if we have tuh rap yuh to sleep with rocks an' pour it down yuh. Ye got no time tuh waste with fool notions. Drink that likker. All yuh kin hold."

"I never," said Cutbank sadly, "seen a man so free with another man's likker as that Tuley Bill. Drink hearty, Buckie."

Buck took a big swallow of the strong stuff. Tuley Bill pulled an anticipating palm across a fire-blackened mouth. Without hesitation he reached for the bottle that Cutbank had deliberately corked and was shoving into his pocket. Cutbank relinquished his most valued possession wryly.

"Hawg!" he growled, and got busy with his slicker.

"Here's worms in yore grave," grinned Tuley Bill.

"Choke, hawg!" grunted Cutbank, and retrieved the bottle.

"Here's nits in yore whiskers," he toasted. And a moment later they were back at their task.

The fire was not gaining so much now. Other riders from the Rolling M, together with some farmers, were coming to swell the number of firefighters. Wagons with filled water barrels came up. Wet sacks beat back the blaze. Nester and cow-puncher fought shoulder to shoulder against their common enemy, the prairie fire.

Riders would soon be coming from as far away as the 7UP, thus following the unwritten code of cow-land that says a man shall fight fire when that fire is within a half day's ride.

Tuley Bill and Colleen had forced Buck to sit down over near one of the wagons. There were plenty of men now to fight fire. An hour and the blaze would be a wide path of black land spotted with smoldering twigs and spots of cow chips.

Now some riders, followed by a spring wagon laden with soaked sacks, came up. At sight of the two foremost riders, Buck shook off Colleen's restraining hand. His hand on his gun he faced the man on the big gray horse and the younger man who rode with him.

"A man," said Buck Rawlins harshly, "that will set fire to the range of his neighbor is a low down snake that needs killing. Murdock, you and your son sure have gall to come here pretending you want to help put out a fire that you set. I'm too crippled to fight with my hands but if you'll step down, I'll shoot it out with you both here and now. Get down and fill your hands!"

CHAPTER VII
WAR CLOUDS

Let me ride, old timer, ride into the west,
Till I'm lost in the sunset upon the crest —
And with it draw down to whatever lies
On the range that's hid till we top the rise.
                              — The Old Cowman.

Angus Murdock, huge of frame, his red face with
its sidecut whiskers as stern as the land that had
given his ancestors birth, stepped down from his
horse. There was no hint of haste in his movement, no trace of anger in his face that was
seamed and weatherbeaten and sternly lined.
Towering above the blood spattered, bandaged,
tight lipped Buck, he stood there, his Scot's eyes
studying the young cow-man.

"Ye're hurt, laddie, an I ken that ye're sick. I
have no quarrel wi' ye, Buck Rawlins, and 'tis
well ye ken it, er should. I heard the words ye
spoke, but a'ready they're forgotten. I've no
quarrel here." He beckoned his son to dismount.

"Wull, can you not take care o' the lad? He's
bad hurt and no doubt oot o' his head. I'll attend
to gettin' my lads to work at the fire."

"Don't trouble yourself, Angus Murdock,"
spoke up Colleen Driscoll. She stepped between

the giant sheepman and the irate Buck. "Take your men and go back to your sheep range."

"I dinna ken what ye're drivin' at, lass. I come here to gi' whatever help we're able. Only to be met wi' harsh words and insults. 'Tis past the understandin' o' decency. Wull, laddie, tell them to turn back and go hame. We'll follow the wagon we fetched wi' the sacks. I'm thinkin' aboot the fence that was cut on Alkalai. We'll be biddin' ye good nicht, Miss Driscoll. Come, Wull."

"Not till I've made Buck Rawlins explain what he meant when he said we set fire to this range. Either he's out of his head or drunk again. If he was sober and right in his mind, I'd call his bragging bet. Even if I had to borrow a gun to do my shooting. Murdocks don't pack revolvers around. What's this about us setting the fire, Rawlins?"

"I saw Angus Murdock on that same gray horse," said Buck hotly, "if you want an answer, I saw him set fire to the range. I've got one of his bullets in my hide right now. And a 7UP cowboy lies in his grave with another of Angus Murdock's bullets in his back. And you say that the Murdocks don't pack guns!"

Bill Murdock had dismounted. He looked at his father in a puzzled way. Then Bill faced Buck. All the old enmity between the two had again boiled up.

"You lie, Rawlins."

"Then call me a liar also," said Colleen

94

Driscoll, her face white and tense, "and include Tuley Bill. We all three saw that gray horse and the man on the gray horse. If Angus Murdock can prove an alibi that we'll believe, then he's as canny a Scot as ever crossed the ocean to put sheep into the cow country. You Murdocks had better get back on your horses. Ride off this range before you get hurt. Stay off the Rolling M range. Git!"

For a moment the stern face of the veteran sheep-man was heavy with wrath. His eyes blazed from under scowling brows while his big hands clenched and unclenched. His son laid a hand on the older man's great arm.

"Don't give 'em the satisfaction of an answer to their dirty accusations, Father. Our fence gets cut, our sheep killed, our property destroyed and now they say we set fire to their range. It's all just a frame-up between the Rolling M and 7UP outfits to run us out of the sheep business. We're not wanted here. If we start anything we'll be murdered, that's plain.

"When Buck Rawlins sobers up and washes his face, when he can stand up and fight, I'll give him a good bellyful of scrapping and make him howl like a coyote. We come here to help and we're treated like criminals. They just don't know any better, perhaps. But I'll tell this for their benefit now: That in five years there'll be plenty sheep on the 7UP and Rolling M ranges. We'll sheep-off your range and we'll hire nesters to herd the sheep. The day has gone by where men like Dave Rawlins can run Montana at the end of a six-shooter. We'll make these cow outfits move on to some other country where they can steal and murder honest men.

"I tell you now, Buck Rawlins, that we'll make you prove what you said to-night. We'll make you prove that your men didn't cut that fence on Alkalai. And when we've found you guilty, we'll put you behind the bars. You and your kind have played hooky from prison a long time. You'll do time along with your good friend the Nighthawk and his lawless gang. Birds of a feather, tarred with the same brush, you cow-men and your hired outlaws. From this night on, the Murdock outfit stands with the farmers. Now, Miss Rolling M and Mister 7UP, good night. If my father and I get shot in the back as we ride away, there is a law that will hang you to the same gallows that will some day hang your friend the Nighthawk."

The Murdocks rode back the way they had come, leaving Colleen and Buck and Tuley Bill standing there a little dazed. Tuley Bill was the one who broke an uncomfortable silence.

"Goshamighty, Buck, the next time yuh go fer to fog-up any man, put some shells in yore gun. I seen it and they shoulda seen that yore hawg-laig is as empty as my belly is right now. Whew, but that was a plumb fool thing tuh do. I'd uh had tuh kill off them sheep folks if they'd called yore hand. I has tuh stand here, betwixt a sweat and a cold chill while you make gun talk with a cutter that's plumb useless excep' fer drivin' staples er bendin' it across a man's horns. And all the time I'm a-wonderin' whether a .45 slug will knock down either of 'em. They're too big fer anything under the caliber of a cannon." Tuley Bill glared about him.

"Now where is that ol' Cutbank thing with that medicine?"

"Go get him, Tuley," said Buck. "And quit running off at the head. I've got both ears ringing with conversation already." And he commenced shoving cartridges into his .45. When Tuley Bill was beyond earshot, Buck turned to Colleen.

He was startled to see tears in her eyes.

"What's wrong, pardner?"

"I just can't make myself believe that Angus Murdock set fire to our range. Somehow, in spite of what my eyes saw, I can't convince myself that a man like Angus Murdock would be that ornery. Well, the well-known milk is spilled now, Buck. The Murdocks will throw in with the nesters, and I'd bet a hat that Bill was making no idle threat when he said he'd sheep us out. Oh, gosh, Buck, I'm going to weep like a woman. And there isn't a clean handkerchief within miles."

More than anything, Buck wanted to put his good arm around Colleen and tell her that he loved her. That there had never been a day in his life, from the day they met as kids, that he hadn't loved her. But he knew better than to say it. Because he knew now, in his innermost heart, that

Colleen did not love him that same way. That the man she loved was the young sheep-man who had just ridden away after his declaration of war against the Rolling M and 7UP outfits. Colleen Driscoll loved big Bill Murdock.

Buck grinned twistedly and patted her shoulder. "It's the first hundred years that are the hardest, little pardner."

Colleen rubbed the tears from her eyes and tried to smile. She had always known that Buck loved her. And she knew now that he understood the cause of her tears.

"Good old Buck. Good pardner. Golly, who's that coming? The charge of the light brigade?"

"I'd say, for a guess," said Buck, squinting through the smoke and the flickering light of the dying prairie fire, "that it is Ike Niland and his posse."

"After the Nighthawk?"

Buck smiled grimly. "After a man that killed a certain conductor in a gambling joint in Chinook night before last. The same conductor that shot Tex Arnold in the back."

So had the two outlaws missing at the meeting at Fancy Mary's when the loot was divided, accounted for their absence. So had the murder of their pardner Tex Arnold been paid off in full. . . .

Ike Niland's bronzed face was grave and he tugged uneasily at his drooping mustache. He looked from Buck to Colleen and from the girl to the cow-punchers who had quit fighting fire and gathered there in the lantern light at the wagon. Among the crowd was a small sprinkling of nesters.

"Buck," said the grizzled sheriff finally, "where'd yuh git that tied-up shoulder?"

"From one of the skunks that set this fire," said Buck. "What else might be on your mind?"

"A-plenty. These men with me are railroad detectives and U.S. law officers. There's bin talk about you bein' mixed up with the Nighthawk and his gang. It's known that the two men mixed up with the killin' of a railroad conductor the other night, rode away from Fancy Mary's road ranch on 7UP horses. These gents want to ask yuh some questions."

"Before I give any answers, tell me this, Ike. Am I under arrest?"

"Sorry, Buck, but it looks thataway. We was on our way to the 7UP ranch when we sighted the blaze and rode tuh see what we could do."

"You could have done plenty," said Buck grimly, "if you'd rode up when those men were setting it afire."

"Who set it?" asked Ike Niland.

"Since you're so busy chasing outlaws," said Buck a little bitterly, "and letting deputized mobs mistreat women and ride around drunk like they owned the country, I reckon we won't bother you with such a small matter as this attempt to burn out the Driscoll range and kill me. It would be too much to ask of the law that men like Driscoll and my father made here in

Montana. Tend to your nesters, Ike. Us cow folks will settle our own problems."

"Now, son," said Ike Niland, a hurt look in his eyes, "yo're flyin' off the handle. If yuh know the men that set this fire and shot yuh, I'll jail 'em."

"Sheriff," spoke up one of the possemen, "if this is Buck Rawlins, then we'd better take care of the main business. This little fire can be investigated later. Rawlins, where are the Nighthawk and his men hiding?"

"Wherever they are, you'll never break any speed records getting there. I understand I'm under arrest. All right. I'll do my talking through an attorney. Nice weather we're having."

"I'd advise you to take a civil attitude," snapped the detective.

"I didn't ask for your advice, mister. I wouldn't have it as a gift. Ike, I'm your prisoner. I'm asking your protection against any third degree stuff. When do we start for the hoosegow?"

"Directly, son, directly. How bad are yuh hurt?"

"He's hurt too badly to make any seventy mile ride, sheriff," said Colleen sharply. "There's a bad hole in his shoulder, and he has a nasty scalp wound. He needs a doctor more than he needs a warrant served on him. For humanity's sake, for the sake of common decency, I demand of you that you let me take him to our ranch. I've already sent for a doctor. Ike Niland, will you permit these men to take Buck prisoner and make him ride horseback clear to Chinook?"

"Young lady, whoever you are," said the detective, "keep out of this. The prisoner goes with us."

"Buck," said Ike, stepping down from his saddle and walking over to the young cow-man, "yo're under arrest as my prisoner. That's a bad-lookin' shoulder and yuh look almighty peaked. I'm takin' yuh to the Driscoll ranch and put yuh to bed. I'll ask yuh for yore gun."

Buck handed his six-shooter to the soft-spoken sheriff. "Take good care of it, Ike. I may be needing it."

"Look here, Niland," snapped the red-faced railroad detective, who looked oddly out of place on a horse, "you can't pull anything like this. You know our orders and what we planned. That man goes with us."

"I reckon not." Ike's tone was calm. "I've been sheriff in this county twenty-odd years and I never give up a prisoner yet to any man. We kin pick up the trail we want without Buck. He wouldn't tell yuh anything ner show yuh anything, anyhow. He stays at the Rolling M ranch till the doc says he kin be moved. That goes just exactly as she lays."

"Thanks, Ike," said Buck. "It's better than I deserve after blowing off like I did."

"Son," said the old sheriff, a curious twinkle in his eye. "I've dangled yuh on my knee when yuh was a yearlin' and seen yuh cut yore fust teeth. Since you was old enough tuh pick up cuss

101

words from sech ornery old bone-heads as Tuley Bill Baker and Cutbank Carter, you've had the habit of blowin' up like a charge uh black powder. I pay as much mind to them hot headed busts as I do to that ol' fool roan hoss uh mine when he tries tuh snort at some booger he sees.

"I'll just turn yuh over to this spittin', crawlin', fightin' young lady who used tuh dangle on my knee, likewise. Yo're a pair tuh put white hairs on any man's head. Take keer uh the young rascal, honey. He's under arrest and I expect him tuh stay at the ranch, same as he'd stay in jail. No traipsin' off, mind."

Colleen nodded, her eyes starry. Buck grinned and held out his hand.

"There's my word for it, Ike. I'll stay there if Bob Driscoll will let me."

Ike stepped back in the saddle, ignoring the scowls of the railroad detectives.

"See yuh later regardin' the fire and the shootin' scrape. Me and these gentlemen has pressin' business elsewhere. So-long."

There was something mighty splendid in the way Ike Niland sat his fat roan horse. Straight backed, his hat tilted slightly with a swaggering slant that was a memento of younger, more active days when he had ridden the cattle trails and had done his share of boisterous fun-making.

There was also something indefinably tragic there in that straight-backed form. The tragedy brought home to him by the coming of the nesters. He must do his duty as sheriff, regardless of friendships strong as tempered steel. He must, before long, align himself with men he despised.

Even as now, to-night, he rode the manhunter's trail to follow the sign made by men who had shared the same camp-fires of bygone days. The Nighthawk and his bitter grudge against the railroad was now leading Ike, who once had been his pardner, along a dangerous trail.

"Darn you, Buck," said Colleen, "won't you ever get that temper of yours halter-broke? Ike Niland would go the limit for you. And what you said hurt him worse than if you'd stuck a knife in him."

Buck nodded. Had another said the hot words that had come from him, Buck would have fought like a panther in defense of Ike. Now, blood-smeared, dirty with the grime of smoke, the pallor of his face like chalk under the smudges, he stood, dumb and utterly, miserably ashamed. Then, as if a black curtain had been dropped, his world about him went black.

"Catch him, Cutbank," called Colleen. "He's passed out."

An hour later Tuley Bill and Cutbank carried the still unconscious Buck Rawlins up the steps of the Driscoll ranch house. Ahead of them strode Colleen. Her father's voice hailed her from his chair on the big veranda where he spent his days and long evenings in his world of eternal darkness.

"Who's with you, honey?" he called, his ears picking up the sounds made by the two old cowboys with their burden. "Who's there?"

"Buck Rawlins, Dad. He's shot, perhaps dying, so I brought him home. You don't mind?"

"Mind?" The voice of old man Bob Driscoll trembled with emotion. "This is Buck's home as well as ours, ain't it? Take him to his old room. Tell him . . . welcome home . . . and send fer Dave. Send fer Dave Rawlins. I reckon the stubborn ol' son will have tuh cave in and come. Git his room tidied up."

CHAPTER VIII

SAGE-BRUSH NAPOLEON

Fer some folks pack a brandin' iron
In places mighty strange,
But only fools brand mavericks
Astray on trouble's range.
— The Cow-puncher's Yarn.

"Well, bone-heads," snapped Onion Oliver, as Tuley Bill and Cutbank rode up to the cabin that Onion was building for his female nester, as he called her, "what do yuh want here on Miss West's ranch? Who sent yuh and why for?"

Onion's nasal voice brought Mazie West from her tent where she was adding up a swiftly diminishing bank balance. At sight of the blond girl in khaki, both Tuley Bill and Cutbank removed their hats with an elaborate and noticeable self-conscious gesture. Onion Oliver glared at them and jerked a thumb toward the Rolling M range.

"Git!" he hissed. "Git, yuh two ol' mallard drakes."

With elaborate unconcern the two visitors ignored Onion's deadly glare and his hissed warning. They sat their saddles with a rakish, if somewhat over-strained attitude of nonchalance. When Mazie smiled, they each stepped down to the ground and in the left hand of each was a small package of mail. "We come past the mail-box, ma'am," said Tuley Bill. "An' seein' that there was some letters for yuh, we reckoned we might fetch 'em over."

"Now wasn't that sweet of these two cowboys?" she appealed to Onion, who was caressing the butt of his six-shooter with meaning gesture.

"Them two things cowboys?" squeaked Onion. "Them two walkin' bone-yards? Shucks."

"I'm Tuley Bill Baker," announced that gentleman, bowing stiffly, "foreman fer the Rollin' M outfit. The old gentleman with me is Cutbank Carter."

"Foreman of the upper and bigger outfit fer the Driscolls, and proud to have the honor an' pleasure uh makin' yore acquaintance," said Cutbank.

"Where's yore crutches an' canes?" snapped Onion. "Gimme the word, ma'am, and I'll run these two ol' things back onto their range."

"Don't quarrel, boys," said Mazie West. "I'm sure I'd hate to see three brave guys like you shooting holes in each other. And gee, it is lonesome enough here without scaring away anybody. We'll all have some lunch and pass around the gossip. Ain't it at the Rolling M ranch that they took Buck Rawlins when he got hurt last week?"

"Yes, ma'am," said Tuley Bill, turning his

back on Onion, "and he is doin' right well. And it's a treat to see Dave and Bob Driscoll sittin' together on the porch, swappin' yarns and sippin' toddies and tradin' hosses. We just fetched the White Cloud stud over and we're takin' the Rawlins Stardust stallion back with us.

"Buck sent word that whatever yuh needed in the way uh grub er anything, ma'am, to just tell pore ol' Onion tuh git it from the ranch. I heered him tell Dave that he reckoned you wasn't any too well fixed fer cash and there was no use in yuh bein' robbed by them stores in town. And he sent word that if Creighton Marley showed up to have ol' Onion shoot the heels off his boots."

"Dunno as the ol' cuss ever shot anything bigger'n a curlew in his life," added Cutbank, "and if this Marley dude ever made a face at him, the pore ol' feller 'ud swaller his upper plate. Whatever Buck had in mind when he sent such a pore specimen to ride herd on yuh, ma'am, is shore a puzzle. Onion was old and harmless and useless when the Little Rockies was sand piles."

"I was a button wranglin' hosses when these two cripples was a-wearin' out their fourth an' fifth sets uh false teeth. What's that on yore flank, Tuley Bill?"

"A dram uh medicine. Tonsil oil. Singin' syrup. Fer my personal use."

"Take Onion down to the crick," said Cutbank, "and rub some on what he calls a head. Go with him, Onion."

While Cutbank began the recital of a bloody battle with a Cheyenne war party, Onion followed Tuley Bill to the creek. When the bottle had been passed, Tuley Bill lowered his voice to a whisper. "Seen Ike Niland since him and the posse went past on the way to the bad-lands?"

"They come back last night and Ike 'lowed they'd had bad luck."

"Then Hook musta reached the cabin on Rock Crick in time to warn the Nighthawk."

"Shore thing. Hook's back in Landusky. His missus is sick, ain't expected tuh live. Guy has bin stayin' with her. The pore thing has gone plumb outa her mind. Thinks she's back in Wyoming. And, goshamighty but things looks bad between Hook and Guy. They ain't speakin' and Hook has an idee that Guy was on Big Warm when Joe Phelps got shot. He's talked plumb open about Guy and hints that Guy's too yaller tuh tell what he knows.

"Hook claims a scissor-bill called Eric Swanson done the killin' and because Swanson has married a sister to the nester gal that Guy taken fer bad er worse, Guy won't tell what he seen. It's mighty bad talk fer any man to make about any other gent, but it's down-right dangerous when a man like Hook Jones makes it ag'in' his own son. Guy is sayin' nothin' but he taken to packin' a gun. It looks bad, Tuley Bill."

"When yuh see Hook, tell him tuh come to the ranch. Dave and Bob Driscoll want tuh talk with him. And don't tell him that Guy thinks Angus Murdock either killed Joe Phelps, er else he knows who did do the killin'. Guy told Buck that much. And here's somethin' else that Hook ain't to be told. Guy is workin' fer the Murdocks as camp tender. This Eric Swanson is likewise tendin' camp fer the Murdocks. Me, I think the same as does Hook about Guy Jones, but Buck says different.

"Murdock is movin' three bands uh wethers onto the forest reserve next to the Rawlins range. He's startin' a range war an he's throwed in with the nesters. Onion, she's gonna be war. Bob Driscoll and Dave Rawlins are askeered Hook might start shootin'."

"He will," said Onion, "if his missus dies, which same she's expected to do almost any day. I'll git word tuh Hook to go to the Rolling M. Anything else?"

"Keep this Marley away from this yaller-haired nester gal. He's set to buy her relinquishment and put one uh his toughs on this place. He thinks she's too friendly with the 7UP. Somebody tipped off one uh our boys in town. These 7UP Springs is worth more money than me and you both ever seen. Marley will try tuh buy her off. If he can't, he'll try to scare her off. There's a letter in my pocket to her from Marley. I wanted to see you before I give it to her. Think she'll sell out to that slick dude?"

"Not for a million," said Onion stoutly. "That gal's a champion. I bin talkin' cow to her like

109

Buck told me. She's eatin' the grub I fetch from the ranch. I got her a spotted pony and a outfit. Nope, she's a square little lady. She won't sell out to Marley. And she don't scare, neither. Not fer one minute. Game as they make 'em. But if you two golblamed ol' fossils think yo're comin' here regular, guess once more. I'm pertectin' the lil'l' 'un ag'in' all varmints, includin' the two-legged kind as shore kin hold a cork in a bottle till it rots there."

Reluctantly, Tuley Bill passed the bottle.

"Here's to the sciatica rheumatism that ailed yuh last spring. I hope the next cold rain that comes, yuh left yore slicker in the wagon." And Onion took a generous swallow.

Tuley Bill hastily recovered the bottle and together they went back to the tent where Cutbank was reciting, with significant gestures, how he had scalped fifteen Cheyennes.

After some minutes of stalling around, Tuley Bill "accidentally" discovered the letter from Marley to Mazie West.

She opened and read it in their presence.

When she finished reading, she smiled at the three old cow-punchers.

"Boys," she said, giving them all a melting smile that each took to be meant only for him, "it looks like I have a chance to clean up some real wampum. Two thousand smackers, to be exact. That might be chicken feed to you high-rolling guys of the great open spaces, but to a stranded chorine that's made a big mistake in ever leaving the Great White Way, it's important jack. It'll take me back on Broadway and keep me in silk stockings and groceries till I land a job. It'll bring back a lot of dreams that were slipping away. It'll take me back among the friends I left behind me. It'll take me home."

Mazie West's cheeks were a little flushed, her eyes bright with dreams, her voice vibrant with emotion. The three old cow-punchers eyed one another uneasily and tried to look like they were sharing her joy.

"Marley, the johnny that located me here, offers that much for my relinquishment," she went on. "He wants me to keep it a secret, but what good is a secret if you can't share it with your pals? This Creighton Marley is a great guy. A regular sage-brush Napoleon, see. He knows what he wants and how to go after it.

"He wants this little homestead of mine and he's waited till he knew darned well that I was getting homesick for elevators and subways and good shows and drug-store salads and pals that spoke my language. Then he sends me this blank form to fill out and make myself by-by money. He knows I'm broke and lonesome and life out here is just like doing time in Sing Sing. Yeh, he's a wise boy, this Marley sketch. Onion, stake me to a match. That's a good boy. And now, boys, watch this little gesture."

Mazie touched the match flame to the letter and the blank form.

"Mazie West's two thousand dollar bonfire,

no less." Her lips smiled bravely, but her eyes were suspiciously moist. The three old cow waddles looked at her with expressions of solemn awe.

Onion gave Tuley Bill a look that spoke volumes.

They all three sensed the sacrifice this homesick girl of the footlights was making, even if they did not know why she was refusing money that meant so much to her.

"Two weeks ago," she said huskily, "I'd have wept all over Onion's new green shirt. But if I'm sentenced to three years here, I gotta quit turning on the tear faucet every time something busts my heart. Now, boys, we'll get out the good old can opener and have a little banquet. Tuley Bill can furnish you boys with lubricating oil, and I'll stir me up a lemonade. Would you believe it, this happens to be my birthday?"

"Honest?"

"This is the day when little Mazie lights the candles, never mind how many."

"When Buck Rawlins and his dad finds out how yuh burned up that offer from Marley," promised Onion, "I reckon you'll be gittin' a real birthday present."

"They're not going to know about it," said Mazie quickly. "If any one of you tell, I'm off you all for life, get that straight. If I'm gonna be a darn' little fool, I don't want it broadcast. This business is a secret."

They looked at her in blank astonishment.

Onion smoothed imaginary cowlicks on his shining bald head.

"But gosh, ma'am," said Onion, "Buck and Dave Rawlins had shore ought to know what yuh done."

"You don't understand, boys, and I can't see myself putting on any monologue explaining why I'm such a little dumbbell. Forget it. Now let's eat. You boys start getting things ready while I do a quick change and powder what I vainly call my nose."

They let her go.

As they were preparing the lunch, there came certain muffled but quite unmistakable signs of sobbing from inside her tent.

"Rattle them pans, Cutbank," hissed Onion. "Tuley Bill, commence singin' 'The Dyin' Cowboy.' Dang yore hide, didn't I tell yuh the young 'un was game?"

"Game?" whispered Tuley Bill, bringing forth his bottle. "She's all uh that, Onion. And likewise the gal's bogged plumb down in love."

"Yuh think so?" beamed Onion. "Gosh-amighty, yuh think she likes me thataway?"

"You?" snorted Tuley Bill. "You? Sufferin' snakes, you? She's stuck on a real man. That gal's plumb gone on Buck Rawlins."

In her little tent, Mazie West dried her tears and skilfully daubed powder on her face to hide the traces of her grief.

She looked at herself in the glass.

"Of all the idiots," she whispered tensely at

her reflection, "that ever lived, you win the good old hand-painted ash-can. You get a chance to stand from under this ghastly mess and what do you do? You toss it away like you was a Broadway play-boy on a drunk. And what for? What's the big idea? What's this cowboy ever going to be to you? Not a thing, dearie, not a darned thing! He's got dough and an education and a gal. And you're just a cheap little bum from the chorus. Just a cheap . . . little . . . bum." She blinked hard and slapped on more powder.

But when she emerged from the tent a few minutes later she wore a sports outfit that she had been saving for some gala occasion, and she was humming a gay little tune.

And she was wholly unaware of the fact that she was not putting over her act.

Nor had she any way of knowing the terrible danger that her defiance of Marley's offer was to bring to her little homestead.

CHAPTER IX

FLESH AND BLOOD

I'm wild and woolly and full of fleas,
And never bin curried below the knees,
Now stranger, if you'll give me yore address
How would you like to go, by mail or last
*   express?*

— Buckskin Joe.

A soft, steady rain came from a sky that was the gray color of lead. Clods of sticky mud soiled the boots of the men who stood there, hatless, heads bowed beside an open grave.

The coffin made of pine boards had been covered with layers of black cheese-cloth. This was the work of the women of Landusky, their last offering of kind-hearted sympathy to the poor, half demented woman who had been the wife of Hook Jones. They had never quite understood her, had these women of Landusky. They had not quite understood the terrible suffering of the white-haired wife of the one-armed Hook Jones who had been a killer in the Wyoming cattle war.

Now death had ended her suffering on this earth and she lay with hands, toil calloused hands, folded across the old-fashioned bodice of a black dress that was the only garment she had owned that was not fashioned from calico, inside the pine board coffin covered with black cheese-cloth tacked here and there.

The women stayed under the shelter of their buggy tops. The hearse was a spring wagon hired from the barn in town, driven by a restless team of half broken horses. The driver, slicker clad, took an occasional nip from a hidden bottle. The various husbands of the women who had come to the funeral sat in discomfort beside their women. Horses stirred restlessly and there were muttered, under-toned words of profanity from the men. Here and there a woman was sniffling. There was the slosh of boots in the trampled mud.

The voice of Guy Jones. He was dressed in cheap black, his hair wet, the rain spotting the open pages of the worn Bible that had been the most prized possession of his mother. For Guy Jones was saying the last words of prayer before the sodden clods dropped in on the coffin. Guy, his face bloodless, his eyes sunken deep in blued sockets, his harassed cheeks wet with tears and the rain that God sends this earth, his voice clear and gentle.

He did not seem aware of the rain, of the people about him. He was delivering the final prayer above the open grave of his mother, reading from the frayed Bible from which she had taught him the words of God. He did not seem to see Hook Jones, his father. Hook, in overalls and slicker, hat-brim pulled across eyes that no man had ever read. Then Hook had re-moved his hat when the saloon man next to him had whispered something.

Hook's face, hard lined, mask-like. Bloodshot eyes that might or might not be shot with grief. Dripping with rain. His eyes staring blindly at the open grave and the black covered coffin within it. The coffin that would soon be covered with wet dirt. The coffin that held the remains of the only woman Hook Jones had ever loved. Mother of the son he now hated with a terrible, heart-chilling hatred. Under the dripping, yellow slicker that Hook wore was a six-shooter in an open holster that was tied by a buckskin thong, low on his thigh. The pocket on the right hand side of Hook's slicker was cut open so that he could easily get to that gun.

"The Lord giveth . . ." Guy's voice, unfaltering, filled the rain-drenched silence. His rain-washed face, white and ill looking, lifted to the sky that was the color of lead. "The Lord taketh . . ."

Somewhere a woman sobbed softly. The saloon-keeper was mindful of a trickle of rain that had leaked through the front of his slicker and was undoubtedly ruining a new red tie. Hook stood like a man stunned. An impatient horse pawed the mud, splashing it on the men who had lifted the coffin from the wagon into the grave and now waited awkwardly for the moment when they could get back to town and a drink.

None of the nesters were there. Only a small

gathering of women who had known the dead woman, and their husbands.

Now the Bible in Guy's hands closed gently. He knelt, bareheaded, there in the mud at the head of the grave. His right hand found a small piece of sodden clay and he let it slide into the open grave.

Then he got to his feet, the knees of his cheap black pants forever ruined. And without a glance at his father, he turned and walked to the top buggy that he had hired. The driver looked at him with an awed expression. Guy carefully stowed the Bible in a canvas sheath and shoved it inside his sodden black coat.

"Town, Guy?" asked the driver in a scared voice.

"Town," nodded Guy.

Now the other rigs, as if at a signal, started for Landusky. Until they had all gone, save the buckboard that had fetched the saloon man and Hook Jones. It stood there, the team of buckskins tied to the graveyard fence.

In the hands of Hook Jones, or rather in the one hand and the hook that served him as a hand, was gripped a shovel that he had unceremoniously taken from the man whose duty it was to fill the graves. Hook held the shovel as he might have held a rifle. Then, without a word, he began filling the grave of the woman who had been his wife. The saloon man looked around until he found a second shovel. He was about to assist in the dreary task when a look from Hook's burning eyes halted him. He put away the shovel and walked over to the buckboard where he crouched in its shelter trying to get some consolation from a rain moistened cigar.

After what seemed a long time the grave was filled. Hook Jones tossed aside the shovel and strode through the mud to the waiting buckboard. He and the saloon man untied the halter ropes and climbed into the rig. Hook handled the lines with astonishing skill as the rain-chilled buckskin team went against their collars with a swift lunge. When they neared town, Hook gave the lines to the saloon man. From under a heavy tarp he took a sawed-off shot-gun.

The saloon man gave him a startled look. "What's the scatter-gun for, Hook?"

"I'm killin' the snivelin' little whelp that laid his mother in her grave." Hook's voice was rasping, scarcely human. The voice of a killer whose heart is drained of mercy. The saloon man was chilled by the terrible coldness of Hook's voice and the slitted glare of the man's bloodshot eyes that burned from a face twisted out of shape with hate.

Hook Jones told the saloon man to drive slowly up the street that was a muddy yellow ribbon that climbed up a rocky gulch lined with pines and brush and boulders. Saloons on each side. Lew Jake's place. Pike Landusky's store. Frame and log buildings with square fronts and plank walks in front. Horses, their saddles covered with slickers, tied at the hitch-racks. The street was deserted.

Hook sat with the sawed-off shot-gun ready, his slitted eyes sweeping both sides of the street. When they reached the end of the street, Hook made the saloon man turn the team and drive slowly back down the gulch. Twice they repeated this before Hook turned the team over to a frightened-looking barn man and strode out of the barn, deserting the saloon man, who gave a sigh of relief as he mopped a moist brow.

Straight up the middle of the rain-swept street, Landusky's one and only street, walked Hook Jones, the shot-gun in the crook of his left arm, right hand gripping it tightly. He walked with slanted hat-brim across his eyes, with a wide spread gait. He had discarded his slicker at the barn and the low tied .45 on his right thigh was ready for use.

Up on to the plank walk and into the first saloon he stalked, a terrible figure of hatred. The men inside the saloon had seen him as he had ridden up and down the street. They had been warned, therefore, of his coming. There were no nesters in the place. Only some cow-men, a bleary-eyed swamper, and a gambler who sat dealing himself hands from a marked deck. There was no trace of Guy.

Hook glared from under his dripping hatbrim. There was a silence. Only the soft slap of the gambler's cards. No man spoke. The bartender polished a whisky glass and set it on the bar alongside a bottle of whisky. Without a word,

Hook strode to the bar and helped himself to a drink. Then, without a word, he went out again. Out into the rain, on up the street to the next saloon.

But there was no sign of Guy Jones. Nor were there any of the Big Warm nesters in any of the saloons. The men who watched him make his sinister search felt the deadly glitter of his blood-shot eyes and gave mute thanks when he had gone on.

Men who had known the one-armed rancher since he had first come to the country, men who had joshed with him and swapped yarns had not dared speak. Hook was like some very dangerous beast, prowling, bent on killing.

This was Hook Jones, killer from the bloody Wyoming war. That brutal, blood-smeared range war that had outlawed Hook, had robbed his wife of her sanity, and had given him his son Guy who to-day had read a passage from the Bible and whose black garments showed no bulge of a hidden gun. This was Hook Jones, deadly killer, on the prowl. Where other men might boast of their toughness, Hook's was a lipless, red-eyed silence more terrible than any boasting.

Mixed with that hatred for his son was a gnawing, aching, terrible grief for the woman who had died so pitiful a death. Hook never wanted to ever again see the ranch that had been their home. He was leaving it behind him for-ever. He would once more ride the outlaw trail, homeless, an outcast, destined to fill some uncared-for grave, doomed to death, a killer with a bounty on his scalp.

He had cursed the man who gave him Dave Rawlins's message. He had told the cowboy that he answered no man's call and that he would come when he was ready and not until after he had done a job he had to do.

Now, when he could not find the son whose life he had sworn to take, he saddled his horse and rode out of town, still without his chaps or slicker, still with the sawed-off shot-gun across his arm. His head was bent and the ugly steel hook that served as his left hand, hooked itself around the saddle horn. So Hook Jones quit Landusky that day. And those who watched him go knew that he had gone to join the Nighthawk. Hook Jones was no longer quite sane.

At the homestead of Guy's over on Big Warm that same evening, a white-faced bride peered anxiously into the gray dusk that was filled with cold, drizzling rain. And when Guy rode up she ran hatless into the rain to greet him.

When he had put up his horse, they went into the house. Guy laid the frayed Bible on the kitchen table and went into the bedroom to change from his sodden clothes. He looked white and ill and strained to the breaking point. Olga busied herself with the supper and brought him a hot lemonade which she made him drink.

"It's mighty tough on you, Olga," he said, smiling wanly. "You must have suffered an awful lot these past few days, waiting for me to come home, wondering if my father would murder me."

"Was he there at the funeral, Guy?"

"Yes. He'd promised to kill me after Mother was buried. I left before he did. He was still standing there by the grave, like a man in a trance, when I went back to town and got my horse. I suppose he hunted for me, but I'd gone. I can only hope and pray that he won't follow me here."

Olga nodded.

She knew what Guy meant. That, if Hook Jones came here to their little home, then Guy would use the six-shooter that lay loaded on the shelf in the kitchen.

While Olga finished preparing supper, Guy read from the Bible that had belonged to his mother. The Bible that she had carried with her from the Wyoming cattle war.

Perhaps the prayers of the white-faced boy and the girl who was his wife sent to God were answered that night. Because Hook Jones swung his horse southward towards the bad-lands that hid the Nighthawk and his men.

"Uncle" Hank Mayberry looked from his swivel chair to the gilt-lettered label on the door that he had left open when he came into his office, there at the Valley Bank.

123

"Henry Clay Mayberry, President."

So he read aloud in an undertone. He studied the lettering with a mingling of disgust and amusement and anger. Then he swore softly at the lettering as if it were able to hear and understand his words.

He tried leaning back in the new swivel-chair and when he almost upset, his comments brought a well groomed and rather patronizing bank employee into the new office.

"Git out!" barked Uncle Hank. "Git outa here and stay out. Go back into the danged monkey cage that fits yuh. And when the Prince uh Wales comes in, tell him tuh lope in here."

"The Prince of Wales?"

"Snodgrass, dang it. And don't lemme ketch yuh wearin' that lavender shirt in my bank again or yo're fired, savvy? Now drag it."

When the confused teller had taken his uncomfortable departure, Uncle Hank opened drawer after drawer of his new desk. His muttering was like the growl of a bear. Finally, after much searching, he found cigarette papers and tobacco and, ignoring the patent lighter on his new desk, he pulled the head of a match across the seat of the trousers made by the tailor his daughter and her husband Howard Snodgrass had taken him to.

A small, white-haired, white-bearded man, Uncle Hank Mayberry. He walked with a limp that was the result of a flint-headed Sioux arrow.

Time had been when Hank Mayberry had been a government scout and a good one.

The feet that he deliberately and defiantly put on the polished mahogany desk were encased in high-heeled, shop-made boots. The hat that he had dropped over a bronze desk ornament was a high-crowned Stetson of finest beaver. He snorted at the onyx ash-tray and scattered his cigarette ashes on the expensive rug. The ashes landed where, until recently, a large brass cuspidor had always stood near his chair. Then he unbuttoned his vest and chuckled.

"What'd ol' Jim Bridger or Liver Eatin' Johnson say if they could ketch me in this danged layout?"

He waited half an hour for his son-in-law. Then he limped out into the front part of the Valley Bank and beckoned the immaculate teller.

"Ring up that sign painter and tell him to fetch along his outfit. When he gits here, tell him that if he don't want tuh git into trouble, he better wipe out that Henry Clay and put in Hank in its place. My name is Hank Mayberry. That's what goes on that door. When the Duke uh Austria gits around tell him he'll find me over at the Bucket uh Blood settin' in a game uh draw poker."

Uncle Hank pulled his hat at a defiant angle and limped out of the bank, tugging with a stubby forefinger at the white collar that always seemed to be choking him.

125

Several times on his way up the street to the saloon, he halted to swap the time of day and a joke or two with overalled cow-punchers. He barely nodded to Creighton Marley and two well-dressed men who stood on the sidewalk in front of Marley's office. He dropped in at the livery barn and for half an hour squatted on his boot heels smoking borrowed tobacco and re-calling the merits of certain horses that he had owned when the barn belonged to him. Quarter horses that had cleaned up the fastest ponies in the country. Then he limped on to the Bucket of Blood, where he joined three cronies in a game of penny ante freeze-out poker.

It was here that Dave Rawlins and Bob Driscoll, the latter with his arm linked in that of his old friend, found Hank Mayberry. Hank looked up from three aces and a pair of treys. He blinked hard for a moment at sight of the two men whose friendship had been severed these past years. Then, with a joyous, if somewhat profane whoop, he got to his feet and greeted his old friends with a manner that certainly could never become the president of a bank.

Others dropped their cards to join the re-union. The white aproned bartender who stood grinning in the doorway of the card room was told to bring in some real champagne.

So it was that Howard Snodgrass, an hour later, looked in upon a gathering that was a de-cided shock to his dignity. Hank called him into the smoke-filled room.

126

"Howard," he said mildly, "what's that high-toned word yuh use when there's a gatherin' of the bank directors?"

"Conference." Howard Snodgrass spoke with annoyed sharpness.

"That's her. Conference. Well, Howard, me and these old cow-hocked, sway-backed, knee-sprung wart-hawgs is in conference. Slam the door as you go out."

"But, look here," said Howard Snodgrass impatiently, "we have an appointment with Marley and the two gentlemen he's bringing over to the bank."

"Tell 'em to wait," chuckled Uncle Hank.

"How long will you be here?"

"Dunno. Mebby all afternoon and all night. Mebby a week if the champagne and bar grub hold out. Hard tuh say. On yore way out, tell Pete we're runnin' short uh champagne."

With an angry scowl, Howard Snodgrass took an abrupt departure. Before he was out of earshot, he heard the laughter behind the closed door of the card room.

"Bob," said Uncle Hank Mayberry, when the laughter had died out, "if ever Colleen fetches home one uh them dudes, set the dawgs on him. Now lemme tell yuh about that sign on the door again. Dave, hang yore head out the door and tell Pete tuh rattle his hocks with that wine. Bin a shore long time since us boys got together. We're about to go the way uh the buffalo, but before we go, we'll holler once more."

From time to time, during the next hours, various and sundry grizzled old timers dropped in and joined the reunion.

Several times during that time, Howard Snodgrass failed to gain admission to the card room.

At the bank, Creighton Marley and his two business associates waited impatiently for the coming of Uncle Hank Mayberry. Marley was in a black mood but dared not show it. The two men who had hoped to leave Chinook on the afternoon train were visibly annoyed.

"It looks like we'll have to wait until to-morrow," Snodgrass informed them. "The old — ah — Mr. Mayberry is busy. He won't be disturbed."

"We came down from Helena, Snodgrass, to get this deal put through to-day. We're losing valuable time. We're in a position to do this bank a great deal of good. If you can't handle our money, we'll go elsewhere."

Howard Snodgrass did his best to smooth out the ruffled tempers of the two men who, at Marley's request, had come from Helena to do business with the bank. Snodgrass and Marley, for many weeks, had been working toward the consummation of this big deal with certain men who were Creighton Marley's backers. Now, on this day of days, when the deal was to go through, Hank Mayberry walked out, foregathered with old cronies who could do the bank no good, and was drinking champagne with those broken-down soon-to-be-penniless stockmen.

It was a bitter dose for Howard Snodgrass. The proverbial final straw was placed when the painter came to change the lettering on the door of Hank's office. Howard Snodgrass had the unfortunate man ushered out with more than necessary firmness.

At three o'clock that afternoon Howard Snodgrass took Marley and the two Helena men to his home for dinner.

At somewhat after three thirty that same afternoon, Uncle Hank Mayberry and Dave Rawlins, with the blind Bob Driscoll between them, walked down the street from the Bucket of Blood Saloon to the Valley Bank. Oddly enough, none of the three showed any visible signs of being intoxicated.

To be sure, their gait was the somewhat rolling gait of men who are more at home in the saddle than on foot. They were in a mellow mood that was as much the result of golden reminiscing as it was the result of the champagne.

"I gotta show you boys that dude office," repeated Uncle Hank. "Even if ol' Bob can't make out tuh see it, he kin feel around. Think of it, not a danged spittoon in the place. A chair that r'ars back like a bronc. It's — it's jest plumb disgraceful, that's all."

Uncle Hank let them in by the side door. The bank was empty. It was with the manner of three school-boys sneaking into a ball game that they entered the stately portals of the Valley Bank.

129

Chuckling, Hank led them into the bank and toward his office. Now a groan came from his grinning lips. He was staring at the gilt lettering on his door. The lettering that had not been changed. He still was, to the public who entered his bank, Henry Clay Mayberry.

It so happened that he was carrying Bob Driscoll's heavy cane. Now, with a growling oath, he smashed the glass panel that bore the offensive lettering.

"Now, boys," he said, grinning widely, "step into Hank Mayberry's office."

Behind Uncle Hank's smile lay a bitter rancor, born of many months' brooding. Howard Snodgrass had, for a long time, run the bank with a snobbish, suave, kid-gloved but firm and effective manner. He had taken the actual management of the bank from hands more accustomed to rope and branding-iron and gun than they were to fountain-pen and legal papers.

Snodgrass had managed to get in a board of directors that smothered Uncle Hank's ideas. Their legal phrases puzzled him, their manner rather awed him. He did not understand banking laws and he reckoned that they must be legally right in their opinions. Though he pointed out that he had always managed to amble along somehow before Snodgrass married his daughter and married himself into the bank.

True, he had been mighty careless about his friends paying off their notes on time and had often made loans to men that could put up little but their names on paper as security. But those men were men with whom Hank had crossed the plains. They were men whose given word was as good as the United States President's bond. They had never beat him out of a dollar. When they couldn't pay off a note, Hank would have 'em make out a new one.

Now, with a new building, new vaults, new employees and new furniture, the bank didn't seem to be Hank Mayberry's bank any longer. It wasn't the bank he'd opened in the old brick building next to the Last Chance, the bank he'd opened with a few thousand dollars and the backing of such old friends as Dave Rawlins and Bob Driscoll.

Nope, this bank was too shiny and cold-hearted and big. It wasn't the kind of a bank Hank liked to run. It didn't feel comfortable to him any more than this danged white collar that choked him. It wasn't the place where he could sit and talk with old-time friends. This was Howard Snodgrass's bank, not Hank Mayberry's. The sign on the door was but a symbol of the rancor in the heart of the old plainsman. He'd smashed the danged thing. And he'd go fu'ther, too.

"Set down, boys. Here's a easy-chair fer Bob. And now, before we go any fu'ther, let's git somethin' off our minds. Both you boys want yore notes renewed, don't yuh? And some money fer runnin' expenses till after the fall shipments and after Bob peddles some uh them hosses. All right. Name yore own figgers, yuh two ol' sons."

"Better we'd wait till to-morrow er some day when Snodgrass kin have his say-so," protested Dave Rawlins.

If Dave had wanted to get money and had wished to use a name that would work the combination, he could not have chosen a more fitting name than that of Snodgrass.

It took five minutes to calm Uncle Hank down and keep him from wrecking the mahogany furniture. At the end of those minutes Hank made Dave Rawlins sign two notes. One, a renewal of the note that was about due, the other a note for money to tide him over until his steers were shipped. And Bob Driscoll made his mark on two similar notes.

"And now," chuckled Uncle Hank Mayberry, "we'll go up to the Bucket uh Blood and see has Pete got that next bottle cold enough tuh swaller."

So, on that day, did Uncle Hank Mayberry, out of loyalty to his old friends, do that which was soon to cause so much trouble. Those bits of signed paper, symbols of the sort of friendship that belonged to buffalo days, were to stand as evidence against a white-haired old man that he had violated banking laws and was therefore liable to a long term behind the bars of State's Prison.

It was the next day that Uncle Hank Mayberry listened to the proposition that Creighton

Marley, Marley's two backers in the land business, and Howard Snodgrass put before him.

Patiently, in a silence that made his son-in-law
uneasy, did Uncle hank listen. And when they
were done talking, the old plainsman got to his
feet and limped to the door of his office. The
door with the smashed glass panel. He opened
the door and held it open. His blue eyes blazed
with anger. When he spoke, his voice was brittle:

"This way out!"

They went. With them went a substantial account. With them also went Howard Snodgrass.
And on the evening of that same day Snodgrass
wired a message to the State bank examiner at
Helena.

CHAPTER X

HAIR-TRIGGERED PEACEMAKER

*Ye Roman-nosed buzzard, yer eye has grown
    dim:*
*Old Time has been rustlin' the lines that were
    trim;*
*Yer joints are as kinked as a rope that's bin
    coiled*
*Since the sheepmen invaded a range they have
    spoiled.*

— To An Old Cow-Horse.

Buck Rawlins looked up from the letter that had
come by messenger from town. He grinned at
Colleen, who sat with him on the big veranda of
the Driscoll ranch house.

"Well, pardner, they've pulled us out of the
bog. Dad and Bob Driscoll got their loans from
the Valley Bank. They'll be home to-morrow.
Dad saw Ike Niland and Ike told him they'd
dropped all charges against me."

"Which don't mean they're through with
you, Buck. Call it woman's intuition or a
hunch or plumb foolishness, but I smell
trouble. Things are quiet. Too darned quiet,
and I'd say it is the lull before the storm. Who
have you got line-riding the range where

Murdock is putting those sheep?"

"Two old heads that won't do anything foolish. Onion Oliver is riding over there every other day. The little West girl goes with him. So far, Murdock is keeping to his own side of the line."

"Where is Hook Jones, Buck?"

"Ask me something easy. Nobody has seen him since he left Landusky. He probably is with the Nighthawk."

Colleen shook her head. "I met Fancy Mary this morning on the road. She says Hook Jones is not with the Nighthawk."

Buck scowled thoughtfully. "That's bad. The Nighthawk is the only man that can handle Hook when he turns bad. Hook Jones is bad medicine. I saw him fight once and he knocked out four big, husky miners before we got him quiet. And for almost a week he sat around brooding, saying nothing to anybody, drinking whisky like it was water. He'd have killed any of us that crossed him. Then he snapped out of it and was all right. But when he's on the prod, he's a devil."

"Hook Jones hates sheep, Buck, and he hates the nesters, especially since Guy got married to that nester girl on Big Warm. Buck, I also found out from Fancy Mary that Guy is tending those sheep camps on the Forest Reserve. He takes their grub to them and is over there at one of their camps half the time. Do you suppose Hook is laying for Guy?"

135

"Hard to say. Gosh, you're getting me worried, now. It would take a man like Hook Jones to start something that it'll take an army to finish. I wish I knew where that big nester roughneck and his gang that tortured Mary are hanging out. They vanished mighty sudden. Gosh, yonder comes our bearer of the evil tidings or I'm a bum guesser."

Buck pointed to a man who had dismounted to open the big pole gate that was the main entrance to the Driscoll ranch. The man was Deacon Nelson, the nester father-in-law of Guy Jones.

Nelson led his mule through the gate, mounted, and rode up to the house. Buck rose to greet the giant Swede, whose rugged face was clouded with trouble.

"What's the trouble?" Buck came abruptly to the point.

"I've come to ask, in the name of God, for the sake of humanity and common decency, that you call off your night-riders. They have run off our work horses and mules, cut our fences, driven cattle across our grain fields. My wife and daughters live in constant terror. Last night Eric Swanson, my son-in-law, was waylaid and badly beaten.

"The dry-land farmers are incensed. They are banding together in order to fight back. Can you not see, young man, what this is coming to? There will be bloodshed, murder. We came here to this country a peaceful people. I am an ordained minister and the pastor of these harassed people who come to me for advice. I have done all in my power to calm them, but the hour has now come when my words will no longer hold them.

"They are holding secret meetings to which I am not asked. They will fight back, once they start. And because we are men of peace, do not think that we cannot fight if the cause is a just one. For God's sake, man, call off your hoodlums!"

"Have a seat, Deacon," said Buck, "and listen to what I have to say. As the God we both believe in is my judge, we have no band of night-riders. The 7UP cowboys are at the other end of the range, ready to begin the calf round-up. The Rolling M riders are almost a hundred miles away gathering horses. You will have to believe me when I say that we are not the breed that uses such methods of attack."

"I was accused by Dave Rawlins of being implicated in the murder of a cowboy named Joe Phelps. I have heard many horrible tales of the methods used by the cattlemen in the Wyoming war. Now, when my property is destroyed, my stock run off, the windows of my house shot with bullets, what else am I to believe? What are my people to believe?"

"I see your viewpoint, Deacon. I don't want war any more than you want it. You are not the only one whose property has suffered. I can take you across the 7UP range and in the course of half a day's ride, show you the carcasses of dead cows shot down and the calves left to the mercy of coyotes.

"We have men scattered around to watch but we'd have to hire an army to guard the amount of range we have. And on the Rolling M range, horses are stolen and chased with dogs until mares heavy with colt have died. Little colts have been so badly crippled that they had to be killed.

"I might ask you, even as you have asked me, that you call off your night-riders. But we've come to the conclusion that, while some of the men who are doing this dirty work are nesters, they don't belong to your clan. They are of a tough breed, put in here by Creighton Marley to make trouble between the cattlemen and the farmers. We have no actual proof, yet, but we're working on it mighty strong.

"I agree with you, things are getting tight. Trouble may come at any time. And nobody but Creighton Marley, sitting safe in his office at Chinook, will benefit by it. Tell your people that. Ask Guy Jones what he thinks of the Rawlins outfit or the Rolling M outfit. He will tell you that we are not murderers or thieves."

"I have already asked Guy and the boy verifies your claim. But the father of that poor, grief-stricken boy is a cold blooded killer who claims allegiance to the 7UP outfit. Can you deny that?"

"I can and I will deny it, sir. Until Hook Jones quarreled with Guy, he was on the 7UP pay-roll and handled our cattle. His ranch was a line

138

camp headquarters in the wintertime. But when he turned bitter, my father sent for him to come to this ranch. He was to be given the choice of obeying orders or quitting. Hook did not come here. He sent word back that he was not coming in to the ranch. Where he is or what he is doing, I don't know. I wish I did. Miss Driscoll and I were discussing the man when we sighted you coming."

"That's true," said Colleen. "If you knew Buck Rawlins as well as I and many other people know him, you would feel safe in accepting his word. Buck Rawlins is not a liar. Nor is he a killer or a bad-man as some folks seem to think. I would accept Buck's word against any man's sworn oath."

Buck bowed elaborately. "Thank you, pardner. But don't give Deacon Nelson the impression that this is a mutual admiration society. There are times, Deacon, when this young lady rawhides me till my hide blisters."

A smile softened the rugged features of the farmer preacher. "I'm finding myself on the verge of being convinced," he said in his deep, kindly voice. "If only you could so convince my people. If you could only aid me in stopping these night-riders by some method that would not necessitate the taking of human lives."

"I'll do my best, Deacon," said Buck impulsively. "Tell you what I'll do. Find out where the nesters are holding their meeting to-night and I'll go there with you. I'm no orator, but if they'll listen, I'll say what I know to be the truth. How's that for a proposition?"

"If you can convince Eric Swanson and the others, then you are doing a merciful and manly deed."

"Your shoulder isn't healed well enough to be riding around, Buck," protested Colleen.

"Shucks, it's as well as ever. That Starlight horse is as easy riding as that rocking-chair. Deacon, I'll be with you in about two minutes."

Colleen excused herself and followed Buck inside the house. She found him shoving cartridges into his belt. He grinned at her boyishly.

"No need to go looking worried, pardner. I might be able to throw a monkey-wrench into this trouble machine if I talk fast to those sod-busters. I'm an envoy of peace."

"Says he, loading his gun. Buck, you'll get into trouble, sure as you're a foot high. The first farmer that won't accept your peace talk you'll want to fight him. You, of all people, going to arbitrate a thing like this. Buck Rawlins, peacemaker. Honestly, if you could only see the humor of it."

"I'm going. And I'll hold my sweet temper choked down. I'll let them smear me and turn the other cheek. Gosh, I haven't been on a horse in a coon's age."

"Not since you declared war on the sheep industry. That was a fair sample of your diplomacy. Buck, for the love of the cow business, stay home."

"For the love of the horse business, quit hen-pecking at me. I'm free, white, and twenty-one."

"And the darndest hair triggered cow-puncher that ever got into a fight. Seeing there's no argument of mine can stop you, go to it. I'll send Tuley Bill over with the wagon to fetch home your remains. Have at it, cowboy."

Buck buckled on his belt with its .45, and reached for his hat. Then he put his arms around Colleen and kissed her, as he had kissed her a hundred and one times.

"So-long, li'l' pardner."

"Good-by, Buck. And hold your temper."

But it was with a heavy heart that Colleen Driscoll watched Buck Rawlins ride away. He turned in the saddle and waved his hat. Never had he looked more handsome, more manly, than he did now. She waved her handkerchief, a lump in her throat. And suddenly she knew that Buck Rawlins meant more than a lot to her.

The nesters had, by popular vote, elected Eric Swanson as their leader. A blond Viking of a man, with eyes the same blue as the sea is blue when the summer sun warms its water. Blue that can change to a cold greenish tint when a storm is brewing. A giant of a man, this Eric Swanson who had taken up a homestead on Big Warm, and possessed of a stubborn brand of courage.

Born in Minnesota and the product of the public high school, he did not lack education, though his intelligence was more stolid than brilliant. What he had learned, he had wrested with stubborn force from his books. Nor was it an easy task to shake his opinion, once he had formed it.

Buck Rawlins, ushered by Deacon Nelson into the little school-house where the farmers had gathered, was met by cold, unfriendly stares. The Deacon had passed Buck through the several guards who surrounded the school-house. Now the young cow-man stood there in the aisle between the desks and benches filled with brawny farmers, facing Eric Swanson, who stood on the platform. Eric, whose face bore the bruises and discolorations of his last night's attack.

Buck's quick eyes swept the assemblage of unfriendly men. Mostly, he reckoned, they were Swedes and Norwegians, with a sprinkling of German and Swiss. They were the farmer type who are grain raisers. Big-boned men, dull of wit, stubborn-minded, slow to make decisions and when those decisions are made, still more slow to give way.

Buck saw the difficulty of his well-meant mission. He saw the antagonism of the farmer toward the cow-man. A word from Eric Swanson and their hands, hard and big and calloused, would be on him. And just now, as the man stood there on the platform, his bruised face hardening, Buck thought perhaps that signal might be given.

"Who sent you here?" growled Eric Swanson.

"I brought him here," spoke the deep voice of Deacon Nelson, who stood behind Buck.

"You take him away before he gets hurt. Nobody here sent for that man. We don't want him."

"He has something to say, Eric," said the deacon. "Something you all should hear."

"He has nothing to say that we want to listen to. He comes here to spy on us. Get out of here, Rawlins."

Buck saw the faces of the nesters become more tense. He heard the whispered mutter that ran like a wave across the thirty or forty men packed in the room. He sensed in Eric Swanson an enemy who would fight without giving way.

Now it was fully revealed to Buck the vast chasm of misunderstanding that separated him and all other cow-men from these invaders. He would never understand them, and they could never see the viewpoint of the cattleman. He saw the folly, the bitter folly of this errand. He hated them, every last one of them, even as they hated him. He hated them because they did not belong here, and because they were heavy-minded and stupid and plodding. Their plows were ripping the very heart from the cow country, their damned barb wire fences were choking the life from this country Buck loved with a reckless passion.

He knew as he stood there that there was nothing he could say, nothing he could do, to make these sod-busters understand. They would never believe him. They would brand him as a liar and a spy. Their looks already condemned him. These men would not listen, as their deacon had listened there on the veranda of the Rolling M ranch. They would only laugh at him, sneer at him, goad him into some rash act that would only precipitate the war that was all but declared between the cattlemen and the nesters. Buck Rawlins had seen their side. But they would stubbornly, stupidly refuse to see his.

Buck, a little white about the lips, fighting back the words that he wanted to say, words that would tell them what fools they were, turned to Deacon Nelson.

"I reckon, sir," he said in a low tone, "that I'll be going. I'm not wanted here. I can't talk their language. There is nothing I can say to that man on the platform or to his friends, that will help matters. I'd better go."

"Yah," leered a big farmer on the aisle who had overheard Buck's words, "ya better go or you be sorry."

Buck's hand dropped to his gun. His temper, white hot in a split-second, swept over him like a flame. His eyes bored into the now startled eyes of the loutish farmer.

"I'm going, you plow shover, but I'm not going because I'm scared. Don't open that loose mouth of yours again. Don't any of you crowd me into a scrap. I'm alone against the pack of you but I'll make some of you sorry. I came here to make peace. You don't want me. All right.

But the first man of you, and the next five that follow him, that tries to lay a hand on me, will be sorry."

Buck backed toward the doorway, his hand on his gun, his steely eyes holding them at bay. Deacon Nelson stood there like a man doomed, as the young cattleman backed out. But as a restless movement passed over the crowd, the deacon's big frame blocked the doorway. His arms upraised, he spoke to them in his deep, throaty voice:

"Stand back. You don't know what you are doing, men. Let that man go his way in peace."

Buck, smarting with helpless rage, stepped up on his horse. His hand on his gun, he rode past the guards. As he rode into the shadows of the night a voice, cautious, desperate, hailed him out of the darkness.

"Buck! Buck!"

"Who is it?" Buck called softly.

"It's me. Guy. Guy Jones. I've been waiting, Buck, since I watched yuh ride to the schoolhouse with the deacon."

"Come on out of the brush, kid. We'll talk while we ride. This place isn't too healthy for me."

"I . . . I can't ride, Buck. I'm hurt . . . I been shot, Buck."

CHAPTER XI
A BREAK IN THE RANKS

Parson, I'm a maverick, just runnin' loose an'
*   grazin',*
Eatin' where's the greenest grass an' drinkin'
*   where I choose;*
Had to rustle in my youth an' never had no
*   raisin';*
Wasn't never halter-broke an' I ain't got
*   much to lose.*

— Crossing the Divide.

There was a bullet hole in the fleshy part of Guy's thigh, so Buck discovered when he had made a hasty examination by match light.

The young fellow's face was drawn with pain, but his eyes were brave and he gamely tried to grin.

"You can tell me how you got this sometime later on, kid. The main idea right now is to get you home and to bed, and get that hole swabbed out."

"I'll get home, Buck. I'll tell you what I found out down on the edge of the bad-lands, then you ride along. I'll hail the first farmer and he'll take me home. Gosh, after me being shot, this nester colony is no place for you to be found by Eric and his cronies. They'll kill you, Buck."

"I reckon not, kid. You let me worry about that. Here, put your arm around my neck. That's it. Lucky I'm riding Starlight. He'll pack double. Up you go, old man. I'll ride behind and hold yuh on."

So Buck took Guy Jones home. Guy's wife, after the first shock that drained the blood from her rosy cheeks, took her husband's accident calmly enough. She heated water and fashioned bandages from clean white sheets. Buck mixed a carbolic solution and bathed the wound. It was a clean hole, made by a steel nosed bullet.

Guy fainted and Buck worked swiftly before the boy regained consciousness. He had just finished his task, there in the bedroom, when he heard men's voices outside. He easily recognized the voice of Eric Swanson. Eric was demanding of Guy's wife where her husband had hidden Buck Rawlins. They had seen Buck's horse standing outside the cabin.

"Where is he, Olga? We want him."

"Eric Swanson," said Guy's bride firmly, "this house is Guy's house and mine. If Buck Rawlins is here, then he is welcome here under this roof and you have no right talking that way to me. Buck Rawlins has always been Guy's friend. He is welcome in this house."

"Buck Rawlins tried to break up the meeting to-night. He pulled a gun and threatened to kill us. Unless you let us in, then we'll class Guy with the cattlemen. I've never trusted him, anyhow.

He's been acting queer around the camps. I sent word in to the Murdock ranch, you bet. I sent word in to Bill Murdock that Guy ain't tending to his job. He ain't been to the camps for two days. He's over on the 7UP range, I bet. Now you let this Rawlins hide behind your skirts, hey?"

Buck stepped from the bedroom into the front room where Olga stood barring Eric's way. Behind Eric stood several other farmers.

"Yah!" barked Eric; "what does he hide there in that room for? Friend of your husband, is he? But your husband ain't home. Yah!" Eric's face was ugly with wrath.

"If there wasn't a lady present, Swanson," said Buck hotly, "I'd knock a few teeth down your throat."

"You?" Eric laughed with an ugly sound. "I break you in two, you fool. With these two hands I break your back."

"I don't think so, fish eater. I'll step outside and try it on anyhow."

"Buck!" called Guy's voice from the bedroom, "Buck, who are you talking to? What's wrong?"

Buck turned to Olga. "Please go in and keep the old kid quiet. Tell him some kind of a lie that will hold him. I'll handle this gent." He almost pushed her into the bedroom.

There was for a moment, a queer look in Eric Swanson's eyes. A startled, almost frightened look. Buck motioned toward the door that led outside.

"After you, snuse eater."

"You got a gun on, Rawlins."

Buck unbuckled his gun belt and laid it and his six-shooter on the table. He flexed the muscles of the arm that had not yet fully healed. He had carried it in a sling made of a black neck-scarf which he now took off and laid beside the gun. Then he stepped outside.

Eric Swanson's companions had found a couple of lanterns. They now formed a circle. Buck sized up the blond giant with a sinking heart. Eric had stripped off his shirt and under-shirt and now stood there, his splendid muscles rippling. Buck, though no light-weight, looked puny by comparison. And he was sadly handi-capped by having only one good arm.

"Let's go, Copenhagen!" He grinned crook-edly.

Eric rushed him. A smile of confidence on his red face, Buck sidestepped and hooked a vicious right into the Swede's mid-section. He figured that to be the big nester's only weak spot.

Eric grunted, whirled, and with a snarling "Yah!" he smashed a big fist at Buck's wounded shoulder. He had done that deliberately. Buck ducked and danced back. That sledge-hammer blow had been like a dull knife stabbing hilt deep into the healing wound. The terrific pain made him sick and faint. He felt the warm blood burst from the reopened wound.

Now Eric rushed again. Buck, covering des-perately, tried to get out of the way. He might have succeeded had not a farmer tripped him. Buck went sprawling. With a victorious, snarling laugh, Eric was about to kick the fallen man when something happened.

A man on horseback had jumped his mount through the ring of farmers. Before Eric Swanson's heavy hobnailed shoe could smash the cow-puncher, a strong hand reached down, grabbed the big Swede by the hair and flung him, yelping with pain, backward. Now the horseman was on the ground.

"My scrap, Buck. Back to the side-lines." And Bill Murdock, for it was he, squared off to meet Eric.

Buck, sick and groggy, got to his feet. Bill Murdock grinned at him crookedly.

"Not because I have any fondness for you, Mister 7UP, but because even a lousy sheep-herder has a sense of fair play. Come get what you have coming to you, Swanson."

"I don't fight against my boss," muttered Eric.

"I'm not your boss, you big cheese. I fired you about half a minute ago. Fight, you big bum."

With the swift foot-work of a pugilist, Bill Murdock stepped forward. Once, twice, his open hands smacked the face of the farmer. Then, poised on the balls of his feet, he smashed a beautiful left to the Swede's nose. Blood spurted. Eric, blinded by the quick pain, shook his head as if to clear it of pain. Bill had stepped back to where Buck stood.

"How's that for tapping the claret, cowboy?"

"Sometimes," said Buck, "when you do something like this, it's hard to smell sheep on yuh. You saved my bacon and I — Watch him, Bill!"

Eric, pretending to be dizzy, had staggered a little. Then he rushed, big fists cocked. Bill did not give an inch. Evenly matched for size and weight, their big bodies crashed together with a terrific force. Bill Murdock grinned into the blood smeared face of the farmer as they swayed together, locked in vise-like clinch.

"I'll teach you a few manners, Swanson, before I finish. And a trick or two. How do you like this, big boy?" Bill's right arm had somehow broken the Swede's hold. It swung in a short, vicious arc, landing on the bleeding nose. With a howl of pain, Eric staggered back.

Bill danced free and with two open handed blows, so loud that his hand against the other's cheek sounded like a pistol shot, he rocked Eric's head. Then, as the farmer covered his face, Bill stepped up, lifted an uppercut into Eric's middle. The farmer, gasping for breath, doubled up.

Bill slid around behind him and kicked him with playful but painful force, in the seat of his bob overalls. Eric went forward on his face.

Some well meaning friend stepped forward. Bill grabbed the man by the waistband of his trousers and flung him ten feet, so that he crashed into others. Now Bill handed Buck a .45.

"Keep 'em out of it, Buck. I'm not finished

with this plow pusher."

And as the crowd stood back, Bill let Eric get to his feet. He slapped the farmer's face a dozen times, until Eric was sobbing and blubbering and begging for mercy.

Finally Bill gave him a final kick in the overalls and then grinned.

"Take him home, the rest of you. And whenever you get snuffy and think about doing battle, take a look at the nose that Swanson will wear from now on. Now drift, the pack of yuh."

When they had taken the sobbing Eric and departed, Bill Murdock turned to Buck.

Buck handed Bill his gun.

"That was dog-goned white of you, Bill."

"You simply furnished me with an excuse to do something I've been itching to do for some time. Keep the change, 7UP. Is Guy at home?"

"He is. And he's got a bullet hole in his leg."

"One of Hook's bullets?"

"Dunno. I was just patching the kid up when the sod-busters showed up."

Bill Murdock looked hard at Buck, who returned his stare. Enemies from boyhood, yet they fought in the open and respected each other's courage and spirit of fair play.

"Well, Buck, got anything to say?"

"About what?"

"About the man that shot you in the wing?"

"Not yet. Only it's hard to make myself believe that Angus Murdock did it."

"Well, let it ride like that, then," said Bill. "If

you don't mind, I'll talk to Guy before you see him again. He's working for me and there might be some things I don't want the 7UP to know. Get me?"

"I'd be thick skulled if I didn't. Go on in and see him. But tell his wife to fetch out my gun and what's left of the bandages. The Eric white hope sure opened up the old scratch."

"Come into the house and we'll patch you up, then."

While Guy's wife bandaged Buck's shoulder, Bill Murdock talked to Guy behind a closed door. Bill came out as the bandaging was finished.

"I've been telling Mrs. Jones," said Buck, "that we're mighty sorry about pulling off this ruckus in her front yard. She's sure mighty decent about it."

"I don't like Eric Swanson," said the girl simply. "I never have liked him. And here of late my father is not quite so fond of him. Two or three times my sister has all but told me that her married life is not any bed of roses. And they've been married only a week or two.

"Eric did all he could to prevent my marriage to Guy. He influenced father, too. That's why Guy and I ran away and got married. No, Eric got just what he needed. But it won't do him a bit of good. It will make him all the more bitter toward the stockmen. I'll tell you this, Mr. Murdock, now that you've broken with him, that Eric has not been the friend he pretends to be.

153

He dislikes you almost as he does Buck Rawlins."

Bill nodded and lit his pipe. "So I figured all along. And that's my only regret. I would have kept him on as camp tender. He's been watched ever since I hired him. So, for that matter, has Guy Jones. But Guy was watched for a different reason. The man watching Guy was supposed to keep the kid from having such an accident as has befallen him. But Guy gave him the slip, not knowing who he was. Mrs. Jones, you are married to a mighty brave-hearted chap. If Buck Rawlins and I had that boy's principles and ideals, there'd be no quarrel between us."

"For once, sheep-herder," said Buck Rawlins, "I can sure agree with you. Guy's one straight shooter."

"Yes, and he's one game rooster, 7UP. Trot in and see him while Mrs. Jones and I have a little business meeting."

Buck sat on the edge of the wounded boy's bed. "Two cripples, kid. Birds of a feather. Now give me the yarn about how you got plugged."

"I'm sorry, Buck, but I can't. Bill made me promise I'd keep shut about it all. But I'm going to tell you this much. The man that shot Joe Phelps was not Angus Murdock. And the man that shot you the night of the prairie fire was not old Angus. He's plumb innocent. Now don't ask me any more. Bill has been awful white to me, Buck. He's going to help me a lot more. Fact is, he aims to stake me in the sheep business. I'll take a band on shares and quit this farming. I got a few hundred dollars saved to put into the deal. It's my big chance, Buck, even if it is sheep I'm handling."

"Don't let that bother you, kid. There's worse things than sheep, even if I can't call any to mind right now. And if Bill Murdock says keep shut, you keep shut. I'm asking only one question. Was it Hook that plugged you?"

"No. No, it wasn't. He'd have done a better job of it. Nope, I was shot by the same gent that killed Joe Phelps and tried to kill you. That's all I can say."

And it was with that bit of puzzling news that Buck Rawlins rode back to the Rolling M ranch that night. Colleen was waiting up for him.

"Well, ambassador, has peace been declared?" she so covered her immense relief at seeing Buck come safely back.

He grinned down at her from the saddle. "Peace? Sure. Just like a flock of hornets when their mud nest is knocked down. If you'll stake me to a cup of java I'll give you the fight, round by round."

CHAPTER XII

DEATH-TRAP FOR TWO

My ceiling is the sky, my floor is the grass,
My music is the lowing herds as they pass;
My books are the brooks, my sermons the
stones;
My parson the wolf on his pulpit of bones.
                    — The Biblical Cowboy.

Onion Jones had seen a ghost. At the edge of the bad-lands, in plain sight against the evening sky-line, he had seen this ghost. No wraithlike, filmy thing that dissolved into thin air. But a burly, thick-necked, blunt-jawed image of a man who had been dead for fifteen years and more. The flesh and blood ghost of that dead man stood with a rifle in his hands, leaning with his broad back against a rimrock.

Onion lowered the field-glasses through the powerful lenses of which he had seen this ghost of a man who had been long dead. His leathery old face betrayed nothing of the emotions that surged through his body. He even smiled at Mazie West, who was finishing the last bacon sandwich they had brought with them.

"See anything important through those over-grown opera-glasses, Onion?"

"Nothin' of any value." He squinted up at the sun. "Time we started fer camp, I reckon. It'll be dark, time we git there."

Together they started for the camp at 7UP Springs. There were times when Mazie West tired of the ancient guardian who guarded her welfare. Onion's odd brand of humor, his wheezy proverbs, his tales of the old West, became rather monotonous. Mazie wanted to be alone. Her only hours of solitude came with nightfall when Onion retired to his canvas tepee down the creek from her camp.

Now, as the slanting rays of the setting sun painted the peaks in ever-changing colors, the girl wanted to ride alone with her thoughts. She wanted to dream foolish, impossible dreams. She wanted to lose herself in those dreams. Braving the chance of hurting old Onion's feelings, she now asked him if he'd mind awfully if she rode on alone.

"Nary a bit," he agreed readily. "You ride on ahead. I'll foller bimeby. Fact is, there was a varmint down there in the breaks that I ketched sight of and I'd like tuh see this varmint closer."

"A wolf, Onion?"

"Kind of a cross between a wolf and a coyote. I'll ketch yuh after a while."

Onion turned back from there. True, Buck had told him to keep a close watch over the nester gal, but shucks, she was travelin' a plain road and no chance to git lost. He'd ketch her before she reached camp. And he shore was honin' fer tuh sight that gent at close range. Over a pair of gun sights, if the play come up right.

"Big Drummond," Onion muttered over and over as he trailed back the way he had come from the point from which he had sighted the man. "Big Drummond, as was killed in Wyomin'. Hook killed him there on Powder River and the wolves et his carcass. I seen the bones, later. Big Drummond, er my eyes is seein' plumb wrong. Drummond, as fought on the other side. As low down and ornery a killer as ever bushwhacked a cowboy.

"Some older-lookin', a heap changed, but I'd know him a hundred years from now. And when he held his head fust one side, then on the other, fer all the world like a dawg a-listenin', there was no mistakin' him. That cuss is Big Drummond and whatever he's a-doin' here, it's bad."

Onion rode with caution. With Big Drummond in the country, it stood a man in hand to ride careful. Drummond had a bad habit of shooting and doing his talking later. Last Onion had seen of him, Big Drummond had been leaning back against the shelving rim-rock, a rifle in the crook of his arm. Like he was watching somebody.

Supposing Big Drummond had come here hunting Hook? Hook had done his best to kill the big bugger, back there on Powder River. It would be just like Big Drummond to trail Hook to Montana, watch for his chance, then plug him. Bust Hook's spine with a bullet and tell it scary to Hook as he laid there dying. That was Big Drummond's way. Skulking, like a yellow-backed coyote. Shooting from the bush.

Onion wondered if Big Drummond could be the roughneck leader of the nester gang that had tortured Fancy Mary. The same big tough gent that had got gay with the West gal and had been run off by Buck Rawlins. Mebbyso. That was about Drummond's style. A big-mouthed bully and coward. Onion wished he'd given the little West gal a look through the glasses at the big son of a gun.

Now, from down in the bad-lands, came the faint crack of a rifle shot, echoing into silence. Onion pulled up abruptly, his hand on his gun. That shot had come from a distance, but there might be other men in these hills just aching to take a shot at a 7UP cowboy. Onion reckoned that Big Drummond was the man who had fired that shot.

Onion pulled his carbine from its saddle scabbard and spurred up. In the heart of the weazened old cow hand was a youthful fire that had never been quenched. He loved the thrill of excitement and had, in other days, been rated as a fast gun thrower. Onion had rattled his spurs in such wild towns as Tombstone, Santa Fe, Dodge City and Abilene. He had trailed long-horned cattle from the Llano Estacado to Miles City. He had fought Mexicans on the Chihuahua border, had swapped shots with the

Chiricahui Apaches, had smelled powder smoke in the Tonto Basin war and looked along gunsights in the Wyoming fracas. And while his bones had grown brittle and his hide wrinkled, his heart was that same reckless fighting heart of the twenty year old cowboy who had come up the Chisholm Trail. The crack of that rifle had stirred his blood.

He stood in his stirrups, his eyes dancing with excitement. If Big Drummond craved fighting, Onion 'lowed he'd give the big son a bellyful. He'd learn the big bushwacker a trick or two. He'd —

"Hold up, mister!" barked a voice.

Half a dozen men with leveled rifles surrounded Onion. They had the drop. Six to one for odds and all of them dangerous enough looking.

Onion swore softly as he raised his hands. This was the gang that had stopped at Fancy Mary's and abused her. This was the gang that was stirrin' up all the trouble. This was the gang that followed the leadership of Big Drummond. Six to one for odds and their guns cocked. One or two of 'em looked half drunk, to boot.

"What's the game, boys?" grinned Onion. "Mebby I'll buy a stack uh chips."

"Yeh?" jeered one of them. "You old fossil, you been on the shelf gatherin' dust for forty years. You buy chips in our game? That's a hot one, that is. Keep them hands up, you old persimmon. Shoot his ears off, boys, if he gets gay. I hope he makes a play for his cannon, just to give you boys target practice."

"Is this the sucker the boss told us to ear-mark?" asked another.

"Naw. This is the old fool they call Onion. The boss knowed him somewhere before. He wants us tuh fetch him into camp all in one piece so he kin work him over in his own way."

"Who is yore danged boss?" asked Onion crisply. His temper was on edge and while he knew himself to be outmatched, still he was making up his mind to go out fighting. He knew the answer to his question. He was simply stalling for time, waiting for that rare break that would let him get his gun and turn this into a short, deadly fight.

"The boss? We calls him Big Meat. You'll know him when yuh see him. He works fer —"

"Shut the gab, fool!" snarled the man next to the half drunken man who was about to become loquacious. "Wanta queer the game?"

"Big Meat's gonna croak this guy," put in another man, championing the drunken one, "so what's the odds? This guy ain't gonna do no talkin' after to-day."

Onion looked them over with frank curiosity. They were not of the cow-puncher clan, these men. Jailbirds, toughs, the scum of city gutters and the product of the hop joints. Onion had seen their type around the gambling houses at Havre and Butte. They made the mining camps that were on the boom and followed the sheep-shearing crews to gamble. Covering their real game with labor in the mines or shearing pens, they worked their cards and dice and when their game was discovered, fought their way out.

They belonged to a new class of men that were coming across the vanishing frontiers. They were gamblers, pickpockets, sluggers and murderers. Men who had no code, no honor, no mercy. Buzzards, jackals. Products of crooked gambling joints and followers of races. Drifters, burglars, thugs.

On foot, the six surrounded Onion, who sat his horse, his eyes hard and unafraid.

He was thinking of Mazie West. If these men had been watching him, then they had also been watching the girl. Now she was riding home alone and unprotected, at the mercy of Big Drummond should he choose to follow her.

Now, as the old cow-puncher tensed, ready to make a desperate gun play, his quick eyes caught sight of something that revived hope in his heart. From a butte spotted with scrub pines there rose a thin column of smoke. For an instant the smoke rose like a gray column into the windless sky. Then it was gone. Now it came again. A third time. Then it vanished.

Onion Oliver relaxed, his heart pounding with hope. He knew that signal and the man who had made it. He knew that it was meant for him. From that butte a man with field-glasses could see Onion and these toughs. His hands in the air, Onion watched the men who stood there on the ground.

"Gents," he said, grinning gamely, "you shore got me. I'm yore bacon. And I'll go along plenty peaceful. I'm just an ol' bald-headed jasper as is past his prime o' life and playin' hooky from the boot-hill. When I cash in my chips, I'll do er without regret. I've seen a-plenty fer one man tuh see, done about all there is tuh do, anyhow. When that boss uh yourn hangs this ol' hide on the fence, he ain't doin' much to be braggin' about.

"Reminds me uh the story about ol' Poker Davis. He was a desert rat and had hunted fer gold in about every country from Nome tuh South Africa. He strikes 'er rich down in Sonora an' he's —"

"Never mind the story, ol' timer," said the man who seemed to be in charge. "Tell it tuh Big Meat. Boys, take his artillery. That's it. Now you kin pull yore hands down outa the sky."

Onion obeyed that order with a sigh of relief. But as he had been talking, his elevated hands had been slowly moving in a crude semaphore signal. Slowly, so that the motion would not attract notice, Onion Oliver had waved three times. Now, as a single puff of smoke appeared, then dissolved on top of the butte, the old cowpuncher knew that the man up there on the butte, the man known as the Nighthawk, had seen the signaled reply to his smoke sign. The Nighthawk was watching and would do what he could to rescue old Onion.

Now the band of hired toughs and their prisoner went down a steep trail that led into a box canyon. At the foot of the trail a man with a carbine halted them. He recognized them and passed them on. And not by so much as the flicker of an eyelid did Onion Oliver betray the fact that he recognized this guard as one of the Nighthawk's crew of outlaws.

At the corral there in the canyon Big Drummond met them. He leered at old Onion with loose lipped, ugly triumph.

"Long time no see yuh, Oliver. I've bin waitin' to have a nice long pow-wow with yuh. We'll drink from the keg and have a medicine smoke, me and you. Old reunion, eh, Onion? A last an' final reunion. It's yore last night on this old earth, Onion, and I aim tuh make 'er shore pleasant.

"Light, yuh bald-headed old skalawag, and rest yore saddle. Come on to the cabin and we'll talk over old times and old friends. Such as ol' Hook Jones as he now calls hisse'f, and some others. And before we commence this augerin' deal, lemme tell yuh somethin'. That yaller-haired gal is locked up in the next cabin. If yuh don't tell me the right answers to a few questions, it'll be her misfortune."

Onion Oliver tensed like a coiled rattler. Big Drummond laughed in his face. Then the old cow-puncher remembered the Nighthawk's signal and the guard who had halted them at the foot of the trail. He'd have to play good poker with Big Drummond. He'd have to play a slick game until the Nighthawk got ready to rake in the big jackpot. Play the cards careful. Play every card for all it was worth. Play the game close to his belly and wait until the Nighthawk showed four aces and raked in the pot.

For himself, Onion cared less than a little. He'd bucked hard games from the Staked Plains to the Canadian Rockies. He'd bet 'em high and rode on to the next game. He'd stake his life and his private horse against any man's bet if they'd let him hold a six gun.

He was undersized and old, he was the human replica of a dried apple. He had never in his life hit a man with his fists. But he owned an old cedar-handled Colt gun that he'd packed for many a year and he could make that old smoke wagon play a tune that was never heard on a fiddle. Give him that old cutter and some loads for it and Onion Oliver would face any kind of a layout from Kosterlitsky's Rurales to Inspector Steele's Northwest Mounties. He had known killers from Arizona to Alberta.

He had, on one occasion, while under the influence of tanglefoot, shot up the Dodge City Post Office with that same old smoke-pole, while Bat Masterson was the law's right arm in Dodge. And he had lifted the same bar bottle that had been tilted by such men as Black Jack, Curly Bill, and the Earp boys, and John Wesley Hardin. He had known, up here in the Montana country, men like Harvey Logan, Butch Cassidy, and others of the Wild Bunch. Sheriffs and outlaws knew the grit that was in the heart of Onion Oliver. Give him his old cedar-handled gun and he would fight anything.

But this was a different game. In yonder cabin was the nester gal. Some time, somehow, the Nighthawk was coming into the game. Better to play 'er easy and place small bets. That was the ticket.

CHAPTER XIII
A HAIR-TRIGGER LIE

*Come, all you melancholy folks, wherever you
    may be,
I'll sing you about the cowboys whose life is
    light and free.
He roams about the prairie, and at night when
    he lies down,
His heart is as gay as the flowers in May in his
    bed upon the ground.*
                            — Old Time Cowboy.

Big Drummond poured two tin cups full of raw
whisky. Onion smacked his lips and accepted his
drink. He knew that Big Drummond was feeding
him the hard liquor in hopes of loosening his
tongue. The two were alone in the small log
cabin.

Next to this cabin was the one where Mazie
West had been put. Onion heard her whistling in
there behind the padlocked door and barred
windows. The girl was whistling to keep up her
courage. The old cow-puncher was mighty
proud of her. She was game, that young 'un. Big
Drummond had likewise heard her whistle. He
grinned crookedly.

"So long as you talk like I want yuh to talk,

Onion, the gal will be safe. But if yuh don't come clean with me, then she won't have such good luck. We got orders to hold her here fer two weeks. That'll be cut to shorter time if she signs some papers the boss sent."

"Marley shore wants that homestead at 7UP Springs, don't he?"

"Who said anything about Marley?" growled Big Drummond.

"I did. I ain't plumb dumb, Drummond. Here's a sty on yore eye, Big Meat." Onion chuckled and lifted his cup.

Big Drummond, sometimes called Big Meat, leered at Onion across his cup of whisky.

"If only you was thick-skulled, Onion, I might not have tuh kill yuh. But as it is, yo're too wise."

"The good dies young," grinned Onion. "What was it yuh wanted to know?"

"Where's Hook Jones?" The big man snarled the question.

"That," said Onion frankly, "is what I'd give a lot to know. He left Landusky the day of his wife's funeral. He ain't bin seen since. They tell me he acted plumb loco."

"Yuh wouldn't be lyin' now, by any chance, Onion? Don't forgit that purty li'l' yaller-haired gal in yonder cabin. I'd shore hate to see her harmed. Yuh shorely wouldn't be so foolish as tuh lie to yore ol' friend Big Meat."

"I got no call tuh lie about Hook."

"You don't look like you was lyin'," admitted Big Meat. "Another thing I'd like to know is this:

168

Who is these two camp tenders that the Murdock outfit has over near here?"

"One of 'em is Guy Jones, Hook's boy. The other is Guy's Swede brother-in-law. They married sisters. Nester gals over on Big Warm."

"Yuh mean tuh say them two is related thataway? Good friends?"

"That's it. They married sisters and live next door neighbors."

"That's odd. Still, I've heard uh such doin's before now. I got some shirt-tail relations uh my own that I wouldn't trust none."

"What do yuh mean, it's odd?" asked Onion casually.

"Well," said Big Meat, "I was watchin' the two of 'em to-day. The big 'un was trailin' the least 'un. While the least 'un was snoopin' around down in the breaks, where he's got no business to be. That's all."

"Swanson was trailin' Guy," mused Onion aloud. "I never did like that big Swede's looks."

"Ner me," admitted Big Meat grimly, as if he recalled some particular incident. "But that kid uh Hook's is gonna match hisse'f plenty trouble if he don't stay outa the breaks. His camp tendin' chores don't include detective work. He's gonna git hurt wuss than he got 'er to-day."

"Guy got hurt yuh say?"

"Yeah. He was shot in the laig while he was off his horse follerin' a trail he had no business follerin'."

"You shot the kid, Big Meat?"

"Don't be so almighty curious. I never said I shot 'im. I said he got shot, that's all. Drink up, yuh bald-skulled ol' hunk uh jerky."

They drained their tin cups and Big Meat filled them to the brim with the fiery whisky. Now Onion knew that the big man had a dual purpose in hitting the liquor. He wanted Onion to talk, for one thing. And now Onion suddenly remembered a habit of Big Drummond's. Sober, the man lacked the courage to carry out any real crime. Whisky gave the man nerve and dulled his qualms of conscience. He was now deliberately getting drunk enough to kill Onion and take the nester girl against Marley's orders. Already an ugly glint was creeping into the big man's eyes.

"Onion," he said, his eyes slitted and his voice a low snarl, "where's the Nighthawk hidin' and where did they cache the money they stole? I want the truth outa yuh er I'll twist that hairless head off that skinny neck uh yourn. You know the right answer tuh both them questions and I'll take nothin' but the truth. Come clean, yuh mangy ol' son!"

"Lemme git outside uh this drink, Big Meat. Then I kin talk. Yuh know what the Nighthawk'd do tuh me if he knowed I squealed."

"No need uh you worryin' along them lines, Onion," leered the big man. "You ain't ever seein' him no more. After tonight, you won't be bothered about meetin' anybody. Drink up and commence talkin'."

Onion choked a little over his cup. He wanted to get the effects of that whisky. With its glowing warmth creeping over him, Onion felt loose of tongue and nimble of wit. Tipsy, Onion Oliver was as convincing a liar as ever spilled a windy yarn. If only he could acquire that stage of mellowness, he could, perhaps, trick this ugly brute into some sort of trap. Onion drained the cup and reached for cigarette makin's.

"Some uh the money is gone," he told Big Drummond. The whisky was warming his stomach now, sending through his veins that delicious warmth that makes a man forget that he is hungry or cold or broke. His brain began to work out plans and pictures. Onion, while not exactly a drunkard, was a lover of good whisky. He liked the raw taste of the stuff, the warm spot it made under his ribs, the dreams and contentment of mind it brought to him.

"Yep, some uh the money is gone. Spent fer this and that. But there's a-plenty left. Not enough tuh split up amongst this gang uh bums you got workin' fer yuh. But if one man had it all, say, he'd be fixed fer life unless he throwed it away."

"Think I'd split with these tramps?" grinned Big Meat. "Not much. Where's the stuff hid, Onion?"

"I kin take yuh to where a part of it is, but I dunno as I could tell yuh the location er even map it on paper. It's in a tin box that was put in under a cutbank and then the cutbank was caved in on it. And there's more hid in an old badger hole near the lone cotton-wood on Second Crick. And another dab is wrapped in a slicker and planted in the road where a lot uh hosses and wagons and freight outfits has passed over it.

"You know how *you* would hide, say, five thousand dollars. Yuh'd pick the right spot. And even if I was tuh be tied to stake an' set on fire, I couldn't give yuh any map uh the spot. I couldn't tell any man how tuh find it. There's that cutbank. There's that badger hole. There's that place dug in the main stage road. How kin I tell any man the exact location. Big Meat, she kain't be done. Nope. I'd have tuh be with yuh."

"How does it come," growled Big Meat, a suspicious glitter in his eyes, "that you know where this money is cached?"

"I kin tell yuh, and I kin add to it that I'd a heap ruther be a-settin' on a few cans uh high explodin' powder than tuh be weighed down with the aforesaid knowledge uh what I know. The play comes up thisaway. There's the Nighthawk, Shorty, Whitey, and the rest. They divvy the proceeds, each man a-sharin' his share, savvy? This was done at Fancy Mary's. Then each man has his share uh the loot.

"They kain't spend 'er all. They don't want tuh spend 'er all. They want tuh hide 'er where she'll be safe till the sign is right tuh quit the country. So each uh the boys figgers he'll plant his share somewheres. They talks 'er all out there at Fancy Mary's road ranch.

"Then this question comes up. Supposin' one uh these boys git killed er sent to the pen? There's his cut uh the money planted where nobody kin ever find it. And they argues pro and con-wise fer a long time till the Nighthawk gits the right answer. He moves that they all agree on the selection uh one man they kin all trust. This aforesaid man will go with each and every gent who has money tuh cache. He'll help plant the money. And he will be the only livin' human alive as knows the correct hidin' place where each uh these boys has hid his dinero. This idee sounds shore good to the boys. But who kin they git that they kin all trust? There's a hard 'un to find answer to. So they names over every man they kin think of that ain't doin' time. And then they take some more likker. After a few rounds uh red-eye somebody begins tuh tells a comical story about Onion Oliver.

" 'There,' says the Nighthawk, 'is yore huckleberry. Onion Oliver cares about money in small dabs. All he asks uh this world is a good private hoss and outfit, a bed that's got enough Hudson Bay blankets under the tarp tuh keep his marrow bones from freezin' up on him, a jug uh licker that'll warm his belly, and a good job with an old time outfit. He's an old hand and a good 'un. He's seen many a wild cowboy planted in the boot-hill. He's pointed trail herds and bin in the midst-part uh plenty stampedes. He knowed Sam Bass and Billy the Kid. He's never told the wrong tale to ary sheriff and he kin be trusted till hell is covered with a skift uh ice. Gents, how does ol' Onion Oliver fit into yore minds as the logical party fer to hold all stakes?'

"So, Big Meat," finished Onion, reaching for the jug, "they elects me, unanimous as the sayin' goes. I'm the trust banker fer this game. I'm the high mogul uh the secret order, a-guardin' the gates to all this coin. And right here an' now, I'll rise on my hind laigs to declare that they shore loaded me with a double pack. There's men a-runnin' in packs that'd kill me fer a plugged Mexican dime if they suspicioned what I bin a-hidin' secret.

"Them jaspers shore let me into a mess. Here's you, with a six-gun and an itchin' finger standin' me up. I gotta come clean er be killed. Mebbyso be killed anyhow, fer I see blood in yore eye, Big Meat. Dagone if it don't make a man feel downright weepy. Here I am, old and stove-up and innercent uh wrongdoin', a-nursin' a secret fer which I may die. And it may be, Big Meat, seein' I'm old and ready tuh be pushed into the nearest hole an' the dirt kicked in on my face, that I'll die a-holdin' that there secret in the bosom uh my heart. I'm weary uh life and sad uh heart. I'm a broke-down ol' rannyhan that kain't never whoop ner holler no more. I'm sad plumb from head tuh foot, an' from fore-top tuh hocks. I bin a-carryin' too hefty a load fer any one man tuh pack."

Onion Oliver pulled a shirt-sleeve across moist eyes.

"Looky here, Onion," said Big Drummond, with a wheedling note in his voice, "there'd be enough fer two of us in them caches. While me and you have bin on wrong sides, still, we ain't got any real grudge between us. How'd yuh like to throw in with me? We'll quit this layout, dig up that money, and pull stakes fer the Argentine country. I'll quit this gang.

"You ain't beholdin' to the Nighthawk ner the other. Anyhow, they'll be out like Nellie's eye before long when the Marley gang gits 'em pocketed. That Marley is a smart gent. He's got book learnin' and he's as slick as a new-born calf. He's gonna run the big outfits out. Then, bimeby, when the nesters feels the buzzards and drouths an' go broke, he'll take over their homesteads fer nothin' excep' their car-fare home. Him and Howard Snodgrass is gonna own this whole dang' country. But me and fellers like me that's takin' the big risks will be sloughed into the discard. I want mine while the sign is right. You string yore bets with mine, Onion, and we'll both be a-wearin' diamonds. You lead me to where them caches is and we'll drift yonderly. Want that game?"

"She sounds shore sweet music to my ears, Big Meat. Let's tilt another 'un. Git dry a-talkin'. Here's tuh crime in general an' fleas in yore blankets."

Half an hour passed, during which Onion Oliver and Big Meat Drummond conjured up oral visions of Buenos Aires and other points south.

All the while the snaky eyes of the big man watched Onion. And Onion, mellow to the core of his heart, talked on and on. Telling many yarns that were, for the most part, rank lies that were so colored as to be taken for the truth. Probably never in his entire life had Onion Oliver lied more convincingly. He was so carried away by his own artistry that he was believing his own lies. In detail he described how he had helped plant each outlaw's share of the loot. How they had argued as to the advantages of this hiding-place or that one. How each of them had given him a handsome reward for his trouble and how the Nighthawk and his men had warned him against ever betraying the hiding-places.

Onion, quite tipsy now, lying with a remarkable glibness, all but forgot the girl in the cabin next door. He nearly forgot the signal sent by the Nighthawk, and that the guard at the foot of the trail leading into the canyon was one of the Nighthawk's men.

It was Big Drummond who first noticed that something was wrong in camp. Big Meat Drummond, filling the two tin cups from the jug, happened to look up at the window. Inside the cabin was candle-light. Outside was darkness. But not too dark for the big man to see that someone was standing out there by the window. A man with a handkerchief tied across his face, masking all save a pair of slitted eyes. In the hands of the masked man were two guns. Both these guns were pointed at Big Meat, who now stood there, his hands slowly lifting.

Onion looked at the big man, followed Big Meat's staring eyes to the man at the window. Onion chuckled softly and stepping in behind Big Meat, lifted the fellow's guns.

"Be quiet, Big Meat," he said in a low tone. "Be awful quiet and peaceful, because I'm rearin' tuh kill yuh here an' now. My pardner outside feels the same way to'rds yuh. So just keep yore paws in the air while I frisk yuh fer the key to the cabin where yuh got the nester gal locked up. Behave, big feller, er yo're gonna be in hell in plenty time fer breakfast."

CHAPTER XIV

DRUMMOND BREAKS

*Hush-a-by, Long Horn, your pards are all
    sleepin';
Stop your durn millin' an' tossin' your
    head,
Wavin' your horns so unrestful an' sweepin'
All of the beef herd with eyes big an' red.*
           — Fate of the Beef Steer.

It was the Nighthawk himself who stepped into
the cabin with Onion Oliver and Big Meat. Across
the lower part of his face was the black silk handkerchief. Above it, his eyes glittered. He motioned
Big Meat back into his chair.

"Onion," he said softly, "here's that ol' cedar-
handled hog-laig of yours. Took it off the tramp
that took it away from you. Supposin' you
unlock the door uh that next cabin. Fetch the
girl in here. I want her to hear and be witness
while we make this big cuss talk."

Onion was back in a few minutes, Mazie West
hanging to his arm as if she were afraid he might
leave her again. This was probably one of the
proudest moments of the old cow-puncher's life.

"That's the big pun'kin roller there, Onion,"
she said hotly, pointing at Big Meat Drummond,

"that brought me here. He said that you were hurt and was askin' for me. The big bum. He's the same heavy character that Buck Rawlins slapped to a peak at my camp. He's Creighton Marley's tough guy. He's the guy that pushed the bull off the bridge, the guy that lives in the last house at the toughest end of tough street. He's a ten-minute egg, he is. I bet he's kicked the crutches out from under more cripples than any bird alive. He's the type that slaps kids and beats up women. He's a heel, no less."

The Nighthawk's eyes twinkled. "The little lady reads you like a gypsy reading a palm. Drummond, you'll talk now and you'll talk plenty fast. I want the names of the men behind Marley. I hope you kin put out the correct answer, because if yuh don't yo're due for some hard luck. Who pays Marley?"

"The Northwest Land and Finance Company pays Marley."

"And who owns the Northwest Land and Finance Company?" asked the Nighthawk.

"Some dudes in Helena, near as I know. Howard Snodgrass and Marley own stock in the layout. They got plenty money behind 'em and they're locatin' nesters on the best land they kin pick where it'll hurt the big outfits. They got 'er planned to grab off the best land here, force the big outfits into a cheap sale, buy up the 7 UP and Rolling M outfits fer cheap money, then grab the homesteads that the nesters will have to let go of when they can't make a livin' off the dry land. I heard Marley say they'd own the whole country in ten years. They're powerful, I'll tell a man."

"Mebbyso. Mebby not as powerful as they figger," said the Nighthawk.

He turned to the girl.

"Lady, it's time that you and my friend Onion was hittin' the trail for home. Better if both of you didn't come down here in the bad-lands again. Tell Buck Rawlins and Dave and Bob Driscoll that I kin ride line on the proposition down here. Ma'am, I reckon this big rattlesnake has bin somewhat insultin'. Well, he won't bother you no more. He's givin' hisself a necktie party to-night. Sorry yuh can't be there, but this is what society calls a stag party. Take a last look at 'im."

"I don't think I quite get the idea," said Mazie West.

"He's aimin' to hang me," said Big Drummond, his voice husky with fear.

The nester girl looked at the three men. Above the black silk neckscarf the Nighthawk's eyes were cold and merciless. Onion looked uneasy under her scrutiny. Big Drummond was plainly afraid. The fear of death was in the big man's eyes, and he licked his heavy lips with a dry tongue.

Here was a crudely hewn cross-section of Western life that the girl from the cities had never seen. Here were three men in a cabin, one of them as surely, as cold-bloodedly, con-demned to death as if his fate had been decided

180

by the ballot of jury and the sentence pronounced by a judge on the bench.

"This man," said the girl, her voice sounding pitifully brave against the ugly silence there in the dimly lit cabin, "has done nothing to me that calls for hanging. He's a big bum, but outside of that, he's not hurt me enough to make me want to see him hung. Can't we call it a day, boys?"

"This Big Meat gent," Onion put in, his voice somewhat apologetic, "is a rattlesnake. He's gotta be tromped out, ma'am."

"He's no worse than the men he works for," said Mazie stoutly. "And if this necktie party is being staged on my account, forget it. Pass out rain checks or something. How do you think I'd feel if I had to go around from now on knowin' that a man had been hung because he'd looked sideways at me? You don't need to say it with guns or a rope around some poor yap's neck. I know I owe you a lot, but I won't leave this cabin till you tell me that this big hunk of Camembert is safe.

"Sorry to be souring the party, boys, but them's my sentiments. I've never had a guy hung yet on my account and I'm too old a girl to pick up new tricks. Jesse James, if you'll take that black rag off your face, and if Onion will quit opening his mouth and shutting it like a patent fly-trap, and if the all-but-corpus delicti will pull himself together, you boys will all take another drink and Onion will escort the lady home. And we'll all finish the act by singing Sweet Adeline

181

or doing a few nifty little steps before we bow ourselves off the boards. What say, boys? Do I or do I not save the life of the heavy?"

The Nighthawk's eyes were bright with amusement and admiration for this girl who could so meet a hard situation. He pulled the black silk handkerchief from his face so that it hung now around his neck.

For a long, tense moment, Mazie West looked at the unmasked Nighthawk whose name had once been Wade Hardin. Her face went white as chalk and she gripped the edge of the table as if to keep from falling.

"You?" she said in a barely audible voice. "You?"

The Nighthawk nodded, his mouth, thin lipped, bitter, spreading in a smile that was not pleasant.

"I figured yuh'd be surprised," he said slowly. Both he and the girl seemed to forget where they were or why they were there. They stood facing one another across the table.

Now Big Meat Drummond took his one chance. His big hand shot out, knocking over the candles that stood in the necks of beer bottles on the pine table. The cabin was plunged in darkness. Onion was sent crashing to the floor under the terrific impact of Drummond's fists. The next moment Big Meat was outside.

Shots crashed there in the darkened cabin as the Nighthawk shot at random aim, hoping to stop the big man's flight. Now, outside, other shots rang out. Men shouted hoarsely. The thud of shod hoofs as Drummond rode at a mad pace into the night.

Now the fighting in the darkness became swift and furious. Mazie West felt the grip of the Nighthawk's arms as he pushed her into a sheltered corner, his body shielding her as he jerked the hammers of two six-shooters. Outside the cabin, sounded the wild yell of a cowboy. That would be one of the Nighthawk's men voicing his battle-cry as he fought against Big Meat's men.

"I gotta be leavin' yuh here," the Nighthawk said in a hoarse whisper. "You lay low while Onion and me do some cap-bustin'. Sorry I give yuh such a shock, kid, but I wanted yuh to know —"

"To know that you'll be swinging at the end of a rope before you're done. Gee, what swell breaks I get outa this life. Just when I'm patching up the old heart —"

The Nighthawk picked her up and set her down none too gently. "Keep quiet, kid, and stay down there on the floor. Them shots is comin' close. Onion, where are yuh?"

"Right here, dang it. Let's git some action." Onion took shape in the dim light that came through the window that was now broken by bullets.

Now Onion and the Nighthawk were outside, crouched in the black shadows of the cabin wall. Dodging, shooting, keeping the cabin defended as best they could, as Big Drummond's toughs raked the night with gun-fire. The outlaw under the Nighthawk's command was putting up a good fight. Onion Oliver's gun spewed fire. The outlaw leader was squatted behind the wood-pile, raking the brush with leaden hail. No sign of Big Meat Drummond. Now the Nighthawk crawled over to where Onion Oliver, cussing and shooting, crouched behind a shallow cutbank.

"I got two horses hid behind the cabin, Onion. You and the girl use 'em while me and Ben hold off these skunks."

"Me leave here now, jest when I'm a-gittin' warmed up?" Onion complained in a husky whisper. "Not by a dang sight. Bin a long time since I celebrated a holiday. She's my night tuh play Fourth uh July."

"We got no time to argue. Do like I say."

Onion remembered, there in the cabin before Big Meat knocked out the lights, the look in Mazie West's eyes when she saw the Night-hawk's face.

"You and the gal drift yonderly," said Onion. "I dunno what else yuh are but yo're shore mighty strong in the li'l' gal's heart. Hop to it."

"She wouldn't travel ten feet with me. Do like I say, Onion, and quit runnin' off at the head. Shake a leg."

Onion, muttering, did as he was bid. Mazie West, crouched on the floor in a corner of the cabin, listened meekly to Onion's advice.

"Better do as he says, ma'am. He knows what's best."

"I'll admit this is no place for a lady and my being here makes it hard on you he-boys. I'll go. But if Wade Hardin don't make a try at squaring himself I hope he has bad luck, that's all. Lead on, Onion."

Getting the horses was no small task. It required all the Injun tricks that Onion knew.

It was nearly half an hour before they could get in the saddle.

"All set?" whispered Onion.

"Give the word. All for one and one for me, as the third musketeer said, wiping his trusty sword on his pants leg. Let's go."

"Lay low along yore pony's neck. Ride like you was goin' to a fire an' let me do the shootin'. Here we go!"

Onion in front, his horse on a run. Behind him rode Mazie West. Horses kicking gravel. Onion's six-shooter belching fire. Now they were climbing the trail. Fifteen minutes and they had gained safety. Below, there in the black canyon, sounded shots as the Nighthawk and Ben fought back Big Meat Drummond's toughs. Then, after a time, Onion Oliver and the nester girl had reached the head of the breaks and were riding across the rolling prairie.

"Big Meat," said Onion, rolling a cigarette, "has done quit the flats. He's headed fer Chinook, if I figger right. How do yuh like 'er out West by this time, as far as yuh've gone?"

"Not so bad, not so good. Onion, I have to get into town as quick as I can. I'm leaving this land of the great open spaces to them that like raw meat and beans. I'm quitting, Onion. I'm going back where I belong and where I should have stayed."

"Yes, ma'am."

"He can hunt me up where he first found me, darn him."

"Yes, ma'am."

"And when he finds me, I'll teach him a lesson in manners, what I mean. Nobody can make a sucker outa me. Out here where he can strut his stuff, he may be the main idea, but he'll find out that he can't make me out a chump. What's his idea in wearing that black rag across his map, anyhow? Who does he think he is, Jesse James?"

"Meanin' yuh don't know who he is?"

"He's Wade Hardin and he's all wet in my estimation. He put on a show to-night that was worth the price of admission, but that don't explain away why he fools a girl with his hot line about a ranch home where a girl can raise chickens and a duck and some kittens and a dog and have roses in a garden and a white cottage with a green roof and morning-glory vines growing over the porch. I let him feed me that line of stuff when he's with that Wild West show in Chicago and I fall hard for his boots and big hat and his cowboy ways.

"Then, when I get ready to leave the show flat and let it go bust because Mazie West in the pony ballet is giving up the two-a-day stuff for a little gray home in the West, what does he do but take a powder on me. He leaves me waiting at the church. Leaves me with my orange blossoms withering and my dreams all shot to pieces. That's what he does. Now he pulls this fast one to inject some drama into the act. He don't fool me. Onion, that whole show was a frame-up. It lacked the right management to put it over. Thanks for a swell evening and I'll say you had me going. But now I see it was all just a lot of old hokum. I'm goin' home on the first train."

"You mean yuh knowed Wade Hardin when he rode broncs with the rodeo outfits? When he was the World's champeen bronc setter? Yuh met him in Chicago?"

"I did, and how. I fell for him hard. Ten years ago, and then some, near as I recall. Me just a kid breaking into the show game."

"And him the best cowboy that ever set a bronc comin' out of the chutes. Goshamighty! Wade Hardin, when he had the world by the tail. When he was top-hand uh all the contest boys. When he could rope, ride, er dog a steer with the best of 'em. When him an' Clay McGonigal an' Henry Gammar an' Lee Robinson was knockin' on broncs an' swingin' the fastest loops in the world. Yeh, Wade sat up amongst the kings them days. And it was right in Chicago that he quit the game an' hit the outlaw trail. Yeppy, right there in Chicago Wade Hardin cut his string an' from then on he's known amongst friends, enemies an' strangers as the Night-hawk."

"What do you mean, the Nighthawk?"

"That's what we call him now. He's outlawed. He's —"

"He's the Nighthawk that held up the train I was on? You mean that Wade is the Night-hawk?" Mazie's voice quivered a little.

"Yes, ma'am. And fer all they got a price on him, he's as square a man as ever helped a friend in a tight. I shore hate tuh hear yuh speak bad about that cowboy. He's all white."

"He give me a run-around. Gee, the Night-hawk. Then tonight's show was the real thing?"

Onion Oliver smiled grimly. "What did yuh think it was, circus day?"

"I — Gee, I didn't know. I was knocked groggy. Kidnapped, listening to a guy get sentenced to hang. Then the heavy guy turns out to be the cowboy that left me waiting at the church door in a new dress that I kid myself into thinking is my bridal gown. What is any girl going to think? He stood me up once and that was plenty. I'll never light no more joss-sticks in front of any guy's picture. Onion, I'm going back to my old act."

"Yo're quittin' the homestead at 7UP Springs?"

"My bank-book shows a balance of one hundred and two dollars and six-bits. I'm using it all on a ticket home. That's final. I'll stake you to

188

that homestead and the good-will that goes with it. You've acted like a champ and whenever you hit Chicago, look me up. I'll show you the town. Out here I'm just a sucker, but back in my own back yard I can get by on a plugged dime. I've covered many a hole in a silk stocking with ink. I've scoffed on slim groceries cooked on a gas jet. I've walked Broadway in December with paper in my slippers to keep my bare feet out of the snow.

"I can beat the game again, too. And when I'm doing my Sarah Bernhardt and bathing in buttermilk I'll start a home for these smart cowboys that feed a girl a line about the sunrise on the Rockies. I never want to see another sunrise unless I've waited up all night to get a look at it. I never want to see another horse or the two-timers that ride 'em. I never want to — Onion, for the love of Pete, slip me a hanky because your nester girl is just about to weep no less than quarts. Darn!"

As Onion Oliver told Dave Rawlins the next morning at the hotel in Chinook, after he and Mazie West had finished a long, hard ride, it was about time that the nester gal got the kind of a deal that was comin' to a woman. And so it was that Dave Rawlins and Bob Driscoll and Uncle Hank Mayberry entertained Mazie West at lunch that noon. With them went Ike Niland who had Uncle Hank Mayberry under arrest, pending the outcome of the bank examiner's findings. The sixth member of that party was Onion Oliver.

And when they had finished the fried chicken and the trimmings that went with it, Mazie West made a short speech.

"Thanks for the two thousand dollars, for the feed, and for everything. I know I should hop the next eastbound train, but somehow I just can't. So I'm returning to Dave Rawlins my check, and we'll let the train go on without me riding the cushions. I'm just a cheap little dame from the chorus, but nobody ever called me a bum. You're all the salt of the earth and I'm for you. I'll go back to my two-by-twice ranch and I'll string my bets with yours.

"Uncle Hank, I have about a hundred bucks in the bank. Take it if you need it. And before we get finished with this Marley burglary syndicate, we'll make 'em all look like fish that have been out of the water about a week too long. I don't remember my dad but they say he was regular, even if he was a cop. And he'd be plenty ashamed if I didn't play my game straight. Whatever I can do in my own childish way, count on me to do it. Put me down as a lodge member."

Uncle Hank Mayberry blew his nose violently. Bob Driscoll, whose chair was next to that of the nester gal's, found Mazie's hand and gripped it hard. Dave Rawlins and Onion blinked hard and said nothing. Like Bob Driscoll told Uncle Hank afterwards, he was reminded of the old days when the pioneer women rode in their covered wagons and took what was their lot. Here was a new type of pioneer woman. Mazie West was homesteading on her frontier. Her heart was as game and brave and clean as ever was the heart of a woman who had come to Montana in the early days.

Gravely, after their manner, they rose, those grizzled veterans of the pioneer days. Their glasses lifted. In a silence that was their greatest tribute to this homesteader girl, they drank.

CHAPTER XV
BIG CHIEF

Let me be easy on the man that's down;
  Let me be square and generous to all.
I'm careless, sometimes, Lord, when I'm in
  town.
  But never let 'em say I'm mean or small!
              — A Cowboy's Prayer.

Saturday noon the Valley Bank closed its doors. Bob Driscoll and Dave Rawlins waited at the hotel for Uncle Hank Mayberry to join them. In the big front room they occupied together, Dave Rawlins paced the floor while Bob Driscoll sat in the big easy-chair, his gnarled hands folded. Bob Driscoll, during these years of darkness that had set him apart from other men, had learned patience.

"Bob, them dudes is out tuh give Hank a whuppin'," Dave Rawlins repeated for the tenth time. "Snodgrass is at the bottom of it, mark what I say. Hank ain't a-tellin' me and you everything he should. Scared he'll be worryin' us with his troubles, I reckon. I'm a-wonderin' if them notes we signed ain't somehow mixed up in the deal they're a-tryin' to hand 'im. I done sent fer Buck to git in here to town. Buck has ed-

192

ucation and plenty of savvy. Colleen might come along. We'll stand by Hank till . . . God!"

"What's wrong, Dave?"

Dave turned from the window where he had been standing. His face was hard and grim-lipped.

"Bob, there's a crowd a-gatherin' at the bank. The news has done trickled out that Hank's bank is in bad shape. Some uh Marley's work, bet on that. He's aimin' tuh hang Hank's hide on the fence. That mob a-gatherin' looks bad. Bob, I reckon I'll have tuh be leavin' yuh alone fer a spell. Some uh that gang is hired by Marley. They're a mangy layout, half drunk and ugly-lookin'. Yeah, they're gatherin' fast. I better step down there."

"What kin you do, Dave? You ain't allowed in the bank and yuh can't do much, single-handed, against that gang. Ike is ridin' herd on Hank and he won't stand fer any kind uh rough work. Set still fer a spell. Hank will be along directly."

"If only Buck 'ud show up. Buck's right handy at a job like this."

"He'll be along, Dave."

"Wish I had yore patience, Bob."

"When a man's been blind as long as I have, Dave, he learns some mighty big lessons. It used to be almighty hard, sittin' always in the black-ness, not knowin' what was a-goin' on, dependin' on the eyes of other folks. I usta think, sometimes, I'd go plumb loco. Colleen hid every gun in the house, fearin' I'd git a-holt of one and

193

finish the job the Injuns begun.

"And then, after while, I begun to see things that I'd never bin able to see when my eyes was good. There's a heap uh things that you folks with eyes never see. And a heap uh things you never take time tuh learn. Things that God meant us tuh see, but we was always ridin' on a high lope an' never took the trouble to pull up and look. A blind man sees a lot uh God's teachin's. Set down fer a little while, Dave."

Dave Rawlins pulled a chair up alongside the window. From there he could see the gathering crowd around the front doors of the bank. Some of those men and women had their life's savings in the Valley Bank. Others in the crowd were the hoodlum element that was there to start any kind of trouble that would give them a chance to destroy property or hurt someone they did not like. They took their orders from Marley.

Marley stood in the doorway of his office. Immaculate, a thin smile twisting his mouth, his eyes watching the crowd in front of the bank. Now and then his manicured hand twisted his trim little mustache. Yet a keen observer would have read a certain vague uneasiness behind his studied calm. His hands were restless and he seemed to be listening. Now, as he stood there, a cautious voice hailed him from the back room that joined his office.

"If I'm stuck here fer the day, get me a bottle and some grub, chief."

Creighton Marley, masking his emotions

behind the leisurely lighting of a cork-tipped cigarette, strolled idly to the closed door that separated his elaborately furnished office from the
back room. He did not open the door, but spoke
in a calm, brittle voice through the closed door.

"Keep that trap of yours shut, you fool. What
do you think you're celebrating, anyhow?
You've messed up things enough without getting
us into more trouble, you clumsy idiot. You and
that Swede farmer make a fine pair of clowns.
You misfire and run to me like a scared baby instead of using that rod you pack. You let a girl
and a dried-up old cow-puncher run you out of
your own yard."

"I told yuh I had 'em dead to rights till the
Nighthawk cuts into the game. Him and his
whole gang attacked me. Lissen, Marley, I want
my dough an' I want a bottle and some grub.
And I kin use a fat seegar. You dig 'em up or I'll
squawk."

"I have a man at the back door, Drummond,"
said Marley coldly. "He has orders to croak you
if you try to pull a fast one. There's another guy
out in front. When you're croaked there'll be
stuff planted on your unwashed carcass that will
prove you were caught robbing my office. Now
get that through your wooden skull, you big false
alarm. I'll give you the bum's rush to-night when
it's dark. You talk nice to me, you big louse, or
you'll have a lily in your hand.

"I'm shipping you out on the midnight rattler
with just one hundred berries in your kick.

You'll take it and like it, and if you don't hop that rattler and do a fade-away, you'll be found stiff in the morning back in the alley. Now pipe down and be polite, Big Meat, or papa will spank. If you need a shot of whisky, look in the bottom drawer of the desk. Hit it light, see. You'll scoff when I get ready to send one of the boys to the Chink's for sandwiches. One more yelp out of you and you'll be caught in there robbing my office. When the law finds you, you'll be as dead as Napoleon. Think it over, big boy."

Creighton Marley lit another cigarette and strolled back to the open doorway of his office. He cursed the luck that had made Big Meat Drummond fail so miserably. Well, the big rat would pay for his mistake before too many hours. He'd put Drummond out of the way. There was a .38 gun equipped with a silencer hidden here in the office. That rod would do the work. Drummond wouldn't be the first man that had tasted the deadly dose from that silent gun.

Now Marley's eyes narrowed a little as he spotted Eric Swanson coming down the street. Swanson, his face puffed and discolored, was with several friends from the Big Warm colony. Marley had heard the story of Eric's whipping at the hands of Bill Murdock. But he knew that the beating Eric had taken had served to antagonize many of the farmers against the stockmen. Eric left his friends and crossed the street to Marley's office.

Marley faked a genial, silky smile. "What's the

196

good word, Eric? Need more money for the homestead?"

"I got money in that bank that I heard was going broke. You told me to bank there. What are you going to do about it?"

"You won't lose a dime. You know that, Eric. I told you when we started that I'd see you through and I'm a man of my word. It happens to be to our advantage that this bank should go bust. Now you sit tight and you'll come out on top, get me? When I withdrew my account from the Valley Bank, I took care of you. You can't lose a dime if you play with me. Where was the wreck?" Marley grinned at the big farmer. Eric scowled darkly.

"Bill Murdock double-crossed me, that's all. He's not the man I thought he was."

"I told you that, Eric. Want revenge?"

"You bet I want revenge and I'll —"

"Hold it, Eric. Hold everything. Let me handle the thinking. You will get satisfaction, and how. Keep your mouth shut and follow my instructions. Now take your friends and get over there to the bank. Make 'em think you're losing your last dollar if that bank closes. Talk some, but not too much. Get the idea?"

"What about my friends, Marley?"

"Listen, Eric, I'm carrying you, but I'm not carrying every half-naturalized farmer in the country. Get smart and look out for yourself. How'd you like to get hold of all that Big Warm farming land and have the jack to finance the crops? How'd you like to make more on the job as straw-boss of that whole district than you'd make out of your three hundred and twenty acres in five years? Ponder on that.

"When I picked you to boss that Big Warm section, I figured you were smart. Now it's time you woke up and saw the sunrise. Let your friends and neighbors book a little losing. You're winning and I'm making you win. This can't be handled in a week or two. It takes time to put over anything that's worth the gamble, don't you see? Now you follow out my orders and I'll see that you come out on top. Play with me, brother, and you'll be the richest farmer in this country. Throw me down and I'll break you. Which way do you go, Eric?"

"You mean I'll have all those farms on Big Warm?"

"You heard me right."

"I don't lose what I put in there in that bank and on my farm?"

"You lose nothing. You're playing the winner in this race. You can't lose. You're cashing in on a hundred to one shot. Want it or don't you want it?"

"I'll take it, Marley."

"It's all under the old hat, see? No tongue flapping."

"I ain't that dumb."

"Then get over in that mob and do your stuff. Here's a century note for drinks. Spend it on the suckers. Stay wise, kid, stay wise."

Eric Swanson put the hundred dollar bill in his pocket and winked a discolored eye.

"I'm wise, Creighton."

"I'm Mister Marley to you, Swanson. *Mister* Marley. Just an old Spanish custom. Get that."

Creighton Marley gave the big farmer a hard look, smiled sneeringly, then turned his back on Eric Swanson and walked into his office.

Something of the worried look was gone from Marley's eyes and he hummed softly as he reached for the telephone.

"Local, Seven Nine. And I want to speak to Howard Snodgrass. This is John Smith speaking. . . . Nobody but Snodgrass. That's the idea, dear. . . . That you, Howard? Okay. Listen, I'm having lunch with you at your house in fifteen minutes. . . . What? . . . No. I said in fifteen minutes. You'll be there, regardless, old man."

Marley hung up softly and snapped open a cigarette case of hammered silver. He looked at his wrist-watch and smiled. Then he slipped a small automatic into his coat pocket.

Stepping to the closed door that led to the back room, he opened it with a pass-key and stepped inside.

Big Meat Drummond sat at a desk, a bottle of whisky in front of him.

"I'll be back in an hour, Big Meat. You stay put. Better not step outside for anything. How do you feel?"

"Lousy."

Marley's right hand held the little automatic.

199

"Just a pea-shooter, Big Meat, but it's potent. Are you taking my orders or not?"

"You're the main gaffer, Marley. I'm licked."

"Still feel lousy?" The small automatic moved a little. Marley's eyes were narrowed, hard, merciless. The lips that held the cigarette were smiling crookedly.

"Naw, I feel like a million."

"That's the spirit, Big Meat. See you later. Do you want your chicken sandwiches plain or toasted?"

"Either way, chief."

"So I thought." Marley backed out the door and locked it. Then, after adjusting his already perfect tie, he walked down the street with an easy, arrogant stride.

CHAPTER XVI
PRISON SHADOW

Those were frontier towns, old pardner;
'Twas a game of take en give,
And the one who could draw the fastest
Was the only one who'd live.
　　　　　　　　　　— Billy the Kid.

Chinook had company. A varied, motley company, that mid-afternoon when the Valley Bank closed its doors at noon. The cow town teemed with a hundred rumors. The farm wagons of a nester gathering stood in the feed yard, the teams eating hay, the women sitting in anxious groups in the meager shade of the wagons. Their faces wore a harassed, wearied, beaten look. Their men were uptown in the crowd that still hung around the bank or gathered in the crowded bar-rooms. They had staked their all on a venture that now seemed doomed.

It was a foregone conclusion that the Valley Bank was broken. That the money they had put in there, together with the money borrowed from Creighton Marley, was lost.

With their crops in the grounds, their pine board shacks, battened with strips of boards, roofed with tar-paper, built there in this land into which they had come with their last dollar and their high hopes, they now stared, blank eyed, bewildered, at stark disaster. A bank that held their money was about to fail. Instead of a bumper crop promised them by the spring rains, they were left, literally and proverbially, holding empty the grain sacks that had been waiting to be filled with the golden grain.

Theirs was a vision of fields of grain, maturing under an autumn sun, ready to be cut and threshed and sacked into wheat and flax that was to be turned into golden dollars to be spent with a farmer's thrift on the necessities of life and the education of their children. The crops were growing under the shelter of their barb-wire fences. They had come here to Montana to make their homes, to live out their lives in a furrowed land that would never gain them wealth but which promised to maintain their simple homes. They asked for little save that hard living wrested from a soil made fertile by rains they had knelt and prayed for to their God.

And now, on the day that was to bring a promised tomorrow, they were faced by stark calamity. Stunned, bereft of proper under-standing, wholly bewildered by a condition that their plodding minds could not grasp, they sat on that hot day in June, in the sweltering shade of wagons left in a stable yard, their hearts pinched with strange grief, their hopes with-ered, waiting to hear that word that would mean to them poverty and the loss of all they had hoped to find in this new land to which they had migrated.

Uptown, tied to the hitch-racks in front of the saloons and stores and the hotel, were saddled horses. Horses that wore the oldest brands in the State of Montana. Saddles that had weathered drouth and blizzard. Coiled ropes that had picked up the hind feet of calves that were stamped with the iron of the men who were pioneers.

Cowboys who rode those horses had never known anything but the unfenced range. They had no home ties, no dreams, no families. They worked for forty dollars a month which they spent with a free hand. Their eyes followed the sky-line that forever receded as they rode. Always, and until their days ended, they would be riding across horizons seeking a better range.

Their lives were bounded by nothing save the four far points of the compass. They claimed their home to be somewhere or anywhere between the sunrise and sunset. They heard the bawl of a new-born calf, rather than the mewling whimper of babies nursing at a mother's breast. Their lives could never be bound by the strands of barb wire. They claimed no roof save the star-light sky, no bed save the tarp-covered roll of blankets spread on the hard ground. They squandered their hard-earned pay across bar and poker table. They emptied their pockets and emptied their guns at the stars as they rode out of town and back to the hard life that they loved and could never leave.

Now a cowboy, weaving on unsteady legs warped bow-legged from years spent in the saddle, came to the barn to see if his horse had been grained. He had seen the children who had been there at the feed yard that morning when he rode into town. Now, under each arm, the cowboy carried bulging gunny-sacks. He halted at the wagons, under the hostile eyes of the women there. Selecting a buxom woman whose face seemed less cold than that of the others, he walked over to her and with an awkward bow, left the bulging sacks at her feet.

"Somethin' fer the young 'uns, ma'am." And he left as he had come, stiff gaited, embarrassed that he should be so caught in an act that might be construed as "chicken hearted." And when he had gone to see that his horse was fed and watered, they had opened the gunny-sacks to discover them filled with candy and fruit and a motley assortment of toys. So had a tipsy cowboy made a gesture typical of his race, and had departed before the woman could give refusal or thanks for the gift.

The woman whose toil-worn hands untied the sacks, a mother of five red cheeked youngsters, stared at the generous supply of things they could ill afford. Tears sprang to her wide blue eyes. The clamor of the excited children brought a wistful smile to her lips.

Uptown, the street in front of the bank was packed from one sidewalk to the opposite one.

For the most part, the crowd consisted of men. Farmers, small ranchers, a couple of sheep-herders dazed with liquor, their dogs cowering between the unsteady legs of their masters. Some pimply, sallow-cheeked youths in wasp-waisted coats and cigarette-holders whose sole aim in being there was to spot a possible sucker for a few games of Kelly pool or poker dice for chips at the pool-rooms. Weak-spined younger brothers of the old-time tin-horn gambler who fleeced the cowboy and trapper and soldier. Some Indians who stood like statues of patience, their squaws sitting on the edge of the plank sidewalk, waiting for something they did not understand, some white man's amusement that would give them food for camp-fire talk when they went back to the reservation.

There were some tough-looking characters in clothes that bore the cinder smudges rubbed off the rods under box-cars. Other human bits of driftwood ready to pick a pocket or start a fight, slinking like underfed, vicious dogs, through the crowd. Oddly, there was not a cow-puncher in the crowd.

On the side street stood a roadster parked within a few steps of the side door of the bank. Now that door opened quietly, emitted Howard Snodgrass, and closed. A moment and Snodgrass was in his car, had started the motor, and was gone before the sheep-like crowd was aware of his departure.

Those who did notice gave his going but small

notice. The man they wanted to see was Uncle Hank Mayberry. They were beginning to mutter his name, coupled with insults and threats. Bolder ones shouted for him to come out and face the music.

Now a lone rider came down the street. Buck Rawlins, his square jaw covered with several days stubble of beard, in shabby overalls, and a shirt that needed changing. His hat was an old one, his boots were rusty, and he looked a little haggard. Buck had quit the spring round-up over on Larb Creek to make a hard ride for Chinook in answer to his father's message.

He had stopped only twice on that ride of over a hundred miles. Once he had stopped at the Rolling M ranch for a fresh horse and a bite to eat and to leave a message for Colleen, who was at the horse camp on Second Creek helping cut out some three-year-old geldings for breaking and sale. Buck's second stop was at Fancy Mary's road ranch. Again he changed horses, was fed by the genial negress, and spent half an hour talking to the Nighthawk, who was hiding out there while a bullet hole in his side healed.

Now, after a long night and morning spent in the saddle, Buck Rawlins rode into Chinook. Around his middle was a sagging cartridge belt and a .45 in its open holster. He carried his left arm a little stiffly.

From the opened hotel window the voice of his father hailed Buck. Buck pulled up, slouching sideways in his saddle, grinning crookedly.

"Step up a minute, son. I'll give yuh the lay uh things."

Buck stepped out of the saddle and dropped the bridle reins over the hitch-rack. He walked into the hotel lobby. The lobby was crowded and Buck had to push his way through. He was conscious of several pairs of unfriendly eyes following him up the wide stairway to the floor above.

He entered the room without knocking. Dave Rawlins greeted his son with a wide smile. "Glad to see yuh, boy. Yo're a sight fer sore eyes."

"And fer blind eyes," added Bob Driscoll as Buck crossed over and gripped the blind horseman's hand.

"Your note said they were trying to throw and hog-tie Uncle Hank Mayberry. I saw the mob milling around the bank. Is it that bad?"

"They're sayin' Hank misused money belongin' to the bank. That he's made loans contrary to bank laws. The skunks are tryin' tuh send Hank Mayberry to the pen. They're houndin' a man that never stole a dollar in his life. Look at that mob down yonder. Hear the talk they're a-makin'. Yuh got here just about in time, Buck. How many of our boys are follerin' you?"

"The Block outfit is in town waiting delivery on some horses. They're just as good as our cowboys and they'll fight to the finish for Uncle Hank. Cutbank Carter and Tuley Bill should be in town later on this evening. We'll have men, if it comes to a show-down. But I don't think that it will come to that. Unless Uncle Hank is too deep, we'll pay off the creditors a hundred cents on the dollar."

"We? Me'n Bob has done all we kin. We're not usin' a dollar uh the money Hank loaned us. But she goes deeper than that, son. Hank has to account fer at least fifty thousand dollars, so the li'l' West gal finds out somehow. There, by gosh, is a woman with the grit of a real fighter. She's downtown somewheres now, keepin' an eye on things and listenin' to what she kin hear. Yeah, the Mazie young 'un says Hank is in the hole to the tune of fifty thousand er worse."

Buck rolled a cigarette. His lips, sun-cracked and marred by the stubble of dust-filled whiskers, grinned. His eyes, bloodshot from weariness, puckered at the corners.

The gray eyes of Dave Rawlins and the gray eyes of his only son Buck met in a grim glance. They understood each other, this father and son. Buck, in overalls and battered hat and whiskers, his hair uncombed, with the dust of Sun Prairie round-ups powdering his clothes and the skin under his clothes, his face showing streaks where the sweat had trickled from under the battered hat — Buck, smelling of sweat and branding fires, was the son that Dave Rawlins worshiped with all the pride of a cow-man for a son who is a real cow-man.

Never had Dave Rawlins been so proud of his son as now. Buck might have finished college a Phi Beta Kappa at the head of his class and Dave

Rawlins would not have thought so much of it. But standing there in the hotel room at the Chinook House, facing Buck, who looked as disreputable as a man can look after a hard week's work on a round-up, he was as proud as ever a father can be.

"There'll be fifty thousand dollars cash in the bank on Monday morning, Dad."

"The days of miracles," said Bob Driscoll gravely, "has passed, Buck."

"Hank Mayberry will have fifty thousand dollars cash Monday morning," repeated Buck softly. "We'll lick these scissor-bills. We'll make Marley and Snodgrass take a licking before we're done. We'll save Uncle Hank's bank."

"Yuh ain't doin' anything foolish, son?"

"No, Dad. Just helping an old friend that is in a tight. Nothing foolish. Now I'll go on down and try to crash the gate there at the bank."

Dave Rawlins motioned toward a bottle of whisky and glasses on the table. "Yuh look kinda laig weary, Buck. Slip up on a drink."

"If you don't mind, I'll just pass it up. When I learn how to take a drink, I'll take one. But until that day comes, count me among the water dogs. Now you two sit down and auger some. I'll be back after a while."

"I'll be watchin' from the window, Buck. When yuh need me, holler."

"I don't think I'll need any help, Dad. So-long."

When Buck's spurs jingled down the hallway,

Bob Driscoll spoke. "Buck is a good boy, Dave, a mighty good boy."

"And Colleen is a mighty fine girl, Bob. We're almighty lucky."

"Mebbyso, Dave, some day, the two young 'uns will git married."

"It's always bin my biggest dream, Bob. Now set there while I pour us a light 'un."

CHAPTER XVII

BUCK RAWLINS LENDS A HAND

With a center-fire saddle and a .45 gun,
And a top cow pony, I'm never on the bum,
Come a ti yi yippy yi yay, yi yay,
Come a ti yi yippy yi yay!

— The Chisholm Trail.

As Buck pushed his way outside the hotel door a girl's voice hailed him cautiously.

"Meet me back in the alley. Important, cowboy. Plenty important."

Buck, with a quick, sidelong glance, saw Mazie West standing beside him. He nodded and walked on outside. Calling a careless "Howdy, see yuh later, boys, at the Bucket of Blood," to two or three cowboys who lounged near the hitch-rack, Buck stepped up on his horse and rode around into the alley. Mazie West was waiting for him.

"Gosh, I'm glad you showed up," she said. "We need help and I ain't fooling. Get a load of this. Marley calls Snodgrass on the phone. Tells him to be at Snodgrass's house. Marley has gone over there and Howard Snodgrass just left the bank. There's dirty work at the cross-roads, Buck. And that ain't the half of it. The Big Meat

211

Drummond, Marley's ten-minute egg, is hiding in Marley's back room. Likewise Marley is ribbing the Eric Swanson guy to stir up the farmers. Things look bad for Uncle Hank."

"You know," grinned Buck, "I wish that there was something I could do to make you think I was not such a tramp. You've acted like a mighty real friend to us folks. I'd like to have you think I'm something besides a drunken fool and a crook."

Mazie West smiled and held out her hand. "Any of us are apt to be all wet sometimes. If I thought you weren't regular, Buck Rawlins, I wouldn't shake hands with you."

"You mean that?" Buck took her hand and held it. She was smiling a little wistfully.

"Sure I mean it. You're okay, cowboy. And we're wasting time right now. Better get on the job."

"Right. I'm moving right now. But say, how did you get all this inside dope on the Marley and Snodgrass combine?"

"From Onion. The poor old dear is hiding under the floor of Marley's office. We tunneled in from the Chinaman's kitchen next door. Took us all last night to dig in. I broke every fingernail I own handling dirt. He's in there now, bless his heart. And we've got enough on that burglar gang to hang 'em. Marley is using Snodgrass. They're old partners in varied and sundry crimes. Can't we call their dirty hands?"

"Keep that contact with Onion. I'm going to

pay Marley and Snodgrass a short visit. Then I'll be back at the bank. We'll whip 'em or take a whipping. And I hope the day will come when we can pay back a little of what we owe you. You're . . . you're a white man, lady."

"Nope, just a darned little chump, Buck."

Buck gripped her two hands in his. For a moment they stood there, in a narrow alley cluttered with ash-cans and boxes and empty beer barrels. He gripped her hands hard, grinned down at her, then swung back into his saddle. He lifted his battered hat, swung his horse up the alley, and was gone. Mazie looked after him with a little smile.

She was thinking of a day, ten years ago, when a cowboy had won first money at the big Chicago rodeo, had bent from his saddle and kissed her, then had ridden away and out of her life. Her hands were clenched hard as she walked back into the hotel and up to the room where Dave Rawlins and Bob Driscoll waited for the coming of Uncle Hank Mayberry.

Buck Rawlins was humming under his breath as he rode boldly up the street to the modern and smart-looking bungalow where Howard Snodgrass lived. Dismounting, he swung with a quick step up the walk and up on the veranda. It was his first visit to the home of Howard Snodgrass who had married Maud Mayberry.

Time had been, years ago, when Buck had carried Maud's books home from school and had taken her to parties. The past few years had separated them, divided their comradeship and their friendship. Maud had married Howard Snodgrass when she was going to an Eastern college for girls. And while Buck had never really cared for her, he resented Maud's desertion of her old friends since she had come home the wife of the suave and polished and formal-mannered Howard Snodgrass.

A colored maid answered the doorbell. In reply to Buck's inquiry she told him that neither Mr. nor Mrs. Snodgrass were home.

"Sorry," grinned Buck, pushing his way past her and into the house, "but I think you're mistaken." Boldly, with a swinging, spur-jingling stride, he walked down the short hallway and, opening a door, stepped into a smoke-hazed room where sat Howard Snodgrass and Creighton Marley.

They gaped at him with a mingled fear and resentment. Marley's hand slid inside his coat pocket. Buck grinned crookedly at him.

"Better not, Marley. I'd hate to kill Howard's friend in here. But unless you let go of that gun I'll kill you where you sit. I've got a few words to say to you two crooks and I'll say 'em. Even if I have to talk after I've put a bullet in the belly of Creighton Marley."

Like a flash Buck's gun was in his hand, covering the two men. His boot slammed the door closed behind him. And as the hands of the two men raised, Buck smiled and nodded.

"Howard, take Marley's gun and lay it on the table. Then relax. Move, Howard, I'm not in a very tolerant humor. That's it. Now sit back, gentlemen, while a cowboy talks. Quite a joint you've got here, Howard. You'll miss it a lot when you move."

"What do you mean, move, you drunken fool?"

"When you go to the State's Penitentiary, Snodgrass. You and your friend Marley."

"Look here, Rawlins. That's about enough of this horseplay. Go on back to your saloons and honkeytonks, where you fit into the scenery. This is my home and you're intruding. I'll have you jailed for this."

"Yeah? Yeah? Somehow, I don't reckon so. I just can't seem to conjure up the picture of me languishing in jail. But I may be wrong. I usually am."

"Right. You usually are wrong," snapped Marley, sneering. "You think you can get away with anything just because your old man and his friends were here before the law and a decent civilization came here. You can't get away with any of that swashbuckling, high-handed, buccaneering stuff to-day. The day of the robber baron of the cattle range has gone. Better take a powder, Rawlins. You're in wrong here."

"Marley," said Buck pleasantly, picking up Marley's automatic and putting it on a black walnut buffet among glittering glasses and decanters filled with wines and liquors, "I'll talk to you in a moment. Right now I'm trying to hold my temper in check while I talk to Howard Snodgrass. One more yip out of you, my little peacock, and I'll push your nose down your throat. You shut up." He turned to Snodgrass, who was getting red, his hands were gripping the arms of his leather chair.

"Snodgrass," said Buck, "in a few minutes you are taking me to the bank. Before you go with me, tell me the right answer to a question. How much is Uncle Hank Mayberry's shortage? I want the truth or I'll bend this gun across your horns. Talk up."

The eyes of Howard Snodgrass shifted under Buck's bloodshot, cold gray stare.

"Fifty-three thousand dollars. He's due to go to the pen."

"Yeah? All right. Now for another question. Does Maud know about this?"

"Yes. Of course she does. The poor girl is all broken up to think her own father is a common absconder, a thief. She's upstairs in bed, with a nurse in attendance."

"Now isn't that just too bad." Buck's eyes hardened. "Snodgrass, send for your wife. What I have to say is also for her to hear. Send for her."

"This is outrageous, Rawlins!" protested Snodgrass hotly, swinging up from his chair with a quick movement.

Buck shoved his gun into its holster. He took one step forward. His whole weight was behind the swing that landed on the point of Howard

Snodgrass's jaw. And as the dazed bank official picked himself up off the floor, his hand held against a jaw that was sending terrific pains into his head, Buck smiled crookedly at him.

"I'm waiting, Snodgrass. Call your wife. Marley, sit still or I'll cave your pasty face in."

Howard Snodgrass pushed a button on his desk. The colored maid answered the call. Snodgrass, his voice a little thick, told her that he would like to speak to Mrs. Snodgrass immediately.

"In heah, suh?"

"In here," said Buck, rolling a cigarette. "And tell her to please hurry."

In a tense silence the three men waited. Buck stood near the door.

"You'd better take a stiff drink, Snodgrass," he said coldly. "You'll be needing it."

Maud Snodgrass, white, her eyes showing signs of recent tears, came into the room. Buck closed the door behind her. She looked at the three men, a bewildered expression in her eyes. Buck held a chair for her.

"Sorry to disturb you, Maud, but it's absolutely necessary. I have something to tell you that may somehow make up for my intrusion here. Uncle Hank is all right. His bank won't go bust."

"Buck" — Maud Snodgrass faced him with tragic eyes — "this is hardly the time or the place for clowning. Please don't."

"I'm not clowning, Maud. I mean what I say.

217

Your dad is to me just about the same as my own. You know that. I've known you since you wore pig-tails and your father's home was my home many times. Do you think I'd come here joshing at a time like this? I tell you that Uncle Hank is in no danger of going to prison, ever."

"Buck, do you mean that?"

"I wouldn't ride all night from the round-up over in the Larb Hills to come here and crack funny jokes."

Maud Snodgrass turned to her husband. There was a flash of quick flame in her eyes that made him wince.

"You phoned from the bank not more than half an hour ago that the bank had failed and they were sending Father to jail. What have you to say?"

"What he says, Maud," said Buck grimly, "he'd better save to tell a jury. Hank Mayberry never made a crooked deal in his life. If the money in the Valley Bank has been misused then Howard Snodgrass is the gent that misused it. It's a hard way to break it to you, Maud, but that's exactly what I mean."

"I'll make you prove what you're saying!" gritted Snodgrass.

"And we'll make him prove a lot of other things, Howard," Marley put in.

"I was always taught never to fight in the presence of ladies, Marley," said Buck, "but it looks like I'll have to go against my teachings if you don't shut up."

"Buck," said Maud Snodgrass, "you're making some rather bold statements that I'll have to ask you to prove. Howard is my husband. Creighton Marley is our best friend."

"And," added Buck grimly, "Hank Mayberry is your father. It looks like I've wasted my time. I'll use the same door where I came in. I'll go alone. But before I leave here I want to talk on the phone to Uncle Hank Mayberry at the bank."

Buck reached for the phone. After a minute's waiting he heard Uncle Hank's voice at the other end of the wire.

"This is Buck Rawlins, Uncle Hank. Cowboys in town. My horse is outside and wrapped up in my slicker is about sixty thousand dollars. Have the side door of your bank open when I ride up. So-long."

Buck turned to the two men and the woman, who were staring at him. He grinned and pulled on his battered hat.

"Never judge a man by the rags he wears. See you all later." And the silence in the room he shut the door upon was more, far more impressive than any words that could be said.

CHAPTER XVIII
BLACKSNAKE LAW

*Now all you young maidens, where'er you
reside,*
*Beware of the cowboy who swings the raw-
hide,*
*He'll court you and pet you and leave you and
go*
*In the spring up the trail on his bucking
bronco.*

— Bucking Bronco.

Sixty thousand dollars in currency wrapped in a yellow slicker. Buck slid his horse to a halt at the deserted side door. He had untied the saddle-strings and was walking across the plank walk with the precious bundle when a man on horse-back, dust powdered, weary, his horse sweat streaked, pulled up and swung off his saddle, a gun in his hand.

"Drop it, Rawlins, and reach for some sky. You're my meat." The man pulled back his dusty coat, revealing a gold badge. His six-shooter covered Buck menacingly. Buck eyed him narrowly. An ugly, twisted grin was on the cowboy's mouth.

"You were at Fancy Mary's road ranch last

night, weren't you?" said Buck contemptuously. "You were tending bar there for Mary. And you sneaked up to the closed door and listened to some talk. You know where this money comes from, do yuh? And you likewise know what it is to be used for. And you were in that posse that was going to take me for a buggy ride at the Rolling M fire. I knew you last night, you sneaking coyote. I knew you would try to follow me." Now Buck grinned and looked past the man.

"Thanks, Onion. If the rat tries to squeak, snuff him out."

The man with the badge whirled quickly. As he turned, Buck's six-shooter rapped against his skull and he went limp. Onion Oliver shoved his cedar-handled Colt back into its worn scabbard and bent over the unconscious man, ripping the gold badge from the man's shirt.

"I'll handle him, Buck. Git in there," he hissed.

"Good head, Onion. See you later." And Buck rapped on the locked door that was opened by Uncle Hank Mayberry. Now the door was closed and locked. Buck was inside the bank with the money.

Out on the sidewalk, Onion Oliver and a Block cow-puncher carried the unconscious man down the street, half dragging, half carrying the limp bulk. The little scene had happened so quickly that not one of the crowd in the main street had noticed. They had not been watching the side door.

"He's taken too much red-eye." Onion grinned at a curious constable. The constable nodded and let them pass along. Onion and the Block cowboy carried the limp man into a card room at the Bucket of Blood and locked the door.

"When Buck Rawlins sets his mind on somethin'," chuckled Onion, "he'll come dog-gone near carryin' 'er through. Lordy, he's quick. But he was shore in a tight there fer a second. This weasel had 'im foul. Lucky we spotted this bugger and was waitin' fer just such a play. The question is, what'll we do with his carcass?"

"He ain't dead, Onion."

"Nope. But he will be when he leaves this room. He's got the goods on Buck and I work fer Buck. He ain't sendin' Dave Rawlins's boy Buck to no pen. Not if I have tuh kill the cuss cold-blooded."

Onion turned the man's head and peered intently at it. A queer smile puckered the old cowhand's mouth. Then he set about searching the man's pockets. A wallet claimed Onion's attention and for some minutes he carefully read several cards and notes he found. Then he tossed the ornate badge over to the Block cowboy.

"You kin keep 'er for a souvenir. This jasper ain't any more of a railroad dick than I am. He's one uh Marley's job-lot, mail-order gun toters. Same cuss that was down in the bad-lands when they tried tuh kidnap the li'l' nester gal. I thought he looked familiar."

"Gonna kill him, Onion?"

"Kill 'im? Mebby, later on. I'll keep 'im on ice fer a spell. Git me a couple uh hoggin' strings and somethin' that'll do fer a gag in his mouth. He's what the Romans usta call a prisoner uh war. Ever read about them Roman fellers? They was fightin' fools. A feller named Cæsar rodded the spread and they was the first layout that ever begun a range war. On a range they called Gall and from what I read, them fellers had gall and plenty of it.

"They swum a river and cleaned up on the tribe on the yonder side, usin' nothin' but big bowie-knives to do their plain an' fancy carvin'. Them as laid 'em down they taken prisoner and holds back in a tight corral. Hostages, is the name they give them mavericks and they holds 'em under close herd. Then, in case one uh this Cæsar's boys gits into a tight an' corraled by the sheep folks across the river, they swaps hostages like we'd swap yearlin's that was branded wrong and so tallied. That's hist'ry, cowboy, and I read 'er last winter in line camp out of a book that didn't have one dang pitcher in 'er.

"Well, we'll hold this flea-bit specimen as a hostage. When Tuley Bill an' Cutbank git in, we'll vivisect the weasel er somethin'. Tuley Bill will know. He's got some uh the greatest idees fer treatin' prisoners as ever was learned off the Apaches er Cheyennes. He kin set aroun' an' nibble at a bottle uh Injun likker an' think up

223

more ways uh dealin' misery to a human than ary man I know. An' when Tuley sets here an' begins tuh orate fancy on sewin' up eyelids er drivin' nails into a man's briskit er openin' his belly with a dull knife, this fake detective is gonna go shore pale an' scary an' he'll give up head like a calf bein' drug to the fire.

"When we turns him loose he'll be acrost the boundaries uh seventeen States afore daylight. He'll hit a high run fer spots uh this earth that is unknown. He'll be a-driftin' yonderly. He'll be headed fer a climate as fits his clothes. And he ain't a-tarryin' here ner there tuh auger er graze. Ner he won't even stop tuh likker.

"Speakin' uh that kind uh fruit, let's git busy surroundin' about three big 'uns whilst we gits our hostage hog-tied proper. Then I gotta go back an' play gopher till the nester gal learns what she aims tuh learn. I'm a-gittin' cramps in my hocks from layin' on the damp ground under that floor, but any man as wouldn't crawl on his belly fer ten miles acrost bog holes an' snow drifts an' prickly pears tuh dust off that gal's shoes with his only good hat, is no gentleman. Here's blisters on yore tonsils, stockhand."

Meanwhile, inside the bank, Buck faced Uncle Hank Mayberry, the bank examiner, and the other bank officials. Uncle Hank's face was gray and lined heavily with worry. He smiled wanly at Buck and his bulging slicker. Now Buck stepped to Hank's desk and spread open the slicker.

There, in thick bundles secured with wide rubber hands, was the currency.

"Count it, gentlemen," said Buck, "I think you'll find it all there. Sixty thousand cash."

Ike Niland gave Buck a long, searching look, opened his grim lips as if to speak, then changed his mind. Uncle Hank sat on the corner of the desk, trying to roll a cigarette with shaking fingers. The eyes of the little old frontiersman were misty. His under lip quivered as he looked at Buck.

"I don't know how to try tuh say 'er, Buck, so I reckon I won't try."

Buck nodded and faced the bank examiner. "This money should be security for notes signed by my father and by Bob Driscoll and the other cow-men around here. Does this clear Uncle Hank Mayberry of the fool charges? Or are you going to try to railroad as fine a gentleman and as honorable a citizen as ever lived in Montana?"

"This is unexpected and irregular, of course," said the bank examiner whose task had, so far, been a most unpleasant one. "If there is cash here in the bank to cover the notes signed by the various stockmen to whom Mr. Mayberry has made loans, then those loans are most certainly covered. It is not an unusual thing for one bank to come to the assistance of another bank in such instances. There is nothing to prevent an individual from doing likewise. Your loyalty, my friend, is splendid."

"This is not my money. Uncle Hank, you will just make out some sort of a statement for me? I'll dictate it, if you'd like, and you write it." He grinned at the little old banker who gripped his fountain pen with stubby fingers.

"To Mary Green," dictated Buck slowly. "Friend Mary: Many thanks for the favor. Your friend, Hank Mayberry."

Uncle Hank wrote mechanically and blotted the fresh ink with the bronze handled blotter. He looked quizzically at Buck as he folded the note and handed it to the young cowman.

"Buck," he said, trying to keep his voice steady, "would it be speakin' outa turn if I asked who is Mary Green?"

Buck smiled a little and put the note in his wallet. "Mary Green," he told them, pride in his voice, "is a lady that we've always known as Fancy Mary."

"Fancy Mary?" gasped Uncle Hank. "Fancy Mary?"

"Yes, Fancy Mary. She's never had much use for banks and her life's savings that she's accumulated, she buried. When she heard that an old friend of hers was in trouble, she dug it all up and told me to give it to you."

For the first time since Buck had opened the slicker with its packages of money, Ike Niland seemed to relax. Buck grinned at him.

"So you thought I'd gone into the road-agent business, did yuh, Ike?"

"I wouldn't uh put it past yuh, son. Hank, step

out an' tell that pack uh howlin' wolves that yore bank will open as always on Monday mornin' and them that chooses kin draw out. I'll tell 'em first and then you kin talk to 'em."

Ike Niland, tall, raw-boned, grim-lipped, opened the front door. Beside him stood Uncle Hank. Together they faced the mob that now went ominously silent.

"Folks," said Ike, his voice harsh and rasping, "you kin go on home. This bank ain't closin' its doors. It'll be open Monday and them as cares to, kin draw out what they got deposited. Most of you will be takin' this as shore good news. There are some other men in this crowd that will be sorry tuh know that Hank Mayberry's bank ain't failin'. I know just about every one uh them same men and if they start anything, it will be to their sorrow." Ike's steely eyes roved over the crowd as if he were singling out the agitators. Then he laid his hand on the shoulder of his old friend. "Tell 'er to 'em, Hank."

"It's like the sheriff says, men. The bank will open Monday, the same as always. Them as is scared of losin' their few white chips kin draw 'em out."

"Yah!" snarled Eric Swanson. "Big talk that ain't costin' you a nickel. If you got money in that bank, pay off now. Pay us now!"

Others took up the cry. There was an ugly, surly, dangerous tone to their grumbled demand. "Pay us! Give us our money now! Pay off!"

Nor would they quit their clamor, even when Ike Niland held up his arm to silence them. Ike's few special deputies were moving quietly toward the ring-leaders. Ike pushed Uncle Hank back behind him and the two, sheriff and banker, were back inside the bank. Even as Ike slammed the door shut, a bullet ripped through the door.

Ike's face was hard and set. He looked at Buck.

"Buck, slip out that side door and git down the street. Gather all the good men you kin pick up. Come up the street a-horseback and on yore way up, stop at the harness shop. Stake yore men to buggy whips an' quirts an' blacksnakes. Don't pull a gun unless I tell yuh to. If them toughs an' farmers git nasty, whup 'em till they quit. No guns unless they make a bad play. Out yuh go, son."

Now Ike Niland again stepped out the front door. In his hands was a short-barreled automatic shot-gun. Alone, gaunt, grim, menacing, he faced the mob, that suddenly went silent again.

"The man that steps forward, gits killed. I'm the law here and I'll be the only law. You can't run this town and you'll mighty soon learn it. Right now I'm coverin' Eric Swanson and some uh the toughs hired to start a ruckus. You'll be the first ones tuh feel what's in this scatter-gun. When I told yuh this bank would open Monday I meant just that. There's money in there to pay off any man that wants to withdraw his account. Hank Mayberry will pay off Monday. Not until

Monday. And I'm here to protect him and his bank. That goes just as she lays."

Up the street, riding at a slow trot, came Buck Rawlins and the Block cowboys. In their hands were long blacksnakes and willow buggy whips that could cut a man's flesh like a knife. All had guns.

They came at a steady gait, quiet, orderly, like soldiers. There was something dangerous about that quietness that awed the more timid of the mob. They commenced to shift uneasily at the approach of the cowboys. Ike's special deputies gripped their clubs and gun butts.

Within a scant five feet of the tightly packed mob, Buck and his cow-punchers halted, at a signal from the sheriff. "If these men don't git in one minute, Buck, whup the hides off 'em." He pulled out a big silver watch.

Buck and his men sat their horses, their whips ready. They looked like they would thoroughly enjoy horsewhipping the mob into flight.

"They got us licked," said a man in a harsh, bitter voice. "I got no gun. I ain't gonna be whipped like a dog. I'm comin' back Monday."

A murmur of assent from the others. Eric Swanson, his swollen face white under its discolorations, was the first to start down the street. Before thirty seconds had passed, the mob was dispersing, jostling their way down the street, headed for the bar-rooms or the feed yard where their women waited. Calamity had been averted. Five minutes later the street in front of the bank was deserted except for the cow-punchers.

Uncle Hank Mayberry and Ike Niland stood there by the door of the bank. Hank grinned crookedly at the sheriff.

"How's chances tuh borry my gun back, Ike? Yo're the only man that ever handled that ol' haw-laig except' me."

Ike's eyes crinkled at the corners as he reached into the waistband of his California pants and pulled out a long-barreled six-shooter which he gravely returned to the little old plainsman.

"I was scared yuh'd git reckless with 'er, Hank."

Ike posted guards inside the bank. Buck dismissed the Block cowboys with instructions to return the unused whips. Then he walked down the street with Ike Niland and Uncle Hank to the hotel where Bob Driscoll, Dave Rawlins and Mazie West waited in the hotel room. They had no sooner gained the room when Onion Oliver appeared. The old cow-puncher's face was grave and taut-muscled.

"Gents," he said abruptly as he shut the door behind him, "I got bad news. Trouble has popped over on the forest reserve. A feller fetched word to Marley at his office. A herder was killed and his sheep run off. Sheep wagon burned an' a camp tender hurt bad. The Murdocks will have the word by now and I reckon war's declared."

"Who had orders to bother them sheep?" Ike Niland's voice was brittle. He eyed Dave

Rawlins and Buck and the blind Bob Driscoll.

"Nobody had such orders, Ike," said Dave Rawlins grimly. "I've got no quarrel with Angus Murdock. We never was friends, account of his bein' a sheep-man, but I never give any man orders to bother his lousy woolies."

"I'm gettin' a posse an' I'm goin' out after whoever did it, boys," said Ike Niland in a voice that sounded tired and a little old. "I'm not deputizin' any man here. I've got my own deputies." He turned and walked out of the room, closing the door behind him. On the table stood the glass of whisky which he had set down, untouched. Onion's cracked voice broke a heavy silence.

"I didn't tell it all. The man as done that killin' was Hook Jones!"

CHAPTER XIX

GUN LOCO

Through progress of the railroads our occupa-
*   tion's gone;*
So we put our ideas into words, our words into
*   a song.*
First comes the cowboy; he is pointed for the
*   West;*
Of all the pioneers I claim the cowboys are the
*   best;*

— The Camp Fire Has Gone Out.

Trouble rode just under the sky-line of the bad-
lands ridges, skulking in the scrub pines and
brushing up in the coulees. Hook Jones, killer, like
a prowling wolf, his gun turned against every man
now, his mind twisted and warped with that
insane craving to kill, would never be taken alive.

Alone, shunning the men he had once ridden
with along many trails, nursing a fancied grudge
against friend and foe alike, he was like a
prowling wild beast. Hating sheep and sheep-
men with a terrible bitterness, hating them because he blamed them for an ill-luck that had befallen him, he had struck in the dead of night.
Struck with an insane ferocity that was like the
lash of a whip.

232

Firing a sheep wagon, he had shot the bewildered herder who had come stumbling, blinded by smoke, flame scorched, half-clothed and unarmed. He had sent shot after shot into the band of sheep that broke from the hillside bedground. With that same wanton killing lust of the wolf, he had slaughtered the frightened sheep, scattering them into the hills to be pulled down by the four-footed wolves.

The camp tender, a downy-lipped boy from the highlands of Scotland, riding to investigate the fire and the shooting that had awakened him from his camp a mile away, had been shot through the arm by the snarling, cursing, red-eyed Hook Jones.

Hook Jones, his carbine poking the wounded boy in the ribs, had gritted his deadly challenge to the sheep outfit.

"Git on yore cayuse an' git fer home. Tell the lousy sheep owner that hires yuh that Hook Jones is wipin' 'im out. I fought yore kind in Wyoming and I'll fight yuh here. Git word to yore sheep folks that I'm here a-waitin'. Git word to that snivelin' son uh mine that I'll kill him when he comes, the same as I'd kill a stinkin' sheep. Git word tuh Big Meat Drummond that I left him fer dead once an' I'll make a real job of 'er this time. Tell the nesters tuh come along. Tell 'em all.

"Tell 'em I'm a cowboy and a killer. I'm a rattlesnake coiled tuh strike. I got whisky in the jug an' meat in my belly. I got ca'tridges enough tuh

233

go around. Git on that sorry lookin' pack horse yuh ride an' git to yore home ranch. Tell 'em all that ol' Hook Jones has opened up this war, an' he'll never be took alive. Git, yuh sheep-stinkin' whelp. Outa my sight!"

The wounded boy had carried the grisly challenge and a gruesome tale to the Murdock ranch. By a man he met on the trail, he sent word to Chinook that the range war had broken out. That news, before dusk of another day, had put a hundred and more men in the saddle. Nesters, sheep-men, cowboys. And in the pale light of a half moon, Hook Jones, mounted on a big white horse, rode his wolf's trail, ready to kill.

At a homestead on Big Warm, Guy Jones got stiffly into the saddle. He rode alone into the night, a carbine across his saddle, his white face stamped with a tragic, terrible look. He had been gone several hours when Buck Rawlins, riding a hard pressed horse, pulled up. Guy's wife met Buck at the lighted doorway.

"He's gone," she told Buck in a lifeless voice. "Guy has gone to kill his father. May God have mercy on him."

Buck, with the picture of that white-faced nester bride in his mind, rode on. He knew that somewhere under that same moon, the two Murdocks, father and son, were riding with carbines in their scabbards. He likewise knew that Big Meat Drummond and a picked crew of nesters and hired gunmen rode for Marley. And that, within a few hours' ride of the sheep camps, the Nighthawk and his men waited.

But Buck did not know that a girl on a big roan horse was at the camp of the Nighthawk now. Colleen Driscoll, at the horse camp where she had been working with her men, had caught news of the sheep killing. The news had been given her by a man whom she had never seen before. Under her level-eyed questioning the man admitted that he was one of the Nighthawk's riders.

"Take me to where the Nighthawk is camped," she told him. "This thing has to be stopped. Hook Jones has to be trapped and taken care of, or killed if need be. I'm going with you."

There was no persuading her otherwise. She rode with him across the hills at a hard pace, tight-lipped, courageous. Born and raised to this range life, trained to think and act quickly, schooled to steadiness of nerves, she was as capable as any man in an emergency and it was with a silent admiration for her grit that the outlaw guided her to the outlaw camp.

The Nighthawk greeted her without surprise. He listened to what she had to tell of Hook Jones. Then he gave a few quiet orders to his men to saddle their horses.

"The man said," Colleen told him, "that Hook Jones was riding Angus Murdock's big white horse."

The Nighthawk smiled thinly. "That don't

mean that it was Hook that killed Joe Phelps and shot Buck in the shoulder. Hook musta found that white horse where the man that rode him before had put him in a little pasture in the breaks. I had a man posted down there watchin' that horse till the owner showed up. Nor it ain't the same horse that Angus Murdock rides. A dead ringer for Murdock's horse, but it wears a blotched brand on the left thigh. I examined that blotched brand careful, I got it traced where that horse come from down near the Dakota border. When the owner of that horse showed up, my man had orders to take him alive."

"That means," said Colleen, "that Angus Murdock had nothing to do with the killing of Joe Phelps and setting fire to our range. That proves it?"

"Plumb, ma'am. Murdock, for all he runs sheep, ain't a sneaker bushwhacker. And the day that Guy Jones got to pokin' around near where that horse was kept, and got shot in the laig, I patched up Guy's laig and told him to git word to Buck Rawlins that the Murdocks was innocent. The feller that plugged Guy was the man that killed pore Joe Phelps. I almost got him that day Guy was shot but he was too slick fer me. But it wasn't Hook Jones.

"There's a saddle hid where that white horse was kept. That saddle had mighty long stirrups. With the saddle was hid a black coat and a black hat the same as Murdock wears. The hat come from a store in Chinook where Murdock never trades. It's a store that has the nester trade. A store owned by Creighton Marley.

"Now, ma'am, you just stay here. I'll take the boys and scatter 'em out. One of us will locate Hook and pull his fangs. Hook, the pore devil, is plumb loco. I've talked to him twice. He snarled at me like a dog and run me outa his camp. He's plumb loco and I reckon whoever takes him will have tuh kill 'im."

"The man has always given me the creeps. His eyes were as cold and yellowish as the eyes of a wolf."

The Nighthawk nodded. "Hook has always been a killer. I never run across any man that could hate like Hook hates. The only human on earth he cared for was that pore wife of his that lost her mind back in Wyoming when her family was wiped out and she fought like a man with a rifle. No job fer a woman.

"There's one woman in ten thousand, I reckon, that has any call to pull a gun trigger. She might have the nerve to kill a man and never weaken. It's afterward that she loses her nerve. She can't ever forget that she's taken the life of a human being. And it bothers her sleep and makes her old and miserable, and sometimes drives 'em loco like it did Hook's missus. She's better off in her grave, because everything in life that a woman cares about is bloodstained by that one pull of a gun trigger. Ma'am, do you pack a gun?"

"Of course I do. I have a .22 high power car-

237

bine and a .38 pistol."

The Nighthawk nodded, a soft smile on his handsome face.

"Would yuh mind givin' me them guns?"

Colleen knew his object in telling her about Hook's wife. He was forestalling another such tragedy in the life of a woman. She knew that he was right, too. With a quick smile she handed him the pearl-handled .38 she always carried, then slipped the carbine from its saddle boot and passed it over.

"Now, ma'am," the Nighthawk said, "I'll send one uh my men along with yuh. You kin do a heap uh good, mebbyso, before many hours, but that good can't be done here in the bad-lands where bullets are kickin' up dust. Hit the trail for either the 7UP or the Rolling M ranch. Git some bandages ready and some hot water on the stove. If this thing comes to a head, somebody is goin' to need patchin' up. You kin do a lot of good by goin' home."

"I'll go," she told him. "But before I pull out for home, I'm going to the sheep camps. I want to say something to Bill Murdock."

For a long moment the Nighthawk looked at her, his eyes searching hers. Then he nodded briefly. "The two Murdocks and about ten riders went into camp about five miles from here. I'll go with you and see that yo're safe."

Colleen nodded. She had seen that swift glint of suspicion in the outlaw's eyes. Even if she was the daughter of Bob Driscoll and an enemy of the sheep-men, he was not trusting her to go alone to the sheep camp. Without a word they rode, side by side, up the trail. Behind them rode the Nighthawk's men, a grim cavalcade, silent, heavily armed, ready to grin at death.

At the head of the breaks, the Nighthawk scattered them. To each man he gave brief, uncompromising instructions.

"Git Hook. Take him alive if yuh kin. But if he begins throwin' lead, kill 'im."

"You think Hook will be taken alive?" asked Colleen.

"No, ma'am. Not a chance on earth to take him alive."

"Didn't you and Hook used to ride together?" she asked. "Weren't you good friends?"

The outlaw leader gave her a brief look. "I am still Hook's friend," he said quietly. "I hope it is someone besides me that has to kill him. But a quick bullet always beat a hangin'."

"Kin you sing, ma'am?" asked the Nighthawk, pulling up.

"Not according to the music teachers, but the cattle I've sung to at night never seemed to mind. Why?"

"Better commence singin' because we're gittin' mighty near the sheep camp. And while there's a moon, still they might not take much stock in this white rag I'm hangin' on my gun barrel. Nobody I ever heard of, not even sheep folks, ever killed a lady while she was singin'. Tune up."

"I can't think of a song to save my neck . . .

239

Yes. Yes I can, and if there's any merit in my singing this song may help."

In a soft, clear voice that carried sweetly across the moonlit hills, Colleen Driscoll sang Annie Laurie.

The Nighthawk, riding alongside her, his white flag held high, listened to the song of the range-bred girl. A tightness came into his throat. He had never heard a voice like that singing under the stars. He had never felt that pinching of his heart until to-night.

The click of steel-shod hoofs. The faint jingling of their spurs. The star-filled night and the smell of the pines and sage. And a girl's voice, clear-noted as the liquid song of a bird, singing that song that has never grown less sweet in the hearts of men who wander. Annie Laurie.

Now, hulking huge against that moonlit sky, the figure of Angus Murdock, a rifle gripped in his hands. In silence the sheep-man let them come on. And now the song was done and the hush that followed throbbed with the sweetness of its memory. " 'Twas a bonny song, lass," he greeted them. "Wi' memories o' a far fairer land than a' this i' the words. But 'tis no time for the song o' Annie Laurie, nor is it the place. Ye'll name your errand?"

"I've come to plead with you, Mr. Murdock, not to carry this terrible business any further. Two wrongs can never make a right."

"Perhaps not." And the old sheep-man's voice burred harshly. "But dinna think for any minute that Angus Murdock sits at home and lets his men be murdered and his property destroyed. 'Tis too late for such talk. We're here to fight, aye, and fight we will. Take your song and your flag o' truce elsewhere, for the Murdocks will ha' none o' it. Get ye gone."

"Can I talk to Bill Murdock?" she asked.

"Ye canna'. Wull is nowhere aboot here. And if he was here, 'twould gain' ye naught. The lad's a Murdock. No song can soften him when he recalls the blood as has been spilled here. Get ye gone, lass, and take yon white flag and the mon that haulds it from my sight."

"Just a minute, Murdock," spoke the Nighthawk, "then we'll go. One man done all the damage to yore sheep and yore men. Give us till tomorrow at sundown to git this man. There's no sense in throwin' this country into a range war. The man that did the harm will pay for it. He'll be dead by to-morrow night."

"Who are ye, mon, to make such a promise?"

"I used to be Wade Hardin. Now I'm called the Nighthawk."

"An' ye'd ha' honest men take the word o' a thief and a killer?"

"I never robbed anything but the railroads, Murdock, and what I take from them ain't half enough to pay for what they've done to me and mine. And I never killed any man that wasn't tryin' to kill me."

"Hook Jones is one o' ye!" growled Murdock.

"No. Yo're wrong. It has been a long time

since Hook rode with me. I've never hurt you or yore sheep. Two winters ago, when a herder uh yours was caught in a blizzard with his sheep and we found him half dead, we nursed him and we herded yore sheep. The snow was crusted and they had to be fed. For ten days those woolies lived on 7UP hay. Another time, during a dry summer, Dave Rawlins let your sheep water at his reservoir, and never charged you a cent. You've done the same kind of favors for him because, even if you didn't lose no love for each other, you was both white men. Murdock, if you take up this thing and start war against the 7UP, yo're all wrong."

"Prove what ye claim, mon. Prove it."

"Give me till sundown to-morrow and I'll prove it."

"Till sundown to-morrow, then. Get ye gone. And whate'er else ye do, take care o' the lass. For a' that she does na' care for sheep, she has a bonnie voice. Good nicht, lassie. God take care o' ye."

So they left Angus Murdock, standing bulked against the moonlit sky, his rifle in his hands, a huge giant of a man, stern and brave and immovable. When they had gone some distance one of the Nighthawk's men met them.

"I'll have to leave yuh here, ma'am. There's a heap to do. This gent will ride home with yuh."

Colleen held out her hand. "You're doing a lot for all of us," she told him gravely. "I wish there was something we could all do to pay back all we owe you."

"Once a man makes his sign along the outlaw trail there is nothin' that anybody kin ever do except bury him where the coyotes can't dig up his bones. It has bin a honor to meet up with the daughter of Bob Driscoll. He give me my first job and he was like a daddy to me when I was a button of a kid. That was before you was born. If ever I kin do Bob or you a good turn, it's only payin' back, just a little bit, all that he has done for me. So-long."

Before Colleen could say anything more, the Nighthawk had turned his horse and was gone in the shadows of the scrub pines and buck brush.

Colleen and the quiet-mannered man who was her escort, rode on toward home. With her she carried the picture of the outlaw's handsome, tragic face, and the hard eyes that she had seen soften. She wondered what could be that bitter secret that had turned him onto the outlaw trail. What wrong, real or fancied, had changed the life of Wade Hardin? No man had ever shared his bitter secret. Perhaps no man would ever know, even after the Nighthawk's bones lay buried in some lonely grave.

While along his trail that led him into the heart of the bad-lands, the Nighthawk kept remembering the song he had heard to-night. The song that had almost melted the bitter, aching lump in his heart. But, strangely enough, the song blended with the vision of another girl. The girl whom he had left back in Chicago that day when his happiness had turned to terrible grief. The day that he had quit the society of honest men and had turned outlaw. The day that Wade Hardin, world's champion rodeo man, had become the Nighthawk.

He wondered what had brought Mazie West out here to Montana. Had she hoped to find the man who had so abruptly left her? Did she still care a little? No, he reckoned not. Anyhow, he'd never know. He'd never see her again. Once he had finished this job here, he would ride on, on southward, never to return. . . . That Annie Laurie song . . . Mazie West with her hair of spun gold and honest, wistful eyes. . . . It was time he was riding on to cross new sky-lines, drifting, dodging, fighting. His heart empty of hope, an outlaw until he filled an outlaw's grave.

The trail dropped deep into the shadows of the canyon. Down there he thought to find Hook Jones. And when he found Hook their guns would perhaps settle the problems of both lives. Hook, the wolf. Hook, who had always been a killer, never trusting, never trusted, even among the outlaws. Hook would commence shooting, without giving warning. Without even that warning that a rattlesnake gives, Hook would open up with his gun. And the two men who had slept under the same blankets would kill one another. Life shore dealt a man some queer hands to play. And it was a poor sort of man that couldn't play the cards that —

"Lift 'em high, Wade!"

The Nighthawk pulled up abruptly. That was

244

not Hook's voice. That was not Hook's way.

There was a small derringer fastened in the sleeve of the Nighthawk's coat. It was there for a purpose. A hole card that no man's gun had ever yet uncovered. With a slight flip of his wrist, that tiny, deadly little weapon could pump its two .44 slugs into a man's heart within a split second. Smiling grimly, the Nighthawk lifted his hands.

With a six-shooter cocked in his hand, the tall figure of Ike Niland stepped from a brush thatch.

CHAPTER XX

SHERIFF AND OUTLAW

*'Way up high in the mokiones, among the
  mountain tops,*
*A lion cleaned a yearlin's bones and licked his
  thankful chops;*
*When who upon the scene should ride, a-
  trippin' down the slope,*
*But High Chin Bob of sinful pride and
  maverick-hungry rope.*

— High Chin Bob.

"Long time no see yuh, Ike." The Nighthawk's
voice was drawling.

"And the same tuh you, Wade Hardin, with
many happy returns uh the day. Use yore left
hand to unbuckle yore gun belt. I'd shore hate
tuh shoot a man I'd once rode with."

"That goes double, Ike. Sorry I can't say I'm
glad tuh meet an old pardner, but you know how
it is. Well, I'm glad it's you that will pull down
the bounty on me."

"Nobody said a word about bounty, Wade.
I'm no scalp hunter. Now unbuckle the belt."

The Nighthawk grinned crookedly and shook
his head. "Ike, me and you need to have a medicine talk. I got a job to do to-night. It's a job that

holds no pleasure for me, but it's one uh those things that has got to be done. I'll need my gun to do it."

Ike Niland's eyes hardened. "I said I'd hate to kill a man I'd once rode with. But I will kill yuh if you don't do like I say. You've done enough jobs down here."

"Meanin'?"

"Meanin' this Murdock sheep business. Yuh'll hang fer killin' that herder."

"Yuh mean yo're layin' that on me, Ike?"

"I'm layin' nothin'. That's fer the jury tuh prove, not me. Unbuckle that belt!"

Slowly, with his left hand, the Nighthawk obeyed that command that had sounded like the crack of a pistol shot. Belt and gun slid to the ground with a dull thud.

"Now step down without lowerin' them hands. I'm takin' no chances. One bad move and I'll shoot."

"I know yuh will, yuh long-geared old sucker." The Nighthawk, grinning, swung gracefully to the ground. Ike stepped up behind him, searching him for extra guns. He gave a little clicking sound with his tongue when he took Colleen's pearl-handled gun from the outlaw's pocket.

"Where'd yuh git this, Wade?"

"From a young lady that kin shore sing Annie Laurie. She gave it to me as a sort of souvenir."

"Sounds almighty fishy. Now turn around so as I kin look inside yore shirt fer any — Look out!"

With a lightning-like move, the Nighthawk had dropped his arms around Ike's middle, had given a terrific twist and jerk, throwing the older man off his feet and on to the ground.

Hardly more than a minute later the Nighthawk was on his feet with the agility of a cat. He held Ike's gun and the pearl-handled pistol.

"Now, yuh darned ol' turkey gobbler," he told the bewildered and gasping sheriff, "we hold that pow-wow. Yo're gittin' too stove up and slow movin' to be trailin' these hills alone. Ike, you couldn't ever take me outa here. One uh my boys would be sure tuh pull a rescue. Now light up a smoke and we'll talk. For once, you and me are goin' to work in cahoots. I told yuh I had a job to do, and I have. I want to be alone and unhobbled when I do it. And if yo're r'arin' for night work, I'll set you on a job that'll keep yuh awake. Did I hurt yore ribs, Ike?"

"All of 'em feel busted. I mighta knowed better than to git that close to yuh. You always was handy thataway. You talk like yo're drunk or loco."

"I'm not either one. When I'm done augerin' and if you kin see sense to my proposition, I'll give you back yore artillery and we'll work a combine on these would-be warriors that I hope will save a lot of blood spillin'.

"First, I want you to git this much into yore skull. I had nothin' to do with that sheep business. Hook Jones has gone loco and he's yore huckleberry. He's started a one man war on the

248

sheep folks and he'll play his string out till he's cut down. Cuttin' ol' Hook down is the job I have in mind. Now, darn yore homely picture, will you listen or won't yuh?"

For several long seconds the two men looked hard into one another's eyes. Then Ike Niland nodded.

"I never knowed you tuh lie, Wade. I'm beginnin' tuh savvy. Hook always claimed you was the only man that ever came any where near bein' his friend. He's gone loco, now. Killin' mad. I bin afraid he'd do that. A strait-jacket and padded cell in the State Asylum would be a heap worse than bein' shot through the heart. I think I savvy, Wade Hardin."

The Nighthawk nodded. Then he tossed Ike's gun to him. The sheriff said nothing as he shoved the gun into its holster. The Nighthawk likewise put away his pearl-handled gun and now buckled on his belt again. Between these two men there was no need of sworn promise. They had known one another in too many hard places for that.

"Ike," said the Nighthawk, "did you ever hear tell of a gun slinger called Big Meat Drummond?"

"The feller Hook killed down in Wyoming?"

"That's the gent, but he wasn't killed. He's here in this country. He's the ramrod that Creighton Marley hired to handle his tough gents. It was either Big Meat Drummond or a Swede nester named Eric Swanson that killed

Joe Phelps. It was either one or the other of 'em that wore a black hat and coat and rode a white horse the night that the Rolling M range was set afire. Somehow, I think that Big Meat is the gent that passed hisself off as Angus Murdock, but I'm almost positive, on the other hand, that Big Meat wa'n't within fifty miles uh that fire.

"It's had me guessin' some. But I know this for shore. Creighton Marley hires 'em both. And Howard Snodgrass, Hank Mayberry's dude son-in-law, is in on the deal. They both own stock in an outfit called The Northwest Land and Finance Company. They're the outfit that sent out all kinds uh pamphlets and such, all over the East, telling how crops kin be raised here on the ridges and pinnacles. They're the dirty outfit that's fooled these pore farmer devils into comin' out here to dry farm the country.

"They loan the farmers a little money. Enough to tie up the homestead. The farmer puts a crop in and fences the place. The Company keep him from starvin' to death till he's proved up on the homestead. Then they cut him off at the pockets and call in the paper. The farmer can't pay and all he kin do is let his homestead go to this Northwest Land and Finance Company. The same Company that's freezin' out the cattleman. Later, when the cow-man has gone and the farmer has gone, the Company will get water on a lot uh the land, put it in grain and alfalfa, and farm it at a big profit. The whole thing is a big steal, Ike, and the law has tuh give 'em protection while they're a-doin' it."

"You say this Big Meat Drummond works fer Marley?"

"Didn't you know that Marley had a gang uh tough hombres ridin' the hills? They tortured Fancy Mary, tryin' to make her tell where I was. Said they was a posse. They taken Mazie West, a little homesteader girl, and Onion Oliver prisoner. Lord knows what woulda happened if I hadn't taken a hand in the game. I busted up the gang and aimed tuh make a good Injun outa Big Meat, but he got away.

"I was goin' to send Big Meat Drummond to yuh for a sort uh Christmas present. He's worth five thousand bucks on the hoof or laid on the block, down in Wyoming. His gun is for hire on any kind of a job. He's bad medicine. And while he high-tailed it fer parts unknown, he's most liable to be showin' his hand again. If him and Hook ever cross trails, they'll burn powder aplenty, if Big Meat happens tuh be drunk enough tuh stand his hand. Sober, the big son is yellow plumb through, but he's no man tuh monkey with when he's got his hide soaked with fightin' likker.

"And when Marley learns about the war bein' on between the Murdocks an' the Rawlins outfit, he's bound to send Big Meat and his toughs into the ruckus. They'll be drunk and some of 'em smokin' marijuana, and they'll be plenty tough. If you've got a posse down here, gather 'em up and head for the sheep camps at the head uh the breaks. Try to head off Buck Rawlins, if yuh can. Buck is a hot headed young colt and apt tuh git into trouble. Me and the Driscoll lady tried tuh talk peace to Angus Murdock and we got him thinkin'. I told him I'd take care uh Hook Jones. Then I sent Colleen Driscoll home."

"Yuh let her go alone, Wade?"

"With these renegades uh Marley's coyotin' all over the hills? I reckon not. Whitey Rance is with her. As long as Whitey kin lift a gun, she's as safe as she'd be in a church pew. I taken her guns because a woman has no business handlin' a gun. I was thinkin' of Hook's missus when I taken this pearl-handled gun and a carbine off her."

There was a long moment of silence. Then Ike Niland spoke.

"Wade Hardin, you got a heap uh good, solid hoss sense. Yo're purty much of a white man. Yo're still young enough tuh go to a new country and make a new start. Mexico or South America will be about the climate to fit yore clothes. Pull outa here and hunt a new range."

"Too late for that, Ike. The railroad outfits would hunt me down, and do me like they did my dad and brother. They'd put their hounds on my trail and some day I'd be shot down like a coyote, or trapped and shut up fer life, er hung."

"They got yore dad and brother?" This was the first time that any man had ever heard Wade Hardin speak of a father or brother.

"Out in California, yeah. They'd never done

any man harm. They had a ranch there. The railroad wanted a right of way through it. But they wouldn't pay anywhere near the price. There was a lawsuit on about it and the railroad had plenty money and top-hand lawyers to win the case. But Dad wa'n't the kind to lay down and take a lickin'. He fought 'em through the courts.

"He was still fightin' 'em in court when, one night, two men stopped over night at his place. Dad asked 'em no questions and took no money for their lodgin'. But the dirty whelps left money, anyhow. Because the next day, when two railroad dicks drove up, they accused Dad and my brother of bein' mixed up in a train hold-up that had happened some weeks before. They searched the house and the barn. And up in the hay-loft these dicks uncovered a gunny-sack with three — four thousand dollars in it. The serial numbers on them bank-notes corresponded to some uh the stolen money.

"They arrested Dad and my brother and starts for town. The team boogered and run away, spillin' the dicks, Dad and my brother out. And when the dust had cleared away, the dicks was handcuffed together and their guns belonged to the two men they'd tried to railroad to the pen. . . . A week later the railroad posse surrounds Dad's camp where him and my brother was hidin'. And the dirty hide hunters shot 'em down then and there. First I knowed of it was a big account in a Chicago newspaper, showin' their pictures and braggin' up the possemen that murdered 'em. And from that day on, I've done my best to even up the debt. There's the yarn, Ike. Yo're the first man that ever heard me tell it."

The Nighthawk was on his feet now, legs spread wide, thumbs hooked in his sagging cartridge belt, his face hard and stern-looking. And somehow Ike Niland could find no words to say to this outlaw.

Wade Hardin was wrong, his attitude toward the railroads was warped and twisted into an ugly shape. Probably some unscrupulous attorney had engineered the deal against the two men who had fought the railroad company in California. But Wade Hardin's opinion would never alter. No man's argument would ever sway him from the tragic, hopeless stand he had taken. There was nothing for Ike Niland to say.

"I'd quit now if I could, Ike. I've dealt 'em misery a-plenty. I'd be willin' to call it a day, but it can't be done. They'll trail me down."

"It's time we was movin', Wade. But before we separate, I'll give you somethin' to think about. There ain't any picture of you, anywhere, except some snapshots taken when you was ridin' broncs and ropin', and even if they was clear, they'd never do a dick any good because you've changed a lot. Yore hair is gittin' white and yo're heavier. With a mustache and city clothes, nobody would ever know yuh. There's no fingerprint records. No dick in the country ever saw yuh close. If you was to board a train in Dakota, say, with a ticket fer New York, or was to go as fer as Chicago on a cattle train, there'd be no man to lay a hand on yuh." Ike Niland looked steadily into the outlaw's eyes.

"Especially, Wade, if it got proved that the Nighthawk was killed down here in the badlands. Yo're doin' this cow country a big favor right now. Them as are yore friends ain't forgettin'. Think that over while yo're on yore way to find Hook Jones. So-long."

Ike led his horse from the brush and mounted. Solemnly the two men, sheriff and outlaw, shook hands. The bitterness was gone from the Nighthawk's face and his eyes were bright with a strange light.

"So-long, Ike. I'll think 'er over. And even if the sign don't come right for me tuh quit the country, I'll be rememberin'. You've give me better than I deserve, ol' pardner."

"Good luck, Wade. Good luck."

"And plenty of the same to you, Ike. So-long."

When Ike Niland had gone on up the trail, the Nighthawk mounted and rode on. His gun was in his hand now, and his eyes were searching the blotches of shadow on the trail ahead.

He was almost certain that he would find Hook Jones at the hidden pasture a few miles beyond. Somewhere an old owl boomed weirdly. Beyond, death skulked in the shadow of the scrub pines.

CHAPTER XXI

MURDER IRONS

I wonder if on that last day some cowboy
Unbranded and unclaimed should stand,
Would he be mavericked by those riders of
   Judgment
Who are posted and know all the brands?
           — The Cowboy's Dream.

Buck Rawlins had followed the tracks made by
Guy Jones's horse until the sign was lost with the
coming of darkness. Now he must take a blind
chance and hope against hope that he was
thinking as Guy was thinking, that Hook would
be found just in south of the sheep camps, there in
the rough breaks between Antelope Springs and
the Missouri River. . . .

A broken, ragged, short-chopped bunch of
scrub pine hills, cut coulees, and small canyons.
A country that it took the round-up several days
of hard riding to work. Here, in these hills, were
a hundred and one places where a man could
hide out and another man could pass within a
stone's throw and never sight him.

In at the head of the rough hills were the sheep
camps. The camps that Hook Jones would be
waiting to attack. Hook would be hidden some-

256

where in those rough hills south of the sheep camps. There he would hide by daylight and from there he would ride forth at night, a sinister rider of crazy retribution, avenging fancied wrongs, killing, burning, slaughtering. "Guy knows where Hook is hiding," Buck kept telling himself. "He'll head for Hook's camp. And Hook will fill him full of hot lead."

What chance had Guy against his father? Guy, whose hand was better fitted to a Bible than a gun.

It would be murder when Hook Jones opened fire. For Guy would ride without taking care to keep in the shadows. He would be skylighted, a target too easy for Hook to ever miss. Buck had one chance in a hundred, perhaps one chance in a thousand of heading off the boy on his way to death.

Buck saw the light of a sheep wagon. The wagon would be empty, of course. Just a lantern burning inside the canvas top. And hidden in the brush around it would be Murdock's men, ready to open fire on the first rider that showed up.

Yet, so Buck Rawlins figured, his only chance of again locating Guy Jones was to find someone who had sighted the boy before dark. It was a desperate chance, riding up on that lighted wagon. A hundred to one chance that some half-scared, quick triggered fool would open up on him with a Winchester.

Better to go boldly. Whistling or singing, so that they'd know he was coming on a neutral

257

errand. It seemed silly, whistling on an errand of this sort, or singing. But it might save his hide from being punctured. But, on the other hand, it might attract a bullet. Those toughs of Marley's might be skulking near the camp. They would not hesitate to shoot, doing their questioning later.

Buck touched the shoulder that was still lame from a bullet that had come out of the night. Better not whistle. When he was within hailing distance of the lighted wagon, he'd call out.

Buck pulled his horse down to a fox trot and kept his hand on his gun. Suddenly he reined up. His alert ears had caught a sound, there ahead. It was the sound of a man moaning as if in mortal pain.

Buck slipped from his saddle. Cautiously, lest it be some clever trap, he crept forward. Now he could make out a man, lying in a cramped position, at the edge of a patch of sage-brush. Keeping the man covered, Buck crawled on all fours up to where the man lay, hands and feet tied behind his back and drawn together so as to bend the man's spine backward in a painful arc. A bandanna handkerchief was tied tightly across his open mouth, so tight as to cut the flesh. Buck's jack-knife freed the man.

"Who are you?" whispered Buck. "Talk low."

For a moment the man, whose face was covered with a heavy beard that almost reached his eyes, did not speak. He moaned through his bleeding lips, his eyes seared with pain. Now

Buck saw that the fellow was bleeding from several ugly looking wounds. His shirt was in shreds and his blond beard matted with blood.

"Work for Murdock, tending camp. Bill Murdock put me here on guard. I guess I went to sleep for a minute. When I woke up that man was on top of me, tearing me to pieces with a sharp hook he had in his hand. Then he knocked me out. I wake up once more tied like this. My back feels broke. I'm sick."

"Come at you with a hook, did he?" Buck's eyes narrowed. That meant Hook Jones was near here. The man could not have lain there long. Even now the murderous Hook Jones might be crouched in the brush, ready to leap on Buck's back. Buck turned his head quickly, then grinned crookedly at his fears. "Can you ride?"

"I think so."

"Then get up on my horse. I'll follow on foot. We can bandage you up at the wagon." Buck lifted the man into the saddle.

"Have you any signal that will pass us to the wagon without getting shot at?"

"Whistle three times. Like this." The wounded man whistled. From the direction of the wagon came an answering signal. They went on.

Under the menacing cover of several rifles held by men who crouched in the brush, they gained the wagon.

"Whoever's in charge here," said Buck impatiently, "step out and lend me a hand with this man." And as Buck lifted the injured man down, he felt the torn body go limp in his arms. Buck laid the man out on the ground and looked up at a man who had come forward. The man had a six-shooter in his hand, pointed at Buck. Buck's eyes narrowed as he recognized the big tough he had fought at Mazie West's homestead. He had not yet learned the big fellow's identity.

There was an ugly, drunken leer on Big Meat Drummond's coarse mouth.

"You got a gall, Rawlins. Knifin' one of our men and fetchin' him in. Yuh shore got a gall."

"So that's your attitude, is it? Where's Bill Murdock or whoever is rodding this spread?"

"I'm the big bull in this herd, Rawlins. What yuh got to say?"

"You? Murdock hired you?"

"Yeah. And he never made no mistake when he did it, neither. I'll show you gents how we treated yore kind down in Wyoming. I'll dish yuh up a mess uh lead that'll make yuh sick."

"Never mind that," said Buck, rising from where he knelt beside the wounded man. "I'll listen to your bragging when I have a lot of spare time on my hands. Take care of this man before he dies."

"Now ain't you the tender-hearted thing," sneered Big Meat. "You cut him all up, then tell me to take care of him. You shore got a gall. Yeah." Big Meat thumbed back the hammer of his single-action .45. He leaned forward from the hips, on widespread legs, his eyes glittering redly in the light that came from the wagon. With a sudden shock, Buck realized that the man was going to murder him.

"Rawlins," he gritted, his lips snarling apart from clenched teeth, "go after yore gun. I'm goin' to kill yuh!"

Buck's gun was in its holster. Before he could ever get it free, Big Meat's finger would press the trigger. At five foot range the heavy .45 slug would tear through Buck's heart. This was to be murder.

Every muscle, every nerve in Buck's body was taut. His narrowed eyes held the slitted, blood-shot glare of the big killer. Then came the crash of a gun.

Buck leaped, his hand dragging out his gun. He wondered, in a split-second's thought, where the bullet had struck him. He felt no pain. What was the matter with the big brute?

Big Meat had spun half-way around, a horrible look of terror on his face. He was sagging at the knees a little. His eyes, wide with fright, stared at the right hand that had held his gun. The hand, limp, empty of weapon, was covered with gushing blood. It hung from a wrist that was a bloody, mangled thing of broken bone and bleeding flesh.

Through the echoes of that gun roar there sounded a laugh, crazy, triumphant. Even as Big Meat Drummond dropped to his knees, moaning and whimpering, holding his maimed wrist. On his knees, swaying to and fro, his staring eyes fixed a horrified gaze on Buck's face.

"Rawlins, don't! Don't kill me! Yuh got me, now! Yuh shot me enough! Don't kill me!"

Big Meat, the bully, was now a groveling, begging wretch. He thought that it was Buck whose bullet had smashed his wrist. Buck stood there dazed, his gun in his hand.

And now Buck Rawlins saw that which seemed to him like some unreal apparition. Just at the rim of light thrown off by the lantern in the canvas-topped sheep wagon, there rode a black coated, black hatted figure on a big white horse. Then, as mysteriously as it had shown, it was gone in the night.

Buck pulled his shattered nerves together. There was the bleeding camp tender at his feet. Just beyond, the kneeling, whining killer with the smashed wrist. Beyond him, several men who stood like dumb statues, their hands raised. It was like some strange, nightmarish dream.

"Pull your hands down out of the sky," he said to the men who seemed terrified, "and take care of this camp tender first. Then look after the big tough boy that was so hard. Come on, men, don't stand there like posts. Lend a hand."

They came now, frightened and timid of manner. They were the sheep-herders and farmers hired by the Murdocks to defend the camps. Buck grinned at them amiably. His own shock of being jerked from the pit of death now took a reaction. He wanted to laugh, or crack a joke or something. But he gathered the frayed ends of his nerves and grinned.

"I'm not shooting anybody, boys. Just take care of these two men."

Now a man rode up out of the night. Buck's gun was back in his hand. Then, with a grin, he shoved it back in its scabbard.

"Howdy, sheep-herder," he hailed Bill Murdock. But there was no answering grin on Bill Murdock's face.

"What's going on here, anyhow?"

"He tried tuh kill me," moaned Big Meat. "He's already killed that camp tender."

"Shut up," snapped Buck. "I shot nobody, Bill. For gosh sake, get off and help me dress this poor devil's hurts. Never mind the hard looks."

Bill Murdock stepped down off his horse. He still had his gun in his hand, but Buck paid the weapon no attention.

"Take his feet, Bill. We'll put him in the wagon."

"And be a target for your sharp-shooters?" rasped Bill Murdock.

"Bill, if you hang around the sheep industry much longer your brains will be all wool. Take his feet. If you're afraid of being a target, you can go back to the bushes, once we get this man on a bed."

Together they carried the wounded man into the lighted wagon. Buck's knife ripped away what was left of the ragged shirt.

"Get a basin of water, Bill, and anything that'll do for an antiseptic. I bet there ain't a clean cloth around."

"It happens that there is. Clean dish-towels washed today. This ain't a dirty cow camp where —"

"We'll do without the oration, sheep-herder. Tell your big plug ugly outside that if he'll come in in a few minutes we'll amputate that hand for him. You shore picked a game guy when you hired that skunk."

"Marley loaned him to me, if you want to know. Here's the water."

"All right, Shep. Now rip one of the spotless dish-towels into bandages and we'll have this bearded lad all done up nice. And listen, Willyum, I was all wrong about you and your dad. What I said, I'm swallowin' now. I just sighted the white horse and the man that rides it. Which reminds me. Throw your guards out further in the brush. It's a great night for murders. And say, where is Guy Jones?"

"Guy? He's home, I suppose. He should be, anyhow."

"But he ain't. He's out gunning for his amiable father. Yeah. Bill, if we don't act fast, there'll be a lot of damage done to-night. Where's the rest of this Marley layout?"

"You'll have to ask Marley that question. He brought the big gent out in his car, then left on one of my horses for somewhere. He said your men and the Nighthawk's outlaws were going to wipe us out to-night."

"You are sheep-brained, Bill. Is Marley alone?"

"No," admitted Bill Murdock reluctantly. "Eric Swanson is with him. Eric is —"

Buck looked up from his surgeon's task with a one-sided grin. "Sheep-herder." And went back to his bandaging.

"I think you said a mouthful, cow hand. I'll post the guards."

"There," Buck told the unconscious camp tender in an undertone, "is one grand gent. The cleanest scrapper I ever knew. Lay quiet, old timer. There, that does it."

Hands and forearms blood-smeared, Buck stepped to the door of the sheep wagon.

"Come in, tough guy, and we'll cut off that mitt. Murdock's blacksmith will make you a new one out of a sheep hook. Step into the operating-room, please."

"Gawd, yuh ain't gonna cut a man's hand off, are yuh?" whimpered Big Meat. "Yuh can't do that, Rawlins. Just tie 'er up tight so's I won't bleed tuh death."

"I was just foolin', big 'un. Come in." He hauled the wobbly-kneed killer into the wagon. Bill Murdock came in. They put Big Meat on the other bunk and examined the maimed wrist. The big man howled with pain. Bill and Buck traded glances. The bullet had torn away the wrist joint so that the hand hung by a piece of ragged flesh. No chance of saving the man's hand. Buck's joshing had turned into grisly reality.

Big Meat Drummond lay back on the bunk,

moaning and sobbing, begging them to do something to ease his pain.

"Whisky!" he begged them. "Gimme whisky. There's a jug under the wagon."

Bill brought it. There was a grim look in the young sheep-man's eyes when he looked from the wounded man to Buck. "Marley brought it." He handed the jug to Buck who filled a tin cup brimming full. Big Meat sat up, his one good hand gripping the cup. He drained it in three big gulps. Buck again filled the cup. And a third time it was filled and emptied. Big Meat's eyes looked glassy now. But it would be perhaps an hour before he passed out.

Again Buck and Bill Murdock exchanged glances. Buck's left eyebrow lifted inquiringly. Bill nodded. Buck's fist crashed against the point of Big Meat's jaw and the man went limp.

"Sheep camp anesthetics, Bill. He'll be out a long time. That water boiling?"

"She boils," said Bill.

Buck went outside. From his saddle pockets he took a compact surgical kit of black leather.

"While I didn't stay long enough in medical school to dirty many shirts," he said to Bill, "still I got the rudiments of the racket. We lack about nine-tenths of the sanitary stuff they preach about, but if this baby is half as tough as he looked when he was about to shoot me in the belly, he'll get over this mere scratch. What's a hand or a little gangrene to a hard-boiled he gun-toter? Hands clean, Bill? Shove 'em in water hot as they'll stand. Here's some whisky to wash 'em in. Shame to waste good likker."

Buck hovered over an open stew-pan filled with boiling water. Into it he dipped shining steel instruments. He worked swiftly, deftly.

"I know doctors, Bill, that'd die of horror if they saw this job. All right, now. That tourniquet is holding pretty. Tie the arteries with thread like this, see. First aid. If he gets to a doctor by to-morrow he'll be all right. Now we apply the — Steady, sheep-herder."

For Bill was swaying a little, faint at the sight of this crude surgery. Buck nodded toward the jug and finished bandaging the wrist.

Bill took a stiff drink and handed one to Buck. Buck shook his head and grinned as he washed his arms and hands in the basin of hot water.

"I got religion, sheep-herder."

A droning, whining, snarling crash. A bullet smashed the basin under Buck's hands.

"Time we put the light out," grinned the young cow-man thinly, and blew out the lantern flame.

CHAPTER XXII

FREE-LANCE LAW-MEN

*Then swing your rope slowly and rattle your
  spurs lowly,
Give a wild whoop as you bear me along;
And in the grave throw me, and roll the sod
  o'er me,
For I'm a wild cowboy, and I know I've done
  wrong.*

     — The Cowboy's Lament.

Tuley Bill Baker looked from the face of Cutbank
Carter to the face of Onion Oliver. Sadness and
annoyance mingled in the eyes of Tuley Bill as he
untied the slicker that was neatly rolled behind his
saddle cantle.

"Some day," he prophesied dourly, "there'll
be a few drops uh strychnine in the bottle. Me,
I'd be shore ashamed if I was either of yuh. I've
knowed yuh both since yuh worked up the trail
with one Mexican spur between yuh and fifteen
dollars a month was good wages. Days when yuh
thought that a man that owned a saddle and a
private hoss was shore a king who had a tail-holt
on the world.

"I've knowed yuh both since the days when I
owned the only overcoat amongst us and we

268

taken turns a-wearin' it when we went on guard of a night. I've knowed yuh both from the Llano Estacado to the rock pile ranch in Canada and never once, never once, durin' all them winters and summers, hard winters and dry summers, have I ever knowed either one of yuh tuh pack so much as a half uh pint. All yuh ever contribute is a corkscrew.

"No sooner do I give in to yore shore pitiful an' tearful pleadin', an' git off tuh untie my slicker, than each of yuh pulls that aforesaid corkscrew quicker than ever Bat Masterson ever drawed a gun. Yuh pore ol' hide-bound things, yuh remind me, fer all the world, of two turkey buzzards a-settin' on their hocks waitin' fer a hunk uh meat."

"What time did me an' Onion have tuh git a bottle?" complained Cutbank. "We was shore occupied in the business uh lockin' up that Snodgrass feller and them two dudes that said they was the Northwest Land an' Finance Company. Onion an' me was doin' chores thereabouts while you leans heavy on the bar at the Bucket uh Blood a-tellin' 'er scary to all as has the fortitude tuh listen. Git that bottle open, yuh ol' hussy."

Tuley Bill tilted a knowing eye toward the eastern sky-line. He pulled the cork out of the bottle that was clamped between his overalled knees. "Daylight in half an hour. We gotta rattle our hocks if we're gonna take a hand in this here game. It's like ol' man Dave Rawlins tells us, we're messengers a-bearin' strong tidin's. We got news tuh spill an' some few an' sundry assorted shapes an' sizes uh job-lot renegades to rope an' hog-tie. Here's yore medicine, yuh two ol' blue nose cranes."

"Here's ring-bones on yore ankles, Tuley Bill," grinned Onion.

Cutbank now captured the bottle. "And a setfast on yore back, Tuley Bill," he added.

"Here's warts on yore ears, bone-heads." And the owner of the bottle pounded the cork in with a callused palm.

The first faint streak of dawn, reddish against the night's gray-blackness, foretold the sunrise. A coyote lifted its howl to the vamshing night, and the echoes caught up the song until it sounded like a dozen of the yapping animals. Now the song was ended, the last echo stilled, and that hush of coming dawn fell like a prayer across the bad-lands.

And there in that changing light, the three old cow-punchers sat their horses. A silence, weighted with a hungry, lonely sadness, held them.

They were old men, past their prime. For them there could not be so many more dawns. They had seen their share together, mounted on good horses, bunched up on some high pinnacle on the round-up's morning circle. Waiting, with other cowboys, for dawn to break and the wagon-boss to scatter them out in twos and threes to drive the cattle to the round-up ground. These three had seen a thousand dawns together. They had sat together smoking on every pinnacle between Milk River and the Missouri. They had shared together the sun and rain and the chill of the first snow that makes the cowboy wonder what has become of his summer wages. Now they sat again in their saddles, riding top horses, waiting for another dawn. They had not changed, those three old cow hands. Leathery, weather-beaten, old — but their hearts were as unchanged as the distant peaks of the Little Rockies. Now they saw, in this dawn, the last frontier of the cow country. Their country, choked to death by barb wire, ripped apart by plowshares. . . . Dying.

As that man who had once ridden range with them, that painter of pictures whose work was to give to posterity the cowboy, said, the farmers were turning Montana with the grass side under. Onion, Tuley Bill, Cutbank, others of the old-time breed of cowboy, were vanishing as vanished the buffalo. Charlie Russell's paintings would record their mark. His pictures tell those who came later how they lived. He had smoked with them and drunk with them and worked with them in sun and rain and snow. Now he was watching them die, as the buffalo had died, their race run, their game finished. There is a saying that nobody knows what becomes of the old cowboy. When they are too old to make a hand, they ride away to die.

Something of that sight of a last sky-line now

held the three old cow hands silent. They knew that it was time to ride on. Montana was no longer their country. They were no longer wanted here. Their ways were not the ways of the people who were coming in. Another fall round-up, riding circle, lazing on day herd, standing guard on black nights, gathering the last of the great herd to ship out of the country, then their work would be over, their job finished. It would be time to ride away.

Their pockets empty, their bones brittle and knotted with old fractures crudely spliced, their hair as white as the snow-drifts, they would ride on. But their spurs would still jingle, their hats would still slant at that reckless angle, and their hearts would be as young as the day when they forked their first bronc. They would ride away to die.

With a solemnity that was like some ritual, Tuley Bill uncorked his bottle. And in a silence, there in the hush of dawn that streaked the bad-lands, they drank. Each of them knew that they would never see another winter here. They would, in a few months, travel yonderly. When the last shipment was made, they would saddle their private horses and ride on.

The first snow would bury their last tracks.

Sunrise found the three near the sheep camps. Tuley Bill sniffed the air and made a wry face.

"Smell 'em, cow hands? Smell the blattin' woolies?"

"A man would think," said Onion, "that you

owned the only nose north of the Pecos. I bin smellin' 'em the last ten miles. Let one sheep cross the range and I kin smell the thing fer forty miles. She looks plumb peaceful hereabouts. Hope they ain't killed off all uh them skunks we come tuh find. Hello. Yonder comes a hossbacker. Who's it, Cutbank?"

"Looks tuh me like ol' Ike Niland. Yuh don't reckon he's after us fer anything, do yuh?"

"Hard tuh say, wart-hawg," grunted Tuley Bill. "Yuh done enough orneriness tuh have a oneasy conscience, I reckon. Me, I'd shore hate tuh pack around a load uh guilt like you got yorese'f weighted down with."

"I bet you stole that bottle yuh keep nursin'," growled Onion. "We better de-stroy the evidence. Ike's a-ridin' like he was goin' to camp fer dinner with a empty stummick."

A few minutes later Ike Niland met them. His face was lined with weariness and worry.

"Glad yuh got here," he said abruptly, and then went on. "Things is almighty tight over yonder. Where is Buck Rawlins?"

"We ain't met him, Ike."

"He left the sheep camps durin' the night. Bill Murdock won't say where Buck went. The rimrocks and brush patches is full uh men r'arin' tuh burn powder. Hook Jones is still loose. Hook was chargin' around all night on a big white geldin', shootin' an' ridin' away before anybody could line sights on 'im.

"Angus Murdock an' Marley an' that Eric

273

Swanson nester has a bunch uh gun fighters hid in the rocks and won't listen tuh reason. Ol' Angus won't listen tuh anybody, not even to his own son's talk. Says he's goin' to stay where he is until sundown, then he's gonna commence to begin or words to that effect. He cussed Bill Murdock out and he cussed me out and he's shore on the prod. Take a man like Angus Murdock, he's slow tuh git mad, but once he does git on the warpath, he is worse than Settin' Bull. And he's sober, to boot. It ain't ary wild whisky talk with Angus Murdock. He's solemn as a preacher an' even his cussin' is solemn. He used words I never heard till this mornin' and I takes Bill Murdock along as interpreter.

"Then Marley comes out with his polite fight talk. Tells me how this will be my last term in office if I don't stand behind the law an' order an' the protection uh property belongin' to citizens. He orates a-plenty about the rights and the legalities uh the sheep-men an' the farmer. He musta had 'er wrote down on paper, the way he went on. Eric Swanson an' this Deacon Nelson is likewise there with Angus Murdock an' Marley. This Deacon nester is a-tryin' to make peace, but he ain't a-gettin' very far. And when I horn in with a word er two, the whole pack of 'em light into me, tellin' me that I'm duty bound to protect 'em against the cow folks.

"Bill Murdock is the only one that seems tuh have any sense. Bill has some judgment, and he's nervy in a tight, even if he is a sheep man. He's playin' a game uh some kind, sort uh lone-handed, and he ain't tippin' his hole card for any man tuh see. He's got me puzzled. This is shore a mess, boys. I need old heads like you three to help me out. How's things in town?"

"Everything is purty and the goose hangs high," grinned Onion. "We got yore jail full and key throwed away. That hoosegow never had such distinguished boarders before."

"What have you three ol' bone-heads bin up to, anyhow? If you bin playin' any of yore old time monkey-shines with my jail, I'll show yuh some lessons yuh never knowed was in the book. What yuh bin up to?"

"Tuck in yore shirt-tail, Ike," purred Onion, displaying the gold badge that had been worn by the man who had tried to halt Buck Rawlins at the bank. "Me, I got a purtier badge than yourn."

Ike Niland remembering certain pranks played in the bygone days by this same trio of old time cow hands, scowled darkly.

"Where'd yuh git that badge, Onion?"

"I taken it off a feller that had no more use for it. A feller that had a bold an' reckless way till us boys gives him a fittin' an' proper initiation into our secret lodge. Ike, that son give up head like a magpie, once he gits goin'. And what he tells about an outfit called the Northwest Land and Finance Company is a-plenty. When we pump his well dry, we takes the proper steps tuh make a general round-up.

"While we are on circle we picks up Howard Snodgrass an' two dudes at Snodgrass's house. We puts Snodgrass an' his friends in yore jail with this talkin' feller. We h'ists a drink and takes the trail uh the others we want. Meanin' this Marley, a feller called Big Meat Drummond, Eric Swanson, and some other dimmer lights, as the sayin' goes."

"Who owned that badge, Onion? Gimme the truth, now."

"The man that owned it died somewhere between the Wyoming line and the Little Rockies, when he was trailin' Big Meat Drummond, the nature uh his ailment bein' lead poisonin', I reckon. Drummond turned in the badge and the feller's papers to Marley, near as I know, and Marley pins the badge on one uh his best men.

"This gent thinks he kin learn somethin' about what become of the money as was lifted from the train robbery at Lodge Crick when the Nighthawk collects his percentage from the railroads, and he hires out to Fancy Mary as barkeep. He's there when Mary gives Buck Rawlins some money tuh give Uncle Hank Mayberry. He follers Buck an' tries tuh pull a stick-up but he ain't lucky. He gits his horns knocked off and he now reclines in yore jail house. He'll tell it to yuh when yuh ask him. He's a squealin' rat. Now let's git Marley an' his pack uh skunks, Ike."

"I hope you three ol' waddies ain't made any bad mistakes. Yuh shore acted like yuh owned that jail. If Snodgrass an' them others is innocent, look at where it puts me. Where'd yuh git the keys to the jail, anyhow?"

"Tuley Bill manages fer the keys. Him an' a bartender slips a drop uh somethin' in a drink that the house is buyin' fer yore deputy. Yuh worryin' about this two-bit job uh yourn?"

"No. But as long as I'm sheriff, I ain't standin' fer a lot uh fool hoss-play. If you three has made a mistake, I'll lock yuh up fer so long that folks will forgit yore names."

"Old Man Afraid of His Hosses," said Tuley Bill testily. "He shore likes tuh rawhide us ol' fellers. Let's ride over an' see the Marley gent, Ike."

Ike nodded and the four men rode on.

It was about half an hour later that they were halted by a shot that kicked up dirt in the dusty trail ahead. They pulled up. The voice of Angus Murdock came from a rocky ledge above.

"Stand where ye be, men. Ye canna advance farther. Name your business."

"We want to talk to Marley," said Ike Niland.

"I've got neither the time nor the inclination," sounded the caustic voice of Creighton Marley from the rocky ledge, "to waste words with a weak-spined sheriff and three drunken men who draw fighting pay from the 7UP outfit."

"We got Snodgrass and yore two other pardners in jail," bellowed Tuley Bill Baker. "They've told a lot about you, Marley. Yore dirty game is all done here."

A rifle shot droned over Tuley Bill's head. The

sheriff and the three old cow-punchers eyed one another in baffled silence. Then, without a word, they turned and rode back the way they had come until they found shelter in some boulders.

"Tuley Bill," said Onion, bestowing a withering glare upon that human object of his scorn, "shore does love tuh tip his hand. Marley, if he's got a lick uh sense, will rabbit on us now. Whatever made yuh pop off thataway?"

"He got me mad," explained Tuley Bill weakly. "He got me mad."

"Yuh don't say so?" put in Cutbank Carter.

"Let Tuley Bill alone," said Ike Niland. "Mebbyso he done just right. If Marley gits scared and pulls out, then his hired hands won't have much appetite fer fightin'. We'll ketch Marley later on. The Big Meat Drummond feller is safe enough at the sheep wagon, where he's hollerin' like a baby about havin' his hand shot off. Let Marley make a run fer it and we'll pick 'im up right now. It'll beat a free fer all fight."

But even as Ike Niland spoke, there sounded the distant crackle of rifle fire. The war was on.

CHAPTER XXIII
"SUPPER IN HELL!"

Sam Bass was born in Indiana, it was his native home,
And at the age of seventeen young Sam began to roam.
Sam first came to Texas a cowboy for to be —
A kinder hearted fellow you seldom ever see.
— Sam Bass.

Hook Jones, ragged, a blood-stained cloth knotted around his head, lay hidden in a buck-brush thicket. His eyes bloodshot and slitted to a pair of glittering lines, watched the wagon where Big Meat Drummond moaned and cursed and begged for more whisky. For hours, hours that had changed from night to dawn and from dawn to daylight, Hook had crouched there in his hiding place, waiting for the chance to kill Big Meat Drummond.

Something of sanity had returned to Hook. His whisky gone, and the hours of jerked nerves due to an abrupt sobering-up now passing away, the killer was almost normal. What tortured hours the man suffered with a dogged, gritting fortitude, only Hook could know.

He was now waiting to kill a man he hated.

The man who had fought on the sheep-man's side in the bloody Wyoming cattle war, the man who had helped murder the family of the girl who became Hook's wife. All the crowded, twisted memories of the Wyoming war now stirred Hook's blood. Crouched in the brush, he enjoyed the grisly satisfaction of his enemy's suffering. He could hear Big Meat curse and whine and cry out in the agony of pain, and the suffering of Drummond was pleasing to the deadly Hook.

Hook, from his hiding place, had shot Drummond's gun from his hand. He had ridden away into the night on the big white horse. And then, his brain working with a terrible cunning, he had swung out of the saddle and let the white horse go on. He had crept back to his brush patch and had watched the shadows of the men inside the lighted sheep wagon. He had sent a bullet into the wagon, the bullet that smashed through the basin where Buck Rawlins washed his hands. He had chuckled in a grisly fashion when the light was suddenly doused in the canvas-topped wagon.

Hook's was a cunning reasoning that pictured the suffering of Big Meat, there in the dark, the pain-ridden man's torture, for pain is many times more intense in darkness than in the light.

From that same brush patch, Hook Jones had watched Buck Rawlins ride away. He knew that Buck was hunting Guy. He knew that Guy was not far distant, even now, and that Guy had been within gunshot range when Hook's bullet had saved Buck Rawlins's life there at the sheep wagon. And because Hook had, for the first time, realized that the son of Angus Murdock was a real man, Hook's trigger finger had not sent Bill Murdock to eternity. And it pleased Hook Jones now to know that his son Guy had been near and had witnessed the fact that Hook had saved the life of Buck Rawlins.

Hook Jones, now, as he waited for the chance to openly kill Big Meat Drummond, was like a man condemned to die before many hours have passed. He knew that he would never leave this place alive. Hating all men, hated by all men, he would die here, fighting until a bullet ended his career.

That was as it should be. That would be the only choice of a man who had been a killer and would remain a killer until he was shot down.

Hook would kill as many men as he could before they dropped him. But, before the odds grew too heavy, he would get Big Meat Drummond.

Buck had left the camp. That was good. Hook had always liked Buck Rawlins. Buck had stood against him, had favored Guy, and he had defied Hook to his face. He had made a bet with Hook that Guy had nerve, more nerve than his father had. Hook, with a certain respect for Buck's opinion, had always secretly hoped Buck was right about Guy.

If Hook could see the proof of Guy's courage,

then he would be ready to pay that bet to Buck, ready to cash in and shake hands. Perhaps, more than anything left in the world for him now, Hook wanted proof of Guy's courage. To know that his son, the son of Hook Jones, was a brave man, that would be all that a dying man could ask. But, with an acid bitterness, the one-armed killer told himself that Guy was a weakling and a coward.

If Guy had nerve, why didn't he come out and fight? Why hadn't the snivelin' little whelp showed the color of his courage when he sat back and seen Hook shoot the gun outa Big Meat's hand? Why didn't he show up now, instead uh hidin' somewheres, scared to come out?

"He knows I'll begin shootin' at him, that's why," gritted Hook. "He's scared tuh face the music. He thinks I'll kill him. Which I will, but I'll give him his chances. I'll give him better than an even break. I'll test 'im. If he's got sand, then it'll be me that drops. But if he is as yeller as I figger, then I'll send him tuh where such coyotes goes when they die. I'll . . . I'll test 'im. So help me, I'll run him through the chute."

Now Hook saw Bill Murdock ride away. It was past sunrise. Hook's carbine barrel covered Bill Murdock until the young sheep-man had gone, hidden from view by a hogback ridge. Then Hook lowered the hammer of his carbine.

"I coulda killed 'im," he muttered, grinning twistedly. "Yeh. I coulda killed 'im. But I want tuh git into that wagon first. I gotta have that talk with my friend in there. My ol' pardner Big Meat. And if I'm stopped by a bullet between here an' there, I'll know that I win that bet with Buck Rawlins. Because Guy will be watchin'. If he shoots from the brush, I'll live long enough to git him, somehow.

"He knows who Big Meat Drummond is because he's bin told by the Nighthawk. He knows that Drummond is the snake that fought us in Wyoming. Big Meat was the one that got away, after me thinkin' I'd killed him. Guy knows that. He knows I'm trailin' Big Meat. He knows I bin on a drunk and I'm sick an' my belly is empty. I need whisky an' some grub an' some sleep. I bin livin' on raw meat because I didn't dast light a fire tuh cook by. I've had the jim-jams an' snakes an' the only water I had was from them gypsum springs down in the breaks. Raw meat an' berries on a belly burned out with rotten whisky. Dasn't sleep of a night for fear I'll be ketched. Vomitin' what meat I ate an' fightin' off crazy notions that work like maggots into a man's brain.

"Now I'm settin' out tuh git a man that hollers because his hand got scratched off. I mind when I lost my left wing. I done my own surgery an' toughed 'er out till I made a fifty mile ride tuh Cheyenne. Held a gun in the doc's belly while he cut off the proud-flesh an' burned 'er with bluestone an' straight carbolic. Now that big son in yonder wagon gives up head like a calf at a brandin' fire. And me out here in the brush with a bullet hole in my head that's shootin' pains plumb into my toes.

"Well, I'll turn a trick now. I'll show 'em that Hook Jones is a better man than any of 'em."

Hook Jones got to his feet. He stood up boldly and walked, his spurs jingling, toward the wagon where the wounded camp tender and Big Meat Drummond lay on their bunks. Carbine in the crook of his left arm, the steel hook looped into the gun lever, in his right hand a six-shooter, Hook Jones strode to the wagon.

A moment later he was inside.

Hook stood there, leering with sun-cracked lips at the staring Drummond. Drummond tried to sit up, then gave up the futile struggle against the strips of blanket that Bill Murdock had used to pin the wounded renegade's head and shoulders to the bunk. The blanket strips were passed across the back of Drummond's neck and under the armpits, then tied under the bunk. Like the wrestler's full-Nelson hold.

"Long time, Big Meat, since my trail an' yore trail crossed. Yuh don't seem proud tuh see me."

"I'm tied down, Hook. Them buzzards cut my hand off. Yuh kain't kill a man that's in the shape I'm in."

Hook gave a quick look toward the wounded camp tender who was conscious, but exhausted, and his eyes fearful.

"Mister," said Hook, "you lay quiet. I ain't a-hurtin' you." He looked in the mess box and found a butcher knife. The keen blade cut the strips of blanket that bound Big Meat. Now Hook spied the jug. He poured out two drinks.

"Throw that into yuh, Big Meat. I'm a-doin' the same. You there, shep, want a shot?"

"I don't drink."

"Then watch the door. If yuh see anybody a-comin', tell me. If yuh don't tell me, I'll live long enough to kill yuh. Me and this big ox is goin' into a pow-wow. Big Meat, this is our last day on this earth. We'll both eat supper in hell. Try tuh die like a man."

It may have been a sort of delirium that gave Big Meat Drummond the courage he now showed. Or it may have been the whisky that put courage into his heart. He swung his legs over the edge of the bunk and forced a grin.

"Give me a gun, Hook, and I'll call the bet. I kin shoot left handed."

"Now," said Hook, "yo're showin' the right spirit. I was a-scared I'd have tuh kill yuh while yuh was kneelin'. Drink up." Hook laid a six-shooter on the bunk.

"Me and you, Big Meat, has played our string out. We'll each have a gun when we leave this wagon. You go around one end. I'll take the other. We'll meet around back. I hope yuh don't weaken."

"I'll meet yuh, Hook."

"Got ary word yuh wanta leave, Big Meat?" Hook jerked a thumb toward the wounded camp tender. "This gent will deliver the message."

"I want 'em to know," said Big Meat, facing

the wounded camp tender, "that it wasn't me that killed Joe Phelps. Tell 'em it was Eric Swanson. Marley fixed it. He give Swanson the white horse to ride when he done it. The same horse I rode the night I set fire to the Rolling M range. Tell 'em that. I reckon that closes my book."

"Then let's git 'er done," said Hook. "I'll foller yuh out of the wagon, Big Meat. I hope that they feed a man good where we're both goin'. And I hope there's a drink in the jug for us both. Pick up that gun, Big Meat."

Those who were there to watch saw that which they could never afterwards forget. They saw Hook Jones and Big Meat Drummond step down out of the sheep wagon. Saw them separate and each start around the covered wagon from an opposite direction. Each man with a six-shooter in his hand.

Now they faced one another at the rear of the wagon. Two guns cracked as one. The two six-shooters belching flame. Big Meat Drummond, sagging at the knees, then falling, laboriously thumbing back the hammer of his gun, trying to send a final bullet into the swaying Hook Jones who was still on his feet.

Hook, a terrible grin stretching his mouth sideways. Hook, bloody, cursing through gritted teeth, his eyes mere slits of glittering red. Hook, pumping bullet after bullet into the dying Drummond, who kept trying to pull back the hammer of a .45.

Drummond, lying on his belly, legs doubled under him, pulling with the last split-ounce of life left him, at that gun hammer. Trying, with the bloody stump of an arm to pull himself up off the reddening ground.

No man who watched made a move to halt that grisly duel. They saw that no living man could prevent that which was to be. Big Meat Drummond, fighting desperately for the few seconds remaining between him and the black eternity beyond this life. Struggling to thumb back a gun hammer and take Hook with him into the black pit.

Hook, his unshaven, bleak face stamped by a sardonic grin, shooting at the dying man. Hook, with a spreading smear of blood on his shirt front, swaying on his widespread legs, cursing the man whose eyes were glazed with death. Now Hook ejected the empty shells from his .45 and shoved fresh cartridges into the chambers of the cylinder.

Big Meat's head sagged forward on his thick neck. The gun slipped from his nerveless fingers. Big Meat was dead. But the gun in his hand was now empty.

Hook's terrible eyes lifted. His lips, snarling away from yellow teeth, were stained with frothy blood. His voice, harsh, croaking, hardly human, went toward the patch of brush and boulders beyond the wagon.

"Come outta there, young 'un! Step out, yuh young, snivelin', psalm-singin' whelp! Come out

287

and git what I gave to Drummond. Stand on yore feet, yuh Bible-totin', mealy-mouthed little coyote! Come an' git it!"

"I'm coming!" Guy Jones stepped from the brush. His face drawn and bloodless, his eyes like burning coals in black sockets, limping slowly as he walked toward his father.

There was a six-shooter in Guy's right hand. Limping slowly, but never once flinching. His eyes steady, his manner that of a man who walks toward death. So Guy Jones met his father, Hook Jones, the deadliest killer of them all, the most dangerous man who had ever ridden the outlaw trail. Hook, dying on his feet, a six-shooter in his hand. Hook, weaving in his tracks, his sharpened-steel hook discolored with dried blood, more deadly than ever he had been.

Yet Guy Jones did not falter. His eyes did not shift from that blood-smeared, terrible figure of his father. Slowly, steadily, the space between father and son lessened. Until but a scant ten feet separated them. Now it was Guy who spoke, his voice breaking the silence with the brittle noise of shattered glass.

"When you call me a coward, you lie! Here I am!"

A sound that was like a sob broke from the throat of Hook Jones as he faced his son. His face twisted from a snarl into a grimace of pain, then softened into a smile.

"Young 'un," he whispered in a husky voice, "here's my gun. Put 'er away, boy, an' let 'er rust. I'll be a-leavin' yuh now, fer keeps. Leavin' yuh. I got no right tuh ask it of yuh, but I'd like tuh be planted alongside yore mother. And mebbyso, young 'un, you'll forgit how ornery I bin. And yuh'll read a few lines from her Book when they bury me. Here's my gun. . . . Tell Buck Rawlins he gits my horse . . . Tell him ol' Hook said . . . said you was a better man than me. . . . Braver. . . . So-long, young 'un. . . ."

CHAPTER XXIV
SHOW-DOWN BATTLE

Let sixteen gamblers come handle my coffin,
Let sixteen cowboys come sing me a song,
Take me to the graveyard and lay the sod o'er
me
For I'm a wild cowboy, and I know I've done
wrong.

— The Cowboy's Lament.

The war was on. Rifles and carbines kicked limerock and sandstone in the faces of the men barricaded behind the strips of rim-rock ledges. Angus Murdock sought to still the guns of Marley, Eric Swanson and the other nesters. Deacon Nelson likewise tried to make Eric and his farmers quit shooting. Eric snarled curses at the Deacon, branding the peacemaker as a coward and a traitor to his own kind.

Deacon Nelson shrugged his big shoulders, turned and left his son-in-law, and heedless of his own danger, walked with steady, long-legged strides toward the spot where Guy Jones was covering the dead Hook with a blanket. Guy looked up at his father-in-law with grief-stricken eyes.

"Come to the wagon, son," said Deacon Nelson gently. "A cup of coffee will do you good. You must help me pray that something will halt this fighting. It's wrong, wrong, wrong!" The Deacon was deeply moved.

Inside the sheep wagon, Guy and Deacon Nelson were to get a shock. From the lips of the camp tender they were to learn that Eric Swanson had murdered Joe Phelps, the 7UP cowboy, thus aggravating this conflict.

But two other men were working on that theory already. Bill Murdock and Buck Rawlins were maneuvering so as to come at Eric and Marley from the rear. That meant a long, laborious and roundabout journey.

"If we can surprise 'em, 7UP," said Bill Murdock grimly, "we'll bluff 'em into laying down. This Eric is our huckleberry. He'll fight. Marley will lay down like a whipped cur."

"Bet a dollar Marley will battle fast and dirty, sheep-herder. You take the Swede, I'll handle Marley. We'll creep up on 'em. Throw down on 'em and tell it to 'em scary. And maybe we can talk some sense at Angus."

"I hope so, Buck. He's a good man, but stubborn. And Marley has him all ribbed to fight. If we can show Marley up for a snake, then Dad will have to give in."

This was before daylight, before the killing of Big Meat Drummond and Hook Jones.

When Guy faced his father, Buck and Bill Murdock were occupying a brush patch behind the Marley gang. They had seen Tuley Bill,

Onion, Cutbank Carter and Ike Niland get turned back. Now they had watched Deacon Nelson walk down and take Guy into the sheep wagon. But, because their shelter was but a skimpy screen of brush, Buck and Bill dared not make a gun play.

By a bad streak of luck the only available shelter was already occupied. Whether the men hidden there were Marley's men or the Nighthawk's men, they had no way of telling. Trapped in their sleazy brush patch, they were forced to crouch, hardly daring to move for fear of drawing deadly rifle fire. The place had looked all right in the dark, but with daylight the two men saw the folly of their venture.

"Just two ostriches, sheep-herder, with their heads bogged in the sand," grinned Buck.

"Yeah. We made great little scouts, cow hand. Great gosh, listen to the argument between Marley and Eric."

"And there sounds Angus Murdock. He's in a ruckus of some sort with Marley and Eric. Listen."

"Ye'll do as I say," roared the voice of Angus Murdock. "I gi' the mon my word I'd no' shoot a gun till sundown. Ye'll guide yoursel's accordin'."

"We'll do nothing of the kind, Murdock," snarled Marley. "We're here to fight and we're going to fight."

"I'll ha' none of it, mon!"

Now came sounds of a scuffle. . . . Then

292

Marley's voice: "Hit 'im again, Eric! Kick his ribs in!"

With an angry growl, Bill Murdock was on his feet, heedless of the bullets that snarled around him. His father was in trouble and Bill was charging to the rescue. Beside Bill ran Buck Rawlins. Now from another rim-rock there came the rattle of gun-fire. That would be none other than the Nighthawk's men, covering the bold move of Bill Murdock and Buck Rawlins. Eric Swanson's men and Marley's thugs were splashing the rocks with bullets.

Now there rose a bellow of wrath. Big Angus Murdock, using a rifle for a club, was standing erect, cracking heads, bellowing with glorious abandon, scattering the farmers under Eric's command with his terrific blows.

Now Bill Murdock, within ten feet of where his sire waged war, stumbled, tried to catch his balance, went down. There was a smear of gushing blood on Bill's chest.

Buck bent over him. His eyes met Bill's. Bill, grinning crookedly, his face twisted with pain. "Don't mind me, Buck, old boy. Get the dirty skunks."

"I'll get 'em. Hang and rattle, shep. If . . . damn 'em, Bill, I'll get 'em! You and I never got along, sheep-herder, but I like you better than any man I ever knew. . . . I'll get 'em, kid."

Buck Rawlins didn't know that he was sobbing. That as he ran on, dry, racking sobs choked from his throat with husky cursing. Now he was with Angus Murdock. Beating at men that seemed to spring from the earth. Now Eric Swanson broke and ran, Marley with him. Leaving their men to bear the scars of the fight. And those men were now howling for quarter. "Bill's hurt!" croaked Buck. "These rats are quitting! Take care of Bill, Angus! I'll handle Marley and his farmer!"

Buck ran, zig-zagging as bullets threw gravel around him. Now he had gained shelter. There sounded the swift thudding of shod hoofs ahead of him. Marley and Eric were making a getaway. Buck saw some horses tied in a brush thicket. A man tried to stop him and Buck smashed his jaw with his rifle barrel. Now Buck Rawlins was in the saddle, riding like a wild man, chasing the two men who had fled.

Behind him he heard shouts and bellowed orders. The voice of Ike Niland declaring the law. The war-whoops of Onion, Tuley Bill and Cutbank Carter. The bellowing voice of Angus Murdock. The snarling drone of bullets clipping the brush.

With a sinking heart, Buck realized that he was poorly mounted. The horse he forked was a collar-marked, stiff-jointed animal that evidently belonged to some farmer. Too late now to get a fresh horse. Down further on he would be able to get a horse. Down at the river.

Now he'd just have to dog along behind Marley and Eric. Cold trail 'em. Follow their sign. Keep a-goin' till he caught up. Two riders broke the brush near him. Buck pulled up his gun barrel just in time. A split-second's action. The two riders were Deacon Nelson and Guy Jones. Buck had come within an ace of opening fire on them.

"I want that horse, Guy," he barked, leaping to the ground without checking the sluggish buggy horse he was quitting. "Quick, kid!"

"But, Buck, I — we —"

"Shut up and get off before I pull you out of that saddle. I got a ride to make."

"After Eric?" cried Guy.

"After Eric and Marley." Buck almost pulled Guy from his saddle. Now he was mounted. He heard the confused sounds of Guy's voice and the voice of Deacon Nelson. Now Buck had a horse between his legs. A horse that wore the 7UP iron, a horse that he had given Guy. Now he would cut down the distance between himself and the two men ahead.

Breaking brush, jumping cut coulees, sliding down slants, floundering through bogs of alkali and skirting the treacherous soap holes that would bog down a horse. Riding as only a cowboy like Buck could ride, with the skill and brains and reckless courage of a Montana cow hand who had ridden since he was old enough to walk.

Buck knew his bad-lands country. He knew that Marley and Eric Swanson must take either one of two trails that dropped down to the river. He pulled up at the forks of the trail. The sign showed that here the two fugitives had split up. Marley had chosen one trail, Eric the other.

Buck pulled a coin from his pocket. "Heads takes the left-hand trail, tails takes the right. . . . And she comes tails. I hope it will be Marley. Marley's the king of 'em all. And it's Marley's hide I'll hope to hang up on the corral."

A rifle cracked. Buck's face felt the rip of a steel-jacket bullet. Now he was shooting blindly at a brush patch, jumping his horse straight through the brush toward the man whose gun was pumping lead. Then he vaulted clear of the saddle and on top of the man who crouched there, jerking the lever of a carbine.

A snarl. A shot that tore past Buck's face. Then Buck was on top of the man, clubbing at his head. A furious, vicious, blood-spattered minute. Then Buck dragged the unconscious Eric on to the trail and tied the man's arms and legs.

"That'll hold you, scissor-bill. I'll just leave you hog-tied till I can get the Marley gent."

Now he was back in the saddle, riding hard, his ripped cheek spilling blood. A mile, two miles. Now he was almost at the river bank. Somewhere a shot crashed, echoed, died into silence. Buck pushed harder. Another shot. Then another silence, charged with a tenseness. The wind stirred the leaves of the giant cottonwoods. Buck was aware of the odor of wild roses. He rode more cautiously now, his gun ready. Who had fired those shots? What had happened down there in the cottonwoods? Now a voice hailed Buck. A steady, gritty voice. "Hold up, stranger!"

Buck knew that voice. It was the voice of the Nighthawk. "It's Buck Rawlins!" he called back to the hidden man.

"Then listen, Buck Rawlins. Turn back. Marley's gone. You stand where you are while I talk. Tell Ike that I done my best. But a skunk named Eric Swanson shot my horse and figgered he'd shot me. I was afoot and couldn't finish my job. Is Hook Jones dead yet?"

"Hook's dead," replied Buck.

"Tell the boys that Fancy Mary has money there for 'em. Tell Ike that he'll find the Nighthawk's horse dead on a sand-bar in the river. The horse Eric shot. Eric killed the Nighthawk. Tell Ike that. If this Eric ain't dead, he'll swear to it.

"In about a month, if Ike or somebody will search the sand-bar close, they'll find the body of the Nighthawk, a hundred yards below where yuh'll find the dead horse he was ridin' when this Eric killed him and the horse. The body of the Nighthawk will be kinda buried in the sand and plumb decomposed. But Ike kin identify it by the gun and the spurs and personal things like a watch and some fool medals that the Nighthawk won at bronc ridin' an' ropin'. Them things will be there with the body that'll be too far gone to identify. . . .

"The Nighthawk is dead. Marley got clean away from yuh. Marley has quit the country. *Nobody will ever see Creighton Marley again.*"

"I get you," said Buck quietly. "But before I turn back, there is a message to a certain gent from a girl named Mazie West. She says that this gent is the only man she ever cared two bits for and that if he don't look her up, she'll find him and marry him or shoot him or something."

"A gent named Hardin Jackson will be in Buenos Aires on the next boat that gets there after he's had about two weeks to square things with some boys that will be joinin' him later on a cow ranch somewhere in the interior. Hardin Jackson. She kin find him at the International Hotel there. If she needs money, Mary will fix her up. Got that right?"

"You bet."

"This same Hardin Jackson would be shore proud to have Buck Rawlins hunt him up some time."

"Buck just might do that same thing, stranger. And I'm wishin' him and the little lady all the best luck."

"And right back at yuh. But if he don't high-tail it fer home and marry a game little girl named Colleen Driscoll, he better not sight hisself on my sky-line. Get that?"

"She don't care about me that way."

"No? Yo're loco. Ask her, yuh bone-head. I know what I'm talkin' about."

"Honest?"

"Honest Injun, pardner. Now I'll be goin'. You might be asked if yuh'd seen me. You ain't seen me, have yuh?"

"No. No, stranger, I haven't seen yuh."

"*Adiós*. So-long, pardner."

"So-long, pardner."

Buck turned back along the trail. He wrapped a bandage around his cut cheek and hummed softly as he rode. At the spot where he had left the tied Eric, Buck found Deacon Nelson and Guy. Eric was cursing them horribly. Deacon Nelson looked grim and a little sad. He was thinking of the news he must take to his daughter who was this man's wife. The news that her husband was a cowardly murderer.

"Shut up," Buck told Eric, "or I'll knock you to sleep with a rock. Let's get going. If Bill Murdock dies, this big hunk of mud will hang. He's a murderer."

"God forgive him, he is," said Deacon Nelson. "He is."

A north wind drove a shift of snow across Montana's brown hills. The last train of cattle had been shipped, and the whistle of a locomotive wailed through the leaden dusk. The last steer in the 7UP iron had quit its range.

For there was no more 7UP range. The Murdocks, old Angus and his son Bill, Bill who had missed death by an inch or two and would bear the bullet scar always, would now run sheep there. The Rawlins outfit now belonged to the

Murdocks. Even as the nester homesteads would go back from flax and wheat to be passed over by the bands of sheep.

But a few days before, Colleen Driscoll and her father had sold the Rolling M to another sheep outfit. The Rolling M horses, together with the tops of the 7UP remuda, had been shipped to California, bought and paid for by a horse owner there.

The big gates of the Deer Lodge penitentiary had closed on Eric Swanson and his hirelings, and Howard Snodgrass had gone through those gates.

Mazie West had gone. Marley would never again be heard from. The Nighthawk, alias Wade Hardin, was marked off the law books as dead.

Over on Big Warm Creek, Deacon Nelson and Guy Jones preached their gospel and followed their plows. Ike Niland would continue on as sheriff, ranching on the side.

Buck Rawlins and his bride, who had been Colleen Driscoll, were on the station platform that night, waiting to take the train that led westward toward Arizona and Mexico. On the next train to follow would be riding three old-time cowmen who hid whatever grief they felt at leaving Montana, behind whimsical, game-hearted grins. Bob Driscoll, Dave Rawlins and Uncle Hank Mayberry were hunting a new range. Maud Snodgrass, so it was told, would be returning in a year to marry Bill Murdock, who had found out where the trail led, by devious route, to its end.

Fancy Mary was gone. Yesterday she had been seen at Chinook. Dressed in tarnished finery, she had taken the train that carried Mazie West. Like the other old-timers, she was moving on.

Down in the bad-lands, three grizzled old cow-punchers, each well mounted, each with his laden packhorse, pulled out, headed for the south. Headed for Mexico, where a man can swing a loop without snagging a fence post.

One of the three old cow hands fumbled in the pocket of his angora chaps and found a bottle. Each of his companions produced a corkscrew.

"Onion Oliver," said Tuley Bill Baker testily, "you an' that Cutbank thing kin pull a corkscrew quicker than ever Bat Masterson drawed a gun. An' I bet when we gits down there on that new spread in Mexico, it'll still be ol' Tuley Bill Baker that supplies what goes with them implements."

They headed the bad-lands and hit the rolling prairie. They skirted a barb-wire fence that held acres of plowed ground and a deserted shack with tar-paper roof. Tumbleweeds lodged against the barb-wire fence. They skirted the desolate, deserted homestead and rode on. Headed for a new range. They did not look back.